Roll Over and Play DEAD

Roll
Over and
Play
DEAD

JOAN HESS

St. Martin's Press   New York

Design by Dawn Niles

Library of Congress Cataloging-in-Publication Data

Hess, Joan.
    Roll over and play dead / Joan Hess.
        p.   cm.
    "A Claire Malloy mystery."
    ISBN 0-312-05956-6
    I. Title.
    PS3558.E79785R65 1991
    813'.54—dc20   90-29882
                                                      CIP

First Edition: July 1991

10 9 8 7 6 5 4 3 2 1

To Gussie

I would like to thank Deborah Robinson, Susan Latta, and the members of COMBAT for providing me invaluable assistance and information.

Roll
Over and
Play
DEAD

1

One of these days I'm going to take a three-day seminar in assertiveness training. Then, with the diploma framed and hung on the wall, I will be able to look potential manipulators in the eye and say, "No." Not "I'm sorry," or "Well, maybe . . ." or even "Gee whiz, I'd like to help you out, but I've got yellow fever."

In my dreams, right?

I was sitting in my cramped little office at the back of the Book Depot, and I was making grumbly noises similar to those made by the boiler on a frigid afternoon. I was doing this because, fanned in front of me like a losing poker hand, were six pages of instructions written in lavender ink by a spidery hand. Said hand belonged to Miss Emily Parchester, who was at that moment heading west in a chartered bus, accompanied by fifty stouthearted members of the American Association of Retired Teachers. Their itinerary included Santa Fe, the Grand Canyon, Carlsbad Caverns, Indian reservations, and other scenic and semiexotic ports of call.

My itinerary for the next twenty-one days included daily visits to Miss Emily's house. While she was busily buying turquoise brooches and postcards, I was to water the African violets, collect the mail, see that a neighborhood boy mowed the yard, and feed two basset hounds named Nick and Nora.

And I was being treated to all this jolly good fun because I lacked the nerve to look tiny, sweet, wispy-haired Miss Emily in the eye and just say no. I'd tried a variety of excuses, but she'd heard them all in her forty years of teaching high school and had smiled patiently at me until I started to squirm, hung my head, and grudgingly agreed to take all six pages and commit them to memory.

So it was all my own damn fault, but that wasn't making me feel any better. When the bell above the front door jangled, I put down the list, ordered myself to stop grumbling, and went to the front of the bookstore to see who might be so bold as to want to buy a book.

My daughter, Caron, and her dearest friend, Inez Thornton, were heading toward the cash register, larceny written across their fifteen-year-old faces. Caron has my red hair and freckles, but while I am mild-mannered and cerebral, she is explosive and hormonal. She has been speaking in capital letters for over a year and has a way of saying "Mother" that gives me goose bumps. In contrast, Inez has nondescript features, limp brown hair, and eyes that seem startled behind thick lenses. She is very much a lowercase speaker, often verging on inaudible, and is still awaiting developments.

"What do you think you're doing?" I snapped.

Caron swung around and assessed her chances. "I was going to get the feather duster and do something about that Filthy Display in the front window. Some of those books look like they've been in the window since prehistoric hippies roamed Thurber Street."

"I was going to help," Inez said loyally, if mendaciously.

"What a wonderful idea," I said. I went behind the

2

counter, found the feather duster, and offered it to Caron. "If you ask politely, I'll let you dust the entire store and even scrub the toilet in the rest room."

I was rewarded with a dark look from my darling daughter. "That's disgusting." She snatched up the feather duster, then forced herself to conjure up a smile. "By the way, I need an advance on my allowance, Mother."

"That's nice. I'll be in the back if you need me—and I know down to the halfpenny what's in the cash register."

"I really, really need an advance."

"And I really, really need to pore over six pages of notes concerning pets, the post, and potted plants," I said, starting for the office.

"Pets?" Inez said blankly. "You don't have any pets, Mrs. Malloy. You don't have any plants, either."

I gave them a terse explanation of the situation, which they found highly diverting, and I once again attempted to achieve the relative sanctuary of my office. It was not to be.

"But what about my advance?" Caron wailed. "It's the most important thing in my life. I May Die."

Telling myself I might require months of assertiveness training, I stopped and looked back at this quivering mass of misery and despair. "What is the most important thing in your life?"

She recovered nicely. "A rock concert. It's a week from Saturday, but the tickets go on sale today and they'll be gone by tomorrow."

"A rock concert is the most important thing in your life? What about developing strong moral values, making rational career decisions, seeking a higher plane of cosmic—"

"I have to see Mousse."

I should have gone straight to the office and buried myself under invoices. Instead, I blinked and said, "Moose? As in Bullwinkle?"

"Mousse, as in chocolate."

"Then go out to lunch," I suggested brightly.

Inez patted Caron's shoulder. "Mousse is the name of the absolutely hottest rock band in the entire world," she explained to her best friend's idiot mother. "They were on the cover of *People* magazine last week."

It was late in the afternoon and I had pets and plants awaiting me. "I'm sure they're the hottest thing since the advent of control-top panty hose, girls. If you want to go to the concert, then raid your respective piggy banks. As for this advance business, Caron, you are already advanced well into the next century and the cash register is closed. As is the discussion."

They were howling at my back (like a pack of wild mooses, I suppose), but I made it to the office and banged the door closed. After a few minutes, things quieted down and the bell above the door jangled as they left, no doubt planning a decorous bank heist. I wished them success, in that there were not enough halfpennies in the cash register for bail.

At the end of the afternoon, I closed the bookstore, and with the six pages in my pocket, drove to Miss Emily's house to find out what I had done to myself. Her house on Willow Street was in what had been a classy residential district back when buggies were in vogue, but now the houses had been divided into apartments and the only buggies in view were of the

4

genus Volkswagen. The elm trees were still magnificent, as were the maples that exploded with color in the autumn. Dogwoods and redbuds were blooming, and some of the houses were almost hidden by ancient azaleas that would soon be laden with rich pink flowers.

Miss Emily lived in the bottom half of what had been the Parchester residence for several generations. She'd told me more than once how her father, a.k.a. the Judge, had presided over the town from the porch swing, swilling mint juleps and offering unsolicited yet piercing insights into the vagaries of Supreme Court decisions. Dear Mama had kept the neighborhood children in sugar cookies and her sewing circle in elderberry wine. Miss Emily had carried on the family tradition of tippling, sometimes before noon, and I dearly hoped she kept a cautious distance from the rim of the Grand Canyon.

The key was in the mailbox, as delineated in page one, paragraph three, the first two having been dedicated to expressions of gratitude. I let myself in, wrinkled my nose at the musty redolence, and went through the living room cluttered with bleached newspapers and exam booklets written by students now crotchety from rheumatism.

The kitchen had a black stove and a cracked porcelain sink. I looked out the window at the fenced yard, expecting to see dear Nick and Nora, but all I saw was a robin hopping about and a half-deflated ball. The yard was ringed with untamed bushes thick with yellow and fuchsia flowers, however, so it was likely they were out there somewhere.

Pages two through four gave explicit instructions regarding the African violets on the windowsill, kitchen table, stool, chair seats, and every inch of countertop. Feeling as though I'd been drop-kicked into the Darkest Continent, I gave them all water, pinches of food, and admonishments to stay happy and healthy (page four, penultimate paragraph).

Page five. I opened a can of dog food, divided it between two plastic bowls, added half a cup of kibble to each, and moistened that with half a cup of water, all in the amount of time it would have taken to whip up a batch of chocolate mousse, let it set, and eat it. And I was going to do this for twenty more days, I thought glumly as I picked up the bowls and, with a bit of juggling, went out to the back porch and looked around for these canine connoisseurs.

The following remarks may be considered offensive to some, or even sacrilegious, but I am not fond of dogs because they tend to snuffle, drool, and attack with either benevolence or mayhem in their small brains. They chase cars, children, birds, squirrels, and pedestrians, to name a few, and those blessed with obsessive dotage do so dressed in sweaters and boots. They also deposit things on the sidewalk.

Moving on to crimes warranting defenestration or perhaps decapitation, I am not fond of cats because they insist on having their own way, and that includes ill-timed intrusions and more arrogance than fifteen-year-olds. I am legally and morally obligated to put up with Caron, but not with a dependent four-legged mammal that sheds. And she never climbs into my lap to lick my face, sleeps on my feet, performs bodily functions in the yard, or attempts to have sex with my leg.

But for the time being, I was obliged to serve dinner to Nick and Nora, after which I could drive home as quickly as possible and seek solace in a glass of scotch and water. I warily looked around the yard. "Nick? Nora?" I called in my best good-doggie voice, which, of course, wasn't good at all.

"Who are you?" barked a voice. It really did, although at this point it was early in the game and I was still in possession of my wits, and therefore made no anthropomorphic leaps.

The man was standing in the next yard, and nearly invisible behind a lush growth of honeysuckle on the fence. He was probably in his late sixties, I decided. His face was harshly lined and weathered, his nose hooked over a bushy mustache, and his gray hair cut in an uncompromising crew cut. "I'm Claire Malloy, a friend of Miss Emily's," I said. "I agreed to take care of the house and dogs while she's on a trip."

"Culworthy here. Colonel, retired U.S. Air Force. Where'd she go?"

"Out West with a group of teachers. Do you have any idea where her dogs might be? I'd like to feed them and go home."

"Couldn't say. Parchester lets them run wild. No discipline, no training. Disgraceful to assume responsibility for animals and then not be able to control them." He shaded his eyes and frowned at me as if my self-control were tenuous. "Damn disgraceful."

"Absolutely," I said absently as I peered around the yard for the pair of undisciplined, untrained disgraces. "Nick? Nora?"

"Silly names, too. I told Parchester she should have given them names with dignity, with significance. Mine's Patton."

I looked back at him, wondering if he was just a teeny-tiny bit schizophrenic. "I thought you said it was Culworthy."

He snorted at me. "My golden retriever's named Patton. He knows the rules. No barking after dark. No chasing squirrels. No digging in the garden."

I nodded, then took the bowls to the porch and set them down. And was slammed from behind by a tank, or so I thought as I tried to keep from nose-diving into the goopy kibble. For a panicky moment, I envisioned Culworthy attacking me, then realized he was hardly the sort to lick my legs or dig his claws into my derriere, or even to make gurgly noises in my ear while drooling on my neck. Oh no, the unseen assailant was not Colonel Culworthy.

"Get off of me!" I yelled, still perilously close to kibble. "Damn it, Nick and Nora, get off of me!"

The gurgles receded and the slobbery tongue stopped slobbering on my leg. I stood up, reeled around, and found myself glaring at two of the fattest, ugliest basset hounds I'd ever seen. Bassets are bred to have heavy chests, but these jokers were walking wine caskets. They had stubby, misshapen legs, gunky brown eyes, wet jowls that almost brushed the ground, ears that did, and woebegone expressions. One of them made a snuffly noise at me but looked away when I frowned warningly.

"Told you so," Culworthy cackled from behind the honeysuckle. "Patton knows his place. Never jumps on people."

"Perhaps he's waiting for the right moment to rip your throat out," I said as calmly as I could, then locked my arms and glared at the miscreants. "Listen, you two, I am not going to tolerate any of that behavior. If you intend to eat for the next three weeks, you'd better watch it."

One of them waddled forward and attempted to lick my foot, but I stepped onto the porch. Pointing a finger at him or her, I said, "That's exactly the kind of behavior I'm talking about. You either cut it out or prepare to go on a long fast."

They both wagged their stubby tails, feigning repentance. I shook my finger for emphasis and stalked across the porch and into the kitchen before they could make another play for my foot. Reminding myself it was all my fault, I used a dish towel to dry my leg and neck.

I was still reminding myself half an hour later, but at least I was doing so at home and with a glass of scotch in my hand. Caron and I occupy the top floor of a duplex across the street from the sloping lawn of Farber College, in loco parentis to a few thousand earnest yuppies seeking enough educational expertise to work for a generous savings and loan or a nice, clean oil company.

From the living room window we have a picturesque view of Farber Hall, with its imposing redbrick facade and towers on either end. Until it was condemned, it had housed the English faculty, one of whom had been my husband. When sprinkles of plaster dust had turned to torrential downpours of chunks, the faculty had mosied over to a bland building, where they worried only about asbestos.

I finally granted myself absolution and was settling down with the local newspaper when I heard an ominous sound. Not the snuffly approach of basset hounds from hell, but the relentless footsteps of an indignant teenager as she came upstairs to our apartment. I managed to freshen my drink and was cowering in the classifieds as Caron marched into the room.

"Everybody's going to be there," she said accusingly.

"Oh, really? Are you interested in a paper route? How about part-time clerical work at a hardware store?"

She flung herself into the chair across from me. I was still cowering, but I could see the newspaper turning brown as she glared at me with the warmth of a laser. "Every last person I know is going to see Mousse. Every Last Person. Even the nerds and the dweebs and the eighth graders. Rhonda Maguire's having a slumber party after the concert."

"Here's an opportunity to start as assistant manager at a fast-food place."

"You are not funny, Mother. This Is Important. Do you realize everyone in school will be there except your daughter, who might as well sit in her room until she's covered with mold?"

"If you keep leaving dirty dishes in there, your whole room's going to be covered with mold," I said, moving on to the real estate section. If I could find a house I could afford, perhaps I could move while she was at school and leave no forwarding address.

"All I need is twenty dollars," she said with a sniffle. More sniffles ensued. "A measly twenty dollars is all that stands between Mousse and utter misery for the rest of my life."

A devastatingly brilliant idea struck. I lowered the paper and said, "I know a way for you to earn twenty dollars, dear."

"Earn? Why do I have to earn it? Inez's father just gave it to her, but my father's dead so I guess that won't work."

"Cool it, Little Orphan Annie," I said, increasingly smitten with my idea. "You want to earn twenty dollars or not?" When she gave me a level look, I continued. "I told you and Inez about Miss Emily's violets and dogs. I will pay you a dollar a day to go over there after school and see to things."

"I have to buy the ticket tomorrow."

Well, at least we were working toward our respective goals. Although I wasn't pleased with the necessity of trusting her, I said, "I'll advance the money so you can buy the ticket tomorrow, but you hand it over to me until the concert, okay?"

"What kind of dogs—little yappy ones or big grungy ones?"

"Somewhere in between," I said lightly, willing myself not to flinch as her laser-eyes bored into me. "Basset hounds named Nick and Nora. They stay in the backyard, so all you need to do is mix up their food and set it on the porch. Their water's in a bowl under a drippy faucet; it needs to be checked every now and then. Feed the dogs, water the plants, bring in the mail, and you're done in less than half an hour."

Caron was no great whiz at math, but I could see numbers spinning around in her head. At last she raised her eyebrows and said, "Fifteen minutes to walk over there, half an hour to mess around, and another fifteen minutes to walk home. You are offering to pay me a dollar an hour, Mother. A Dollar an Hour. What about minimum wage? What about child labor laws, for that matter?"

"What about being the only person in all of Farberville High School who won't get to see Mush?" I countered.

"Mousse. The group is named Mousse." She stood up, gave me a calculating look, and started for her room. "I'll think about it. It sounds like a lot of work for a dollar an hour. It's supposed to rain this week, you know. I'd get totally drenched."

She strolled out of the living room and down the short hallway to her bedroom door. I remembered the sensation of paws on my derriere and drool on my neck.

"Oh, all right!" I called ungraciously. "Two dollars a day, and I'll drive you if it rains."

"Payable in advance?" she said from the hallway.

"I hope you grow up to be a labor negotiator for a bunch of dockworkers."

"Interesting idea." Her bedroom door closed very softly.

The next afternoon it was raining, naturally. Not sprinkling or drizzling, but raining hard enough to fill the gutters with satiny brown water and send the few pedestrians darting from doorway to doorway as they worked their way up Thurber Street toward the campus of Farber College. Occasional claps of thunder broke up the monotonous rhythm on the roof of the bookstore.

Caron and Inez were breathing heavily as they arrived under the protective portico of the Book Depot. While Inez stopped to struggle with the umbrella, Caron came inside, her expression leaving no question as to the identity of the party responsible for the rain. To some extent, this was my fault, having exaggerated maternal powers to an impressionable toddler, who readily believed I had the unlisted telephone numbers of everyone who mattered, including Santa Claus and the Tooth Fairy (who left several testy notes about sloppy dental hygiene).

I gave them a minute to recover and then herded them out to my car. After a brief debate about who was going to drive (we were dealing with the dreaded learner's permit), I handed them the six pages and we pulled out of the parking lot.

"What's all this?" Caron demanded.

"Instructions. As in what to do and how to do it. Just read through them."

"I'm not reading anything, much less doing dogs, until I have my ticket," she announced.

I drove them to a music store and waited in the car for an eternity while they battled a long line of Mousseketeers. Once the ticket was in my purse, I drove to Miss Emily's house and parked. "I'll wait here," I said as I took out a book.

Inez tried the same ploy, but it met with scathing comments about fair weather friendship, craven cowardice, and other less charitable sentiments, and the two dashed to the front porch. I watched to make sure they found the key, and was about to escape into my mystery novel when a young man came up the sidewalk and turned toward the house. He had long, black hair plastered on his head like a bathing cap, and I caught a glimpse of dark, angry eyes as he passed my car. His lips were thin, his jaw sharp and angular, his cheeks strikingly concave. He wore a stained trench coat that might have come off the back of Sam Spade, and he carried a briefcase.

Caron and Inez looked alarmed as he approached, but he ignored them as he checked his mailbox, stuck a few envelopes in his coat pocket, and went around the corner of the house to an exterior staircase. According to page six of Miss Emily's instructions, he was Daryl Defoe, the upstairs renter and sometimes "a wee bit irritable, but basically a good boy."

Caron and Inez made it inside the house, so I settled back to outwit the bumbling inspector and identify the wicked soul who'd laced the souffle with cyanide. I was quite confident that I would succeed;

13

this was, after all, mere fiction and I'd outwitted the Farberville CID on more than one occasion. Not that I would describe Lieutenant Peter Rosen as a bumbler. We'd met a while back when I'd been sus-pected of murder—just one of those annoying little things that happens to us all, I suppose. I'd been obliged to solve the mystery, and in the process had become interested in the hawk-nosed cop with curly black hair, molasses-colored eyes, and ferociously white teeth that hinted of vulpine ancestry.

Peter is a man of great charm, although he lapses from grace when he implies (a mild word) that I meddle in official investigations and stick my hand-some nose into police business. He does this quite often, since I do try to take an interest in his work, as any good friend should.

Lately he has been bringing up the M-word. He is divorced and I am widowed, and we have been keep-ing company in the contemporary sense of the word. My deceased husband ran afoul of a chicken truck several years ago, and I have become settled in my singlehood and protective of my territory, both phys-ical and intellectual. However, the idea of marriage is not loathsome, and at idle moments, such as this one, I allow myself to debate the relative merits.

I was trying to envision the division of closet space when a hand rapped on the window. I jerked my head up and found myself staring at a face only an inch from the car window. The face belonged to an elderly woman with a great cloud of uncombed gray hair somewhat restrained by a scarlet scarf, faded blue eyes, enough makeup to unhinge a Mary Kaye saleswoman, and a wide smile that seemed to con-sume the lower part of her face. A gold tooth glinted at me.

"Hello," she shouted.

I rolled the window down a cautious inch. "Hello."

She seemed unaware of the rain splattering down on her. She stepped back, giving me a better view of the tangled mass of plastic beads and gold chains, a frilly blouse and peasant skirt, a pink fringed shawl, and a leash in her hand. At the end of the leash was the most enormous black cat I'd ever seen. From its malevolent gaze, I deduced that it was not pleased to be taking a stroll in the rain.

"You're Claire Malloy," the woman said.

"I'm Claire Malloy," I said, noting the car door was not locked and wishing I could push down the button without seeming alarmed, which I was.

"I'm Vidalia Lattis," she continued in a melodious trill, "and a very dear friend of Emily's. She told me you had agreed to take care of things while she was off on her tour. I think the Southwest is so intriguing, don't you? I'm very sure those old caves must be haunted by brooding Indian spirits, and of course the desert is so dramatic. A veritable stage for the unfolding of the struggle between life and death, the survival of man in the most brutal environment."

"Oh, yes," I murmured.

She gestured at the cat. "This is Astra. In an earlier life, she was a pampered pet of Cleopatra. Can't you imagine her on a barge on the Nile, sitting regally on a pillow and surrounded by dark-skinned servants with platters of caviar?"

I nodded, although it was easier to imagine the cat starring in a Stephen King movie. It is best not to contradict a gold-toothed woman oblivious to buckets of rain being splashed on her. "Nice to have met you," I added.

"You must come by for a cup of tea some afternoon. I live in the red-brick apartment house right there on the corner. It's terribly cozy, Astra thinks, and so convenient to the library and grocery store, and it is important for us to have—"

She stopped as a large yellow dog shot out of the side yard and came at her, barking like a banshee. She snatched up the cat and darted around to the passenger side of my car. Before I could determine what was going on, she was sitting beside me and the dog had his muddy paws on my window.

Vidalia smiled brightly and said, "As I was saying, the location is good but the neighborhood is not exactly what I'm used to. When I worked at the insurance office, I had my own bungalow, but the yard work became too arduous and I opted to rent an apartment."

She continued to rattle on, but I was missing most of it because the dog was barking its brains out, rain was pounding on the roof of the car, and a great boom of thunder added to the confusion. And at this point, Caron and Inez reappeared on the porch, assessed the situation, and were now shrieking about what they were supposed to do with that monster attacking the car. Caron was, anyway; Inez's mouth was moving.

I reacted in a mature fashion by covering my face with my hands. Vidalia dribbled into silence, perhaps appreciating the implications of my gesture, and the dog stopped barking and sat down on the sidewalk. The rain eased up.

As I removed my hands, I saw Colonel Culworthy striding toward us, his khaki jumpsuit protected by a black umbrella. "Did you open the gate?" he demanded.

I rolled down the window an inch. "I haven't stepped foot out of the car," I said.

"Someone did," he said. "Patton's out. It's not allowed. The town has a leash ordinance, and a damn good one. Don't like to see dogs roaming." He bent down and glared at my companion. "You open the gate?"

Vidalia clutched her cat so tightly its eyes bulged and its tongue poked out. "Of course not, Colonel. I was merely having a chat with Ms. Malloy when that animal came bounding at me."

"Who opened the gate?" Culworthy demanded.

I remembered the upstairs renter had gone around the side of the house that adjoined Culworthy's yard, but I had no desire to offer the information. "Maybe you left it unlatched," I said.

"Nonsense. I always latch it."

Vidalia leaned forward to stare at him. "Then how did Patton get out twice last week? He scattered my garbage all over the alley, and it took me the entire morning to clean it up. Astra was so alarmed that I had to entice her out from under the divan with the tuna fish salad that I'd saved for lunch."

His face turned red. He straightened up, and in a gruff voice, said, "Must have slipped out while I was setting out my garbage cans. Pure accident. Gave him a dressing-down he won't forget. Sorry about the mess in your alley, Vidalia."

I was relieved to see we were not headed for open warfare conducted over my body. Culworthy grabbed Patton's collar and marched him back between the two houses. Once the coast was clear, Caron and Inez came down the sidewalk and waited impatiently while Vidalia thanked me effusively for protecting her and Astra from the certain death, reiterated her invitation for tea, and removed herself from the car.

"Good grief, Mother," Caron said as we drove away, "this neighborhood is thick with weirdos. Did you see that serial killer come at us on the porch? I was sure he was going to pull out a dagger."

"He was so glowery," Inez added in a whisper.

"He's a graduate student," I explained.

Caron was unimpressed. "That doesn't give him an excuse to look at us as though we weren't there."

Inez shook her head. "He didn't look at us, even though we were there. That was what was so incredibly unnerving."

"And that gypsy who threw herself in the car," Caron said to me, ignoring the minor dissension. "Who on earth was that? I mean, really—didn't that sort of peculiar clothing go out in the Sixties?"

"She's a neighbor of Miss Emily's. She seemed pleasant enough, although I may not make it over for tea." I braked in time to let a truck run the light. "How'd it go inside? Did you find everything you needed?"

Caron took a deep breath, and in the pained voice of a martyr with flames licking between her toes, said, "Do you realize there are seventy-seven African violets in the kitchen? And those dogs are disgusting. One of them licked me on the hand. I'll probably get mange or rabies."

"They drool," Inez said.

"They were covered with mud—and who knows what else!" Caron, front seat. "It was nauseating."

"The dog food smells terrible." Inez, backseat.

"And it's looks like vomit when it's mixed up." Caron, front seat.

"Then it's a good thing you only have nineteen

more days," I said brightly as we headed down Thurber Street. I tried not to think of the quantity of complaints I would be forced to endure, and with a properly sympathetic expression. For a person who was not fond of dogs, I was going to hear a great deal about them. But at least, I told myself, I could do so at a civilized distance.

2

Things settled down over the next few days. Caron sighed a lot and compared everything she ate to the dog food she was mixing on a daily basis, but the weather was on my side. A poster of three boys with spiky orange hair and sneers appeared on her bedroom wall; neither of us commented on it. Peter was off dealing with a family crisis, so I spent my evenings outwitting a series of bumbly inspectors and Caron spent hers gushing about Mousse on the telephone.

I was working on a fictionalized account of my monthly sales tax report for the state government when Caron and Inez invaded the store late one afternoon. They came in so tentatively, though, that I closed the ledger and gave them a bemused look.

"It's the dogs," Caron said morosely.

"The dogs," Inez echoed.

"Surely it's getting easier by now," I said. "You must have a routine worked out."

"We did," Caron said. She drifted behind the science fiction rack, where all I could see was the top of her head. "They're missing."

I went around the other corner of the rack. "What did you say?"

"I said they're missing, as in gone. We went to Miss Emily's like we always do. The dumb flowers didn't need water, so we mixed up that disgusting stuff and took it to the back porch. They usually come out from under the bushes when they hear us, but today they didn't. Inez and I called and called, and then both of us crawled around and looked everywhere in the yard."

Inez peeked around the opposite end. "Don't forget about the gate being open," she said, her eyes blinking behind the thick lenses. "I think it's a clue."

I was blinking as hard as she, if such a thing were possible. "Nick and Nora are missing, and the gate was open? Is this what you're telling me?"

"It wasn't our doing," Caron said. Or whined, to be more accurate. Her repertoire is quite extensive. "We don't ever set foot off the porch, because of the dogs trying to drool on our feet. We didn't even know there was a gate until Inez found it. It's sort of hard to see under the stairs."

"It's behind a forsythia," Inez explained.

"But you're quite sure it was closed yesterday?" I said.

Caron took a book off the rack and studied the lurid cover, which involved a nubile warrior in a leather bikini being sucked into carnivorous crimson slime. "Why wouldn't it have been?" she said nonchalantly.

I'd had only fifteen years of motherhood, but I was adept enough to read between the words. I snatched the book out of her hands. "You did go to Miss Emily's house yesterday afternoon, didn't you?"

"Well, sort of."

"What does that mean?" I said in the ominous voice of a maternal warrior in jeans and a T-shirt.

"It was Rhonda Maguire's fault." Caron was edging backward, licking her lips and shooting desper-

21

ate looks at the front door. "She absolutely insisted that we come over and help her paint this incredibly neat banner to take to the concert. We worked out in the garage so we wouldn't—"

"You were at Rhonda's all afternoon?" I interrupted. "You didn't bother to go to Willow Street and feed the dogs?"

"Oh, it's not like that, Mrs. Malloy," Inez said. "Caron paid Rhonda's little brother to do it."

"And he did it for fifty cents," Caron tossed out, in case I wanted to praise her financial acumen rather than throttle her.

I did not. "So what do you intend to do about Nick and Nora? Miss Emily trusted me, and I was foolish enough to trust you." I gave her an evil smile. "But not so foolish as to trust you with the concert ticket."

"Mother, it's not My Fault that the stupid gate wasn't locked and the dogs made a break for it. Rhonda's brother didn't crawl under a bush to open a gate, for pete's sake. I told him how to go through the house to the kitchen. He's not that dorky."

"He's only eight, though," Inez began. She caught Caron's glare and scuttled around the end of the rack.

"What are you going to do?" I persisted.

"Read the lost and found ads in the classified?"

"Try again, dear."

"Go look for them?"

"That's right," I said through clenched teeth. "You are going to search the entire neighborhood, knock on everyone's door, literally beat the bushes, call them until your voice is completely gone, and find those dogs. Do you understand?"

"But I have all this algebra homework, and . . ."

She noticed my expression, sighed loudly, and said, "Come on, Inez. Let's go find the dogs and put them back in the yard. On the way home, we can swing by Rhonda's house to pulverize that stupid little dork."

On that cheerful note, they left. I tried to reimmerse myself in the tax figures, but all I could see was Miss Emily's face as I told her the dogs were gone. She would maintain her dignity, of course, and gaze sadly at me. She might have to dab her eyes with a lacy handkerchief. Her chin might tremble. She might have a heart attack and die on the carpet.

"Oh, hell!" I said as I threw down the pencil (the red one). I grabbed the fly-speckled CLOSED sign, set it in the door, locked the store, and drove to Willow Street.

There was no sign of the search party. I went around the side of the house and found the open gate beneath the exterior staircase. I was about to leave when I saw a footprint in the mud. It did not have the distinctive tread marks of a sneaker, I thought as I placed my foot alongside it. It was longer and wider than mine, and therefore likely to have been made by a man.

The open gate might be a clue, but this most definitely qualified. It had rained five days ago. This area was shady and the ground was still somewhat wet, and it was clear that a man had come under the stairs and walked to the gate. With easy ingress blocked by a forsythia on the other side, it seemed more likely that he had flipped up the U-shaped latch and pulled the gate open a foot or so. Nick and Nora had chanced upon this fortuity and made their escape, but not necessarily immediately. The gate could have been opened four days ago or within the last few hours, I reminded myself.

Lieutenant Rosen might have his fingerprints, but Claire Malloy-Marple had a footprint. All she had to do was figure out what to do with it. I was standing over it and frowning when I heard dry leaves crackle in the adjoining yard. Culworthy's retriever loped to the fence, sat down, and stared hopefully at me, as if anticipating a doggie treat to appear in my hand.

In his dreams, right?

It did give me an idea, though, and I went around to the front of Culworthy's house and rang the bell. He had a martini in his hand as he opened the door, and an unfriendly look on his face. "Ah, yes, you're the Malloy woman. Need something?"

"I was wondering if you might have a bag of plaster."

"What for?"

"Someone opened the gate in Miss Emily's yard, and the dogs are loose. There's a footprint by the gate. I'd like to make a cast of it."

"Good idea. Can't have hooligans opening gates in the area. Dogs run wild, get in the garbage, that sort of thing." He took a sip of the martini. "Yes, bag of plaster in my garage. Wait here, Malloy; I'll take care of this for you. We can use evidence in court to convict the hooligans."

I resisted the urge to remind him whose footprint it was, or belonged to, anyway, and waited on the porch until he came back with a bag of plaster, a plastic bucket, and a long wooden spoon. I led him to the side yard and showed him the footprint. "It looks very much as if it was made by a man," I said. "And the only reason for him coming here is to open the gate."

"Can't have open gates," Culworthy said. He splashed some water into the bucket from the faucet on the side of his house, and we discussed the quantity of plaster necessary to secure, as he insisted, the evidence for court.

It was rather entertaining, and I was beginning to be accustomed to his staccato speech. He was stirring the white mixture when the door above us opened. The renter, Daryl Defoe, came out to the landing, leaned over the railing and said, "What do you think you're doing, Culworthy? This is private property."

"Damn draft dodger," Culworthy muttered without looking up.

"I heard that!" Daryl said, his dark eyes glittering with poorly disguised anger. "I did my year in 'Nam. You want to see the shrapnel scars on my leg, Colonel Culworthy? How about my stay in the Hanoi Hilton? You want to hear about the room service?"

Culworthy stirred more vigorously, splattering plaster on his creased khaki trousers. Agreeing with Caron's assessment of the neighbors, I looked up and said, "Someone opened the gate and the dogs got out. Did you notice anyone in this area?"

Daryl came down the stairs, the Sam Spade trench coat now replaced by scruffy jeans and a slightly soiled dress shirt. His feet were bare. I realized he was not as young as I'd assumed when I first saw him. There were fine lines around his wide-set eyes and a crease in his forehead as sharp as the one in the colonel's trousers. There were a few traces of gray in his collar-length hair, which looked as shiny as it had when I'd seen him in the rain. Then it had been wet; now I assumed it was simply dirty.

"So you're playing detective," he said to Culworthy's back. "I didn't know you'd been in military intelligence, if you'll excuse the inherent contradiction of the phrase."

Culworthy's neck turned red; the spoon clattered in the bucket. I gave Daryl a stern look and said, "Did you see anyone down here in the last few days?"

"There were a couple of girls who've been in the house several times. They must be taking care of the dogs for the old lady."

"Why didn't you volunteer to do it?" I asked. "After all, you're right upstairs, and it wouldn't have been much trouble to feed the dogs for your own landlady." Thus relieving wishy-washy bookstore proprietors from the obligation.

"I sometimes stay in the computer room at the college for two or three days at a time, surviving on stale sandwiches and coffee from the vending machines. Miss Emily knows it and was worried that I might forget the dogs." He gave me a concerned look. "She's devoted to them. I hear her out in the yard, talking to them and tossing a ball and that sort of thing. I hope you get them back before she comes home."

"Nice you noticed," Culworthy growled. "The plaster's thickening. Back, both of you. Must proceed cautiously and follow proper procedure in order to secure the evidence."

Daryl and I obediently stepped back so Culworthy could proceed cautiously, etc. We were all standing around the white puddle when Vidalia appeared.

"Have any of you seen Astra?" she demanded shrilly.

"In your window yesterday," Culworthy said. "Looked like she was napping."

"I mean today," Vidalia said. She was dressed

pretty much as she had been when I first saw her, and now the hem of her skirt was threatening the puddle of plaster.

I caught her arm. "Your cat disappeared today?"

"Oh, yes, and I am so very distraught. I've had Astra for twelve years, ever since she was a tiny kitten no bigger than a ball of fuzzy yarn. She's always had the finest food, and she has her own wicker basket right by my bed with a matching bedspread. Whatever shall I do?"

Unlike my imagined scenario with Miss Emily, Vidalia had no intention of remaining dignified in the face of disaster. She was twisting her hands together and moaning steadily; tears clotted in the mascara and ran down her face in black ribbons. Culworthy and Daryl looked totally bewildered by this histrionic display, so I tightened my grip on her arm and pulled her around to the front yard.

"Tell me about Astra," I said.

"At dawn this morning I let her out for her playtime. She loves to chase the birds; her little eyes are so very merry when she comes to the door and demands to be let inside. Even her yowls are merry."

"And she disappeared?"

"It's entirely my fault," Vidalia moaned, beginning to rock back and forth and hiccup like a coffee percolator. "I was doing her chart. With Virgo rising, it's been an exciting month for both of us, and I was making an adjustment when I realized I'd been working all morning and it was almost time for our lunch. I went to the backyard, but Astra wasn't anywhere to be seen. I called for her, and then walked all the way down to the library and over to the supermarket. What do you think could have happened to poor Astra? She's delicate. Do you think some vicious dog could have. . . ?"

She began to crumple. I caught her, realizing under all the ruffles and accessories that she was very small and thin, and helped her to the porch. She sank down and buried her face in her arms, yowling but not at all merrily.

Culworthy appeared. "What's wrong with the woman?" he barked, although I could hear concern under his gruffness.

"She let Astra out this morning, and she ran away," I said.

"No, she would never do that," Vidalia said between sobs and hiccups. "Astra never leaves the yard. Well, once she chased a squirrel into the next yard, but she came back and apologized."

"Damn shame," Culworthy said. He sat down next to Vidalia and patted her shoulder. "Shouldn't think she went far. She'll be back for dinner."

"I have a nice piece of fish for her. She does so love it broiled with a bit of butter."

I frowned at Culworthy. "Could Astra's disappearance have anything to do with Miss Emily's dogs? It's hard to overlook the coincidence."

Vidalia wiped her face with a tissue from her cuff. "Emily's dogs have disappeared, too? This is dreadful, simply dreadful. Whatever will she do when she returns home?"

Before I could think of a response, Caron and Inez trudged up the sidewalk to the porch. In that they were unaccompanied by basset hounds, I sighed and said, "Did you knock on every door in the neighborhood?"

Caron nodded. "Nobody's seen the dogs. There's a lady up the street who says her dog is missing, too."

"I wonder," I said slowly, "if the animal control officer might have been in this area."

"Like the dogcatcher?" Caron said, turning pale. "He took the dogs to the pound to asphyxiate them?" She sounded seriously upset, but I suspected it had more to do with the upcoming rock concert than the fate of anyone's pets at the local Auschwitz.

"And poor Astra—she's dead?" Vidalia began to cry again.

"Nonsense," said Culworthy, giving me a dirty look. "No one asphyxiated Astra."

"Of course not," I said, then stopped as I heard a thud, followed by an expletive inappropriate for my daughter's tender ears. We all hurried around the house to the side yard. Daryl Defoe was sprawled in the mud. All around him were fragments of plaster, ranging from hefty pieces to pebbles.

"What the hell?" Culworthy demanded.

"The plaster had set, so I was going to bring it around front. I didn't realize how heavy it was and how slippery the ground is," he said, embarrassed.

I stepped over his legs and searched for the footprint. All I saw was smushy mud. "You managed to destroy not only the mold, but also the original print," I said.

"It was an accident."

Culworthy snorted. "Damn convenient one."

Daryl got to his feet, slapping at the mud on his jeans and shirttail, and sending angry looks at all of us. "I don't know what Colonel Culworthy meant by that, but if you think I made the footprint when I opened the gate to let the dogs out, and then destroyed the evidence by staging a fall, you're wrong. Dead wrong."

It was a terse yet accurate description of my

thoughts. However, there was no point in mentioning as much, so I told the girls to wait in the car and led Vidalia back to the sidewalk. "I'm going to the animal shelter now," I said. "I doubt there's an animal control officer on the planet who's capable of catching Astra, but I'll make sure that she's not there."

She gave me a watery smile. "How very kind of you. I think I'll pop the codfish in the broiler and study Astra's chart for a clue to her behavior. Virgo rising can make her mischievous, especially as we approach the cusp. You can imagine how animated she is when Pisces intrudes; I tend to believe she thinks she can catch the fish somehow. But you know how cats are, don't you?"

"Oh, yes," I said vaguely, having no idea how cats were and not eager to learn. I assured her I'd report if I learned anything about Astra, then went to the car.

"We are going to the animal shelter," I said as we pulled away from the curb.

Caron shook her head. "You may be going to the animal shelter, but I have this incredible amount of algebra homework. We are talking pages and pages of these screwy quadratic equations. It's going to take hours and hours—minimum."

"I thought we were going to Rhonda's," Inez contributed from the backseat. "Didn't you tell her we—"

"I have all this algebra homework," Caron said hastily.

"And I have your ticket in my purse," I said.

Caron stuck out her lower lip, but she had enough sense to avoid further self-incrimination and we drove to the animal shelter at the south end of Farberville.

The building was made of concrete blocks and was set in the middle of an unpaved lot. Someone had made an effort to lessen its general aura of starkness with pots of begonias on either side of the door. I parked beside a small pickup truck with a covered bed and grilled windows. There were two other vehicles in the lot, one a hatchback and the other a much-abused, ancient Cadillac with the soaring tail fins of the fifties.

"I'm waiting here," Caron said. "I'll throw up if I have to look at a pile of dead animals."

"No, you're both coming with me," I said as I dropped the car keys in my purse and clicked it closed. "This is an animal shelter, not a death camp. They pick up runaways and take care of them while the owners are being notified."

Caron stared at the building. "There's probably this big oven they kill the dogs in. And the dog-catcher looks like Quasimodo, only worse."

"What do you think he does with the dead bodies?" Inez said in a hollow voice.

"I'm sure he'll give you some if you ask sweetly," I said as I got out of the car. The two followed reluctantly, and we went inside to meet Quasi.

There was a small reception room, with standard office equipment behind a counter. Directly in front of us was a door that, based on the cacophony coming from behind it, led to the kennel. The door on our left had a sign that read DIRECTOR.

As I hesitated, a petite woman with sensible dark hair opened the door, looked over her shoulder, and with a scowl, said, "You're driving me crazy, and I don't know how much longer I can put up with this. You might as well go sleep it off. If you show up in this condition one more time, you're fired. Finito. History. Understand?"

Muttering to herself, she continued into the office and saw us. Her dark eyes narrowed for a moment, then relaxed. Her scowl was replaced with a pleasant smile. "I'm Jan Gallager, the director. We're closed, but I'll do whatever I can for you."

"We're looking for a couple of canine criminals," I said. "The gate was left open. I thought they might have been picked up by the animal control officer."

"Not today," she said with a trace of tightness. "He hasn't been out and he's incapable of picking anything, including his nose. When did your dogs get loose?"

I glowered at Caron and Inez, who were still waiting for a hunchback to come through the door with a wheelbarrow of carcasses. "We aren't sure," I admitted. "Any time in the last forty-eight hours."

The scowl wasn't back, but the pleasant smile was gone, too. "Let me get this straight, please. You say your dogs could have disappeared any time in the last forty-eight hours, right? You haven't seen them since then, or bothered to feed them?"

I felt as though I were facing a parole officer who'd heard rumors. "They're not my dogs. I was taking care of them as a favor, and then my daughter took over the job. She reported their absence this afternoon."

Jan put her hands on her trim hips and looked at the guilty party. "You last saw the dogs forty-eight hours ago? You didn't feed them and supply water yesterday? Animals deserve proper treatment. How would you like to skip two days of meals?"

"I had someone go by yesterday to feed them," Caron said.

"Was the food still in the bowls today?"

Caron shook her head. "No, so they must have gotten loose last night or today."

"Unless," Inez said, always eager to help, "Rhonda's brother just pocketed the money and didn't feed them."

Jan looked as if she were about to launch into a well-deserved lecture when we heard a crash from her office. Wincing, she said, "I'm having a bit of trouble with one of our part-time employees. Go have a look at the dogs in the back and see if yours are there."

She went into the office and slammed the door. Caron and Inez gave me piteous looks, but I squared my shoulders and said, "Come on, girls. Let's get this over with." I ordered myself to open the door, recoiled as the miasma of urine and disinfectant enveloped me, and led the way into a room with cages on either side.

Most of the dozen cages held several dogs. Some were barking, while others lay despondently on the concrete floor. A litter of fluffy brown puppies began to dance about, yapping excitedly and floundering into one another.

"Aren't they precious," Caron said as she bent down to look at them.

The sound, the smell, and the quickly discovered information that Nick and Nora were not present resulted in a headache. "Precious," I muttered as I went into a smaller room. Here I found cats in boxes. I did not find Astra. The final room had boxes of supplies, brooms and mops, and an army cot with a gray sheet and a limp pillow.

Jan was looking through a notebook when we returned to the reception room. "No luck, huh?" she said sympathetically. "Maybe we'll pick them up tomorrow and impound them. Give me a description, the address from where they escaped, and your telephone number. I'll call you if they show up."

I did so, but when I mentioned Miss Emily's street, she flipped to the previous page in the notebook and said, "I thought that sounded familiar. Here's another report of a missing animal from that area this morning. Damn that man!"

"You know who it is?" I said, startled.

"I don't know who's stealing animals, but I know where they're likely to end up," she said in a fiercely cold voice. "I'll bet my skinny paycheck that Newton Churls is back in business. He swore he wasn't buying local animals, and the sheriff was more than eager to believe him."

"I don't understand."

"Newton Churls is the owner of NewCo. He's a Class B dealer and has a place out east of town." She caught my blank look. "He's licensed to sell random source animals to laboratories and medical schools for research—and we're not talking which dog food tastes better. The National Institute of Health gives away over three and a half billion dollars of your tax dollars so researchers can cut animals up, cripple them, blind them, burn them, infect them with diseases, and in general torture them. Over seventy million animals die this way every year so that someone can determine that you really shouldn't drink paint solvent or put it in your eyes."

"This is legal?" Caron gasped. "They can do this to people's pets?"

"Yes, indeed. The dealers are licensed by the USDA, but rarely inspected. They're not allowed to knowingly buy and later sell stolen pets. Every now and then one is reprimanded for filthy conditions and inhumane treatment. Churls no doubt has a wonderfully repentant expression when he's promising to do better. It doesn't stop him from selling someone's beloved pet to a med school so they can see how long the dog can live with nails in his skull."

"That's horrible," I said, struggling not to visualize Nick and Nora on an operating table. "But medical research is necessary, isn't it? That's how we develop and test new drugs that will save people's lives. A child with leukemia deserves all the help he can get."

"Some of it may be necessary," Jan said. "However, the NIH is eager to give away money and not at all eager to ascertain if the proposed research is duplicative, inapplicable, irrelevant to humans—or if it's conducted in a humane fashion." She held up her hands and smiled. "Sorry, I'll get off the soapbox now."

"What about that Churls man?" Caron demanded. "If he stole Miss Emily's dogs, we've got to call the police."

"He doesn't steal dogs; he's much too cunning for that. He buys them from people and doesn't ask questions about the source. When we see a pattern of thefts in a neighborhood, we suspect there's a buncher working it."

"A buncher?" I said.

Jan grimaced and said, "A middleman who picks up strays and answers 'free to good home' ads and notices. When things get lean, he may start collecting pets from backyards. He sells them to someone like Churls, receiving twenty to thirty dollars for a dog and half that for a cat. Churls then sells the animals for as much as a hundred dollars for dogs and seventy-five for cats. Last year Churls dealt with nearly five hundred dogs; we estimated he made forty thousand dollars."

"And you think a buncher might have sold the

Willow Street animals to Churls?" I said. "What do we do now? Should we call the police?"

"It's not that simple," she said, sighing. "It's the county's jurisdiction, so you'll have to call the sheriff. He'll tell you that he can't search NewCo without probable cause. He's wrong, because the USDA guidelines say that the dealer must cooperate with any citizen who suspects a pet is there, probable cause or not. The sheriff will refuse to send a deputy with you, which means Churls won't let you inside the property and might come at you with a shotgun. It's happened before."

"Mother," Caron said. That's all she said, but the implication was that I'd best do something about this dreadful mess.

"You have to do something, Mrs. Malloy," Inez said earnestly.

I shrugged at them. "I suppose we could stage a commando raid at midnight. Scale the fence, open the cages, and run like the wind."

"He has pit bulls that he lets out at night," Jan said. "I suggest you talk to the sheriff and—"

The door of the office banged opened, and out staggered a man with unfocused eyes, wet, flaccid lips, a nose that might have shamed Rudolph, and an overall aura of seediness. His wrinkled cowboy shirt was missing half its snaps, and his jeans were so baggy they threatened to slide down his skinny hips. He moved in a haze of alcohol.

To my regret, I recognized him. To my deeper regret, he recognized me and lifted up a whiskey bottle in salute.

"Wowsy," he managed to say, "it's the senator."

3

Jan, Caron, and Inez were staring at me as if I'd grown a horn in the middle of my forehead. This was not an inappropriate response to hearing me being identified as a senator, and by this rather poor product of mutant genes and dedication to alcohol.

"Hi, Arnie," I said weakly.

"You know this man?" Caron said, as scandalized as only a teenager can be when confronting a parent's foibles.

"'Course she does," Arnie said as he stumbled around the counter and collapsed in a chair. "The senator and me go way back, don't we? Just the other day I was saying to myself, Arnie, I said, you ought to give her a buzz and see about doin' lunch one of these days. Got some questions about the capital gains legislation."

Inez was peering at him from behind the safety of the counter. "I know who this is," she said in a thoroughly awed voice. "And so do you, Caron. It's that man who was supposed to drive the convertible in the Thurberfest parade. He was so drunk that your mother had to drive, and somebody tried to assassinate the senator and that beauty pageant queen."

From Jan's expression, it was clear she was making some distasteful connections between her drunken employee and yours truly. I managed a faint smile and said, "It happened a long time ago, and I was assisting the local authorities in a murder investigation."

"That's not what Peter said," Caron said. "He said you were meddling and that one of these days you were going to find yourself in a cold cell—"

"It was a little joke," I said.

"I don't think so, Mrs. Malloy," Inez said thoughtfully.

An explosive snore caught our collective attention. Arnie's chin was on his chest, and the bottle was tilted at a perilous angle. He was in no condition to make further inquiries about potential luncheon engagements. More snores rattled the blinds on the window and set off the dogs in the adjoining room in a frenzy of barks and howls.

Jan gazed at him for a minute, shook her head, and said, "I must have been out of my mind to hire him, but our budget was slashed right down to the carotid and he was the only applicant willing to work for minimum wage and a cot in the back room."

"He's not an animal control officer, I hope," I said, remembering his penchant for early morning tippling and erratic driving.

"He was hired to assist with the animals and serve as a night watchman. But I'm down to two trained officers, one of whom is scheduled for major surgery, so Arnie has responded to a few emergencies. When he's sober. A very few emergencies have met that criterion, I'm afraid, but there's nothing I can do until I get the staff reorganized."

"He's the dogcatcher?" Caron said.

"The mind reels," I said, nudging her into motion. "Thanks for letting us in after hours and telling us about NewCo. I'll call the sheriff and do my best to elicit some help."

We left Jan to deal with Arnie. Once we were in the car, Caron lapsed into moral outrage. "What are you going to do about that terrible Churls man, Mother? You can't let him sell poor Nick and Nora to a laboratory where they'll be subjected to torture. This is worse than Nicaragua—or El Salvador or one of those places. Nick and Nora are political prisoners, you know. They have rights."

She kept it up all the way home, with occasional mumbles of support from the backseat. It was a refreshing break from Mousse, I thought glumly, but an erumpent social conscience in a postpubescent mind can be a dangerous thing. I was trying to decide on a course of action, but I was also battling with tendrils of pain between my temples and increasing sore ears.

I finally assured them I would take definitive action in the morning, shooed them into Caron's bedroom, and mused over scotch, water, and aspirin. I went so far as to devise a scheme in which three lads with spiky orange hair, armed with amplification speakers the size of refrigerators, descended on Newton Churls's property. It worked with Noriega, after all.

The following morning, however, I made a quick detour by Miss Emily's house in hopes the dogs had returned, ascertained they hadn't, and went to the Book Depot to call the sheriff.

Said person, one Harvey Dorfer, listened to me until I ran down, then said, "We can't go onto the property without a search warrant, and we can't get a search warrant without probable cause. Sorry, but it's the law."

"What about the USDA regulation that says you can?"

"State law says we can't, ma'am. Now if you'll excuse me, I got to see a man about a horse."

"Wait a minute," I said. "Federal law supercedes state law. Remember that little altercation back in the middle of the nineteenth century? It was called the Civil War, although I'm quite sure there was nothing civil about it."

"Seems I heard tell about it. Our side lost, didn't it? Well, those things happen, and as I said, I got to see a man about a horse." He hung up on me before I could get out a mere sputter, much less an eloquent tirade.

I fumed while one of my favorite customers, a glazed hippie of indeterminate years, wandered around the science fiction rack and ultimately bought the book with the warrior and the slime. I dislike catch-22 situations, and this one was a doozy. The sheriff wouldn't cooperate, and the vile Churls person did not sound as if he would be eager to give me a guided tour of his facility. All the while, Miss Emily was on a guided tour that soon would arrive at its zenith and start back to Farberville, where she presumed she would be reunited with Nick and Nora—since she had entrusted them to a responsible bookseller.

Keenly aware I would have to face self-righteous indignation when school was dismissed, I locked the store and drove to Miss Emily's house with an obscure hope. The dogs were not in the front yard. I went through the house, frowned at the untouched bowls of dogfood on the back porch, and was heading for my car when I heard the abbreviated version of my name, as in, "Malloy!"

"Yes, Colonel Culworthy?" I said, stopping reluctantly.

He strode across the yard, his face as gray as his stubbly hair. He was wearing the khaki jumpsuit with bedroom slippers, which hinted of the level of his distress. "Patton's gone."

"Did you—ah, inadvertently let him out of your yard?"

"No. After what happened around here yesterday, I made sure the gate was secured. Did the final inspection myself, before retiring. Patton was in his doghouse. Now he's gone." He was attempting to bluster, but I could see he was deeply upset.

I repeated what the animal shelter director had told me the previous afternoon and the sheriff's less than encouraging response, and this did nothing to slow the twitch in his eyelid or add color to his face. "I guess I'd better talk to Vidalia," I concluded.

"Must take action. Must organize, devise a strategy, force entry," he said, looking more lively as he no doubt formulated overt military action involving howitzers and tanks.

"Right," I said. We went across the street to the red-bricked apartment building that Vidalia had told me she inhabited. Culworthy seemed to know the terrain; he marched up to the door on the end and rapped his knuckles on it. After a moment he rapped again with the fury of a machine gun.

"Colonel Culworthy and Claire," a voice trilled from behind us. Vidalia was coming down the sidewalk, accompanied by a man and a woman. "You must speak to the Maranonis about this dreadful situation."

I was introduced to Helen and George, who were both in their sixties. George was tall and lanky, with

41

impressive silver hair, and his expression was as mild as a sleepwalker's. There was, however, a glint in his eyes behind thick lenses as he appraised me from head to toe, and his smile seemed a shade wicked. Helen was short, busty, and forthright.

"Vidalia told us about Astra and Emily's bassets," she said briskly. "Let me tell you what happened to us yesterday. Juniper, our standard poodle, slipped out of the fence some time back and engaged in an illicit liaison with an unknown male dog. It resulted in a litter of six."

"Cute little things," George said, wiggling his eyebrows at certain of my anatomical protrusions. He reminded me of an emcee on a Las Vegas stage. I didn't find myself overcome with dislike, but I wasn't about to wander down a dark alley with him, either.

Helen gave him a dark look, then said, "When the pups were six weeks old, we ran an ad in the paper, offering them for free to good homes. Juniper's pedigreed, but we had no theory of the paternal influence. Yesterday afternoon a man who claimed he lived in the country came by and took the whole litter. He was very interested in Juniper, and asked questions about her age, weight, and general health. This morning she vanished, too." She gave George another dark look. "None of this would have happened had I been at home. I spent the day visiting a dear old friend in a nursing home."

"Patton's gone," Culworthy said.

I repeated Jan's dire prediction, which resulted in much handwringing and moist blinking, and eventually demands from all concerned as to how to proceed.

"The sheriff refused to cooperate," I said.

"Surely you know someone, George," Helen said. "You were in government until retirement."

"I worked at the post office for forty years," he explained to the rest of us. I alone was blessed with a wink. "I'm not sure the postmaster can intercede."

"Can't see that'll do any damn good," Culworthy growled. "Need a show of firepower. Force this dealer to allow us to inspect the facility."

We were back to howitzers and tanks. Before he could elaborate, I said, "The primaries are coming up next year. Perhaps if we met with the sheriff as a group, and then threatened to contact the media, we might pressure him into action."

"We can stage a demonstration," Vidalia said, clapping her hands excitedly. "We'll take our lunches and refuse to leave until he relents."

"Demonstration!" Culworthy snorted. "Lot of that in the late sixties, early seventies. Pinko liberals and commies, if you ask me. Lacked courage to fight for their countries. Sat around and whined like babies."

Vidalia fluttered her hands in protest. "They were very sincere in their beliefs, Colonel, and dedicated to the cause of peace. I don't think it's fair to categorize them as communists and babies. You never see babies crawling down the street with picket signs."

"Didn't say they were babies," he sputtered.

The one person who could really liven up this escalating brawl came around the corner, heard us, and crossed the lawn in front of the apartment house. "Any luck finding Miss Emily's dogs?" he asked.

Culworthy snorted and turned his back. Helen and George had retreated earlier, but now they both began to tell Daryl about Juniper and her offspring.

Vidalia told him what I'd learned at the animal shelter. Culworthy made staccato remarks about draft dodgers and commies who were like babies, not actually babies. Although Daryl was listening to Vidalia, he was managing to toss out acerbic responses to the colonel.

The yapping, barking, growling, and whining reminded me of the noise at the shelter. "Stop it, all of you!" I said sternly. "This isn't going to get your pets back!" When everyone quieted down, I reiterated my suggestion that we descend on the sheriff en masse and demand his assistance.

"Do you think it'll work?" Vidalia asked.

"I know it will," I said grimly. "I'll bring Caron and Inez."

Two hours later we had formed a caravan and were driving out the highway east of Farberville. Sheriff Dorfer had proved to be more astute than I'd surmised from our previous exchange; when confronted with the mob, he'd quickly decided that one of his deputies who lived in the vicinity of NewCo could, and would, accompany us. Deputy Rory Amos was to meet us at the turnoff and protect us from Churls's renowned ill temper.

Vidalia had promised to bring the sheriff a plate of cookies the following day. She was now riding with Colonel Culworthy in his vehicle, which was the civilian version of a green military jeep. Daryl was riding in the Maranonis' station wagon. I wasn't sure why he had aligned himself with us, but I wasn't opposed to increasing our bulk.

Beside me, Caron was working herself into an exquisitely shrill dither. "He ought to be shot. The idea of taking puppies makes me sick, literally sick."

"We don't know that the puppies are there," I said

mildly. "We don't know that Nick, Nora, and the other pets are, either. I don't think we should shoot him on first sight."

"Well, I do," she huffed.

"Are you going to tell your mother about biology?" Inez said from the backseat.

"Later," she snapped.

I braked slightly to allow a sports car to pass, then resumed a mundane speed. "We have plenty of time right now, and I like to take an interest in your academic progress."

"It's no big deal," she said, taking great interest in the cows in the pasture. "You may get a telephone call in the next day or so, that's all."

"That's all?" I murmured. "Someone at the high school desires to chat with me?"

"Sort of chat."

I gave her a quick look as I settled behind a pickup truck loaded with concrete blocks. "Sort of chat about what?"

"Oh, you know."

"But I don't, and I'm beginning to wonder if I do want to know." Before I could turn on the full maternal thrust, I spotted the dark blue pickup truck I'd been told to watch for. I pulled over to the shoulder, as did the two cars behind me. Telling the girls to wait, I went over to the driver's side, where a young man in sunglasses sat impassively, and said, "Are you Deputy Amos?"

He gave me a thin smile. "Yes, ma'am, and you're the . . . the woman Sheriff Dorfer called about?" It was clear Dorfer had used a more colorful description, but I chose not to pursue it and nodded. "Okay, then," he continued, "you all follow me. Churls's place is a good six or seven miles down the road.

When we get there, everybody needs to park outside the gate and stay together. And I mean it."

We drove down a degenerating dirt road, winding past sloping pastures, a few surly houses and mobile homes with no mobility (except, perhaps, during a tornado), and finally arrived at a steel gate blocking the road. In the middle of it was a crudely painted sign: Pit Bulls Loose Three Days a Week. You Guess Which Three.

Caron and Inez were subdued as we got out of the car. The others arrived, and they seemed equally disinclined to comment on the gate and its sign. Deputy Amos, thin and inclined to twitch, studied the group, then said, "Churls has a nasty temper, and he's liable to be hostile about allowing us on his property. I know you folks are worried about your animals, but stay with me and don't challenge Churls. Let me ask the questions, okay?"

Everybody nodded. Amos went to the gate and shouted, "Churls! We're here from the sheriff's department!"

Beyond the gate was a narrow dirt road, little more than a path through the weeds, and at the end of it, a stark house. A white Lincoln was parked alongside a pickup truck in the yard, and on one side of the house was a satellite dish to suck in shows from the sky. A whisp of smoke drifted out of the chimney.

The only response to Deputy Amos's call was a dispirited bark from an unseen dog. He waited for a minute, repeated his message, and shrugged at us. "Sheriff Dorfer said he'd called Churls to let him know we were coming."

"Did he remind Churls of his legal obligation to allow us to search for the missing animals?" I asked.

The group nodded and muttered similar sentiments, although no one looked as if he were prepared to climb the gate and march up to the house.

"I'm sure he did," Deputy Amos said. He went to his truck and honked the horn several times. "Maybe he's inside and can't hear me. The one thing we can't do is set foot on the property until he admits us. I don't want to run into any pit bulls roaming around."

"Probably bluffing," Culworthy said.

"He's not bluffing," the deputy said with a wince. "We've had reports that he breeds and trains them here, and takes them to Oklahoma for the actual fights."

"That's illegal!" gasped Caron.

"It sure is, little lady. Only the fights take place in another state, so it's out of our jurisdiction. There's nothing illegal about owning pit bulls."

The little lady was about to respond when the door of the house banged open and a man came out on the porch. He looked at us for a long time, then went back into the house. When he returned, he was carrying a shotgun and wearing a cap. He came across the yard and approached the gate.

"Newton Churls, at your service," he said with a sneer. He was elderly, and dressed in dirt-encrusted overalls and a stained shirt. A potbelly jiggled as he shifted his weight from foot to foot, and tufts of oily gray hair stuck out from under the cap and protruded from his ears. With his lip curled back to expose brown teeth, he reminded me of a shriveled monkey.

"Sheriff Dorfer called?" said Deputy Amos, advancing from his truck.

"Reckon he did." The sneer slipped for a brief moment, and Churls looked startled. "Reckon he did," he repeated lamely, "but he didn't tell me who all was coming. I didn't expect to see . . . a crowd. Upsets the animals." He took a pinch of tobacco from a can and deposited it in his cheek, but he seemed puzzled by our presence.

I wasn't sure if I'd witnessed something or not. When Deputy Amos remained silent, I said, "And the sheriff explained that according to the USDA regulation, you must allow citizens to search for their missing animals?"

"Reckon he did. But there ain't no reason, because I don't take stolen animals." He spat on the ground. "It's against the law to traffic in stolen animals."

"Then exactly where do you get animals?" I said in my most withering tone.

"I pick up strays on occasion, and I buy animals from the shelter in the next county. Every animal on the place has a USDA registration number, missy, and I got a right to sell it to anybody willing to meet my price."

"Let us in, Churls," Deputy Amos said. He was attempting to sound authoritarian, but his voice was on the high side and I realized he was closer to twenty years old than thirty. A grizzly, overweight veteran would have been more comforting.

"If the animals were obtained legally, then it shouldn't disturb you too much," I added.

Churls spat again. "You're doing plenty of disturbing already," he muttered, "but let's get this damn thing over and done so I can get back to work." He used a key on the padlock, opened the gate, and gestured for us to enter.

"What about the pit bulls?" Colonel Culworthy said from behind Vidalia.

"I've heard they can be vicious," she said as she scuttled behind him. If they kept it up, they were likely to end up at the highway, I told myself as I glanced nervously around the yard and woods surrounding it, having heard horror stories about pit bulls myself.

"Suit yourselves," Churls said. He tossed the padlock up and caught it. "I ain't got all day."

Helen Maranoni gave her husband a push. "Let's go look for Juniper, George. She's apt to be terrified."

"She's apt not to be here," Churls said, cackling nastily.

Daryl Defoe's cackle wasn't much politer. "What's the matter, Colonel Culworthy? I guess they don't call 'em chicken colonels for nothing . . ."

Enough, I told myself. I smiled grimly at Caron and Inez, stuck out my chin, and walked through the gate. When a pack of crazed dogs failed to beset me, I continued up the rutted driveway to the yard. Everyone drifted along behind me; from their murmurings, I knew they were keeping a lookout for the pit bulls.

In the side yard was a low metal structure with a corrugated tin roof and heavy chain-link fencing. Concrete walkways went between rows of cages, each with a crude doghouse or metal drum to provide shelter. Most of the fifty or so cages held three or four dogs, some silent and others making a peculiar wuffly noise as they jumped against the fence.

"Why don't they bark?" Caron said.

Churls replenished the chewing tobacco in his mouth and said, "The vet comes out every week and we cut their vocal cords. The racket'd drive me crazy."

"You do what?" I said, horrified.

He spat once again. "You heard me. Now look for your dogs and get the hell off my property."

Helen looked at her husband. "If he's done that to Juniper, I shall never forgive you."

"Neither will I," he said quietly.

Vidalia took the colonel's arm and they went down one of the concrete walks, looking sadly into the cages. The girls and I went down another. The fence rattled as the dogs flung themselves at us, and the pathetic noise grew louder as we passed the cages. The smell was unspeakable. A few dogs lay in mud and filth, their coats matted and spotted with mange. Flies buzzed about and settled on eyes, snouts, and dishes containing the dried remains of food. A small beagle wagged his tail at me for a second. At the end of one row, Vidalia despondently studied the cats.

"This is disgusting," I said angrily to Deputy Amos, who was on my heels. "This place passes inspections and is licensed?"

"The state doesn't have an inspector at the moment," he said. "To tell the truth, I've seen worse. But I'll fill out a report and give it to Sheriff Dorfer, and maybe he'll send it to one of the regional offices."

The group came out of the labyrinth and stood in a huddle, mute and horrified. Churls waited nearby, spitting on the grass and cradling the shotgun in his arms like a puppy. I started toward the back of the house.

"Where the hell do you think you're going?" Churls snarled as he hurried after me and grabbed my arm. His black fingernails bit into my skin.

I stopped. "Take your hand off me this instant or I

will shove your teeth down your throat," I said without inflection. "I am aware you have a gun. If you so much as glance at it, I will take it away from you and put it in a place that will prove most uncomfortable." As the words came out, I realized I was courting death, but I was so incensed by the man and his captives that I didn't even blink.

The hand was removed. I continued around to the backyard, where I saw a large pen constructed of the same heavy chain-link fencing. Three pit bulls paced the concrete floor, each watching me with suspicious yellow eyes. Considering there were only three, there seemed to be a large quantity of teeth contained in lethal jaws. From the roof of the pen dangled a rope, and as I drew nearer, I saw that its end was frayed and stained with blood.

Deputy Amos joined me. I pointed at the rope and said, "What's that for?"

"Training." He glanced over his shoulder, then continued in a low voice. "It can get real bloody."

I was getting real nauseous myself. "How dangerous are these dogs?" I asked, watching them pace in the pen.

"Plenty dangerous," he said, keeping a watch over his shoulder. The others had come out of their zombielike trances; I could hear Culworthy harrumphing and Caron opining loudly about the conditions. No one else had followed us, though. "Churls raised them, so he can handle them unless they're agitated. Don't take much to do it, and he's real leery about going in there. Personally, I wouldn't set foot in there with my weapon drawn and a bullwhip. Those jaws lock onto your neck, you're a goner."

Shuddering, I moved away from the pen and looked around to see if there might be more dogs in view. All I saw was a rusted car on concrete blocks, a shed with broken windows, piles of weathered lumber, beer cans and plastic wrappers, and a lone chicken pecking at hard earth.

I started to turn back when I saw Daryl move to the shed. He stopped and crouched down for a minute, as if anticipating an assault, then opened the door and vanished inside it. Seconds later he came out, a cardboard box in his arms, and went around the far side of the house.

"Guess we're done, huh?" Deputy Amos said. "No one recognized a pet, so Churls must be telling the truth when he says he doesn't deal with stolen animals anymore."

"If he buys dogs from bunchers, he wouldn't know, would he?" I heard a bark in the distance; it seemed to originate from the wooded hillside beyond the fence. I started for the back of the yard, but a loud argument erupted in the area where I'd left the others, and I veered toward them.

Helen Maranoni was advancing on Newton Churls, her face contorted with rage. She was holding the box, and from within it came excited yaps. "You perverted, evil monster! How could anyone think of hurting these innocent babies?" Flecks of spittle spewed out of her mouth like a mist of acid rain.

Churls was backing up handily. "You got no business looking in my shed. I bought those pups."

"To bait your pit bulls! How could anyone do such an evil thing!" Helen demanded so loudly I suspected the entire county could hear her.

"They ain't stolen," said Churls as he backed into the side of the house. "Besides, none of them is hurt."

I hurried to Caron's side. "What's going on?"

She looked at me, her eyes spilling over with tears. "He had Juniper's puppies in the shed. Daryl says sometimes the trainers use poor little puppies to give the pit bulls a taste for blood."

As I gaped, Culworthy and Vidalia moved to Helen's side, and a second later Daryl and George swelled the ranks. All of them began to berate Churls, who was trapped by the house and looking increasingly frightened. His eyes were narrowed to slits, and his snarls were now bleated avowals of innocence.

I would have been quite pleased if the group tore him to pieces, but Deputy Amos appeared to have reservations and shoved his way to Churls's side. "Stop this," he snapped.

"This man is a murderer," Helen said. "He planned to kill Juniper's puppies. I demand to know how the litter came to be here."

Churls had found some courage from the deputy's presence. He spat, barely missing Helen's shoe, and said, "Some guy or other brought 'em last evening. He told me they was given to him, and I had no call to disbelieve him. I thought they were cute little things, and I was going to keep 'em. If you're claiming they were stolen, your beef's with him, not me."

"Arrest this man," Helen said to the deputy.

"That's right," Vidalia added, although without a trace of trill. "It must be illegal to treat animals this way."

"I was going to keep 'em for company," Churls insisted.

I believed that the same way I believed the solution to all my problems was aluminum siding. However, I wasn't surprised when Deputy Amos said,

"There's no proof that he was going to do something bad to the puppies."

Helen bristled and said, "We demand that he return the puppies to us right now. Furthermore, I want the name of the man who brought them here. I intend to file charges with the police."

Churls had found enough courage to juggle the shotgun into prominence. "I didn't know him from dog piss. First time I ever saw him, and most likely the last. Now, I've had enough of you folks. I let you look around, and you didn't find your animals. Take the runty things and get off my property—it's time for me to let the pit bulls have their daily exercise."

We trudged back to the gate. Helen was crying, with her husband holding one arm, and Vidalia clutching the other. Daryl carried the box. Culworthy marched behind him, his expression thoughtful. Even Caron and Inez seemed too distressed by the scene to offer editorials.

Deputy Amos and I were at the tail end of the processional, which was as lively as any funeral. In a low voice, I said, "Isn't there anything you can do to stop him?"

"No," he said, sighing. "We've had complaints before, but there isn't any way to catch him in the act and we've got to have proof before we can move in. Like I said, I'll write up a report. Maybe the boys in the regional office will do something. Most likely they won't."

"I heard a dog barking in the woods. Isn't it possible he took our animals away from the main area?"

"Possible ain't probable cause."

"But if we came out here unannounced," I said, becoming excited, "he wouldn't have an opportunity to relocate the animals. If we found them in pens, we'd have proof he's dealing in stolen pets."

"If you come out here unannounced, you're going to find three pit bulls running loose," he said flatly.

"There is that," I said under my breath. I realized Culworthy was staring back at me. He looked away quickly, but not before I noted his pursed mouth and the unnaturally bright eyes of a warrior.

I wasn't sure if he'd overheard my conversation with Deputy Amos. If he had, I was quite sure it meant trouble for a mild-mannered and unassertive bookseller.

4

On the way back from NewCo, we stopped at Miss
Emily's to see if Nick and Nora were lying on the
porch. They weren't. While Caron and Inez made
small talk with the violets, I went into the living
room and sat down on a prickly puce settee, or whatever it was, dug through a decade's accumulation of
magazines and catalogs for the telephone directory,
and called the animal shelter.

Jan reported that none of the missing animals had
been picked up and brought there. I told her about
the confrontation with Newton Churls, adding that
he was by far the nastiest human being I'd encountered in my thirtysomething years. "Helen Maranoni
was demanding his death," I concluded, "and although I'm opposed to the death penalty, I didn't
hear myself protesting."

"He is vile, isn't he? I'm opposed to the death
penalty, too, but if ever anyone were to change my
mind, or at least cause me to question my position,
Churls is the one. I've heard stories of him bragging
about how lucrative his business is. He claims the
Lincoln was bought from profits from dogfights, and
he's been known to drink a lot of whiskey and carry
on about all the cash he's got squirreled away at that
filthy place. Talk about blood money . . ."

Shuddering, I said, "He mentioned that he bought

dogs from an animal shelter in the next county. Has he ever tried to acquire animals from you?"

"He tried once," she said with a harsh laugh. "I grew up out that way and I recognized him. The first thing I did when I took over was raise the adoption fees and require a lot of paperwork and a personal interview. I think Churls had a deal with the previous director or one of the officers. The records were haphazard at best, nonexistent at worst. Strays, and sometimes pets, were picked up but not logged in. Churls or one of his bunchers would come by at night, select the animals, and pay a small gratuity that never made it to the petty cash box. Now every animal is assigned a number when it's brought in, and we track it through its departure. A tail count is performed every morning and every evening."

I tried to imagine one of her less sober employees on his knees in front of the cages, trying to count a bouncy litter of puppies. "How's Arnie?" I asked. "Did he straighten up?"

"He wouldn't straighten up if someone inserted a ramrod in his rear," she said, sighing. "I desperately need to replace him, but the salary's low and not too many people want to wash down dog pens for minimum wage. And we must have a night watchman to make sure someone like Churls doesn't try to pull a fast one. We have drugs on the premises, too."

"He's not armed, I hope?"

"Only with those developed in the womb, presuming he didn't crawl out from under a rock."

She promised to call if she learned anything, and we ended the conversation on a gloomy note. Caron and Inez had passed through the room earlier, so I called farewell to the violets and went out the front door.

What I saw was enough to stop a herd of buffalo in the middle of a stampede. Caron and Inez were in the adjoining yard, and included in the group of Culworthy, Daryl Defoe, Vidalia, and the Maranonis. George held the box of puppies, and his wife periodically leaned over to smile at them. Daryl was talking—and Culworthy was listening intently. Odder and odder, I thought as I walked toward them.

Seven faces went blank and Daryl stopped talking. It was not the warmest reception I'd had, and was in fact cooler than my last interrogation at the Farberville Police Station, when I'd been obliged to admit to a lack of candor in an official police investigation.

"Well?" I said.

Culworthy snapped to attention, catching himself before he actually saluted. "Ah, Malloy. Any luck at the shelter?"

"No, Jan hasn't seen any of the missing animals, but she promised to call if the officers find them." I looked at each of them in turn, on the off chance my ESP had improved greatly in the last day. "What were you discussing?"

There was a pause fraught with awkwardness, and therefore hinting of impending deceit. "The stolen animals and that horrible man," Helen answered, but not at all briskly.

Vidalia sniffled. "And he might get his filthy hands on Astra. She has never been kept in a cage, and she'll be badly frightened. I can't bear to think about it." She sniffled more loudly as she fumbled in her cuff for a handkerchief.

"Then don't think at all," Culworthy snapped. He looked at Daryl and said, "Talk to you later, Defoe. Come by at nineteen hundred hours." He muttered a generic good-bye and marched into his headquarters.

"Why did you look in the shed?" I asked Daryl.

"Too many cages." He went up the stairs to his apartment.

After another awkward pause, Vidalia trilled something about searching once more for Astra and wafted away, her scarf fluttering behind her like a gossamer blue ponytail.

"Come along, George," Helen said. "We must feed the puppies. I'm sure that man gave them no attention. Aren't they sweet?"

I put my hand in the box and let it be attacked by rough little tongues and teeth as sharp as knitting needles. "Can you describe the man who took the puppies?"

"I was at the nursing home when he came. Otherwise, this never would have happened, I can assure you. I'd have asked questions about this farm and demanded to see his driver's license. I'd have required references." She gave us a moment to appreciate her purported efficiency, then gazed stonily at her husband. "George dealt with him."

George smiled benignly. "Yes."

"The baseball game," she prompted him.

He looked down for a minute and scratched his head. "That's right. I was watching the game and dozing when he came. Ordinary fellow, said he'd parked down the street a ways, said he liked dogs."

"But what did he look like?" Caron said abruptly.

"Ordinary."

In a steely voice, Helen said, "Go on, George—tell them the truth."

I would have felt some pity for him, if he hadn't looked so guilty. About what, I had no theory. He shuffled his feet, rubbed his jaw, and finally said, "I wasn't wearing my glasses. I took them off and was sound asleep when the doorbell rang." He put the box down on the grass, took a pair of wire-rimmed bifocals from his pocket, cleaned them with a handkerchief, and settled them on the bridge of his nose.

"He couldn't bother to find them," Helen said.

"And I'm blinder than a bat without them," he continued. His expression reminded me of Nick and Nora after they'd beset me the first day. Repentant, but not necessarily with measurable sincerity. "The man was average, and he sounded like a regular guy. I told him how Juniper had escaped while in heat and that the puppies were half poodle and half whatever was loose in the neighborhood that day. He asked me some questions about Juniper; I just thought he wanted to make sure she'd had all her shots and was in decent health. When I told him the puppies were in the backyard, he said he'd get them himself so as not to disturb me anymore."

Helen crossed her arms. "Thus giving him an opportunity to examine the gate and consider how best to steal Juniper during the night."

"You don't keep her in the house at night?" I asked, surprised that Juniper didn't have her own bedroom and private bath. This was my first serious encounter with pet owners, and I was beginning to grasp their devotion to their animals. Astra had a basket with a matching bedspread and preferred her fish broiled with butter. Patton no doubt had an air-conditioned doghouse, carpeted in khaki. Nick and Nora's daily dinner took twenty minutes to prepare, and Miss Emily had noted in a postscript that a nice piece of filet mignon might brighten them up if they seemed depressed by her absence.

With an edge of accusation, Helen said, "George put in a doggie door so Juniper could go out whenever she wanted. She was very restless all evening, missing her puppies, and went outside numerous times to look for them. I attempted to soothe her with warm milk, but when we retired, she was pacing fretfully. I slept late the next morning. George discovered Juniper was gone after he returned from the grocery store."

"The doggie door was your idea," George said defensively.

I realized how simple it would be to stick a piece of meat through the doggie door in order to lure the dog outside. Unlike Churls's pit bulls, all the missing animals were friendly and accustomed to kindness (and little treats) from humans.

A shiver ran down my back, as if Miss Emily's bus had driven over my grave. I told the Maranonis to call me if anything noteworthy happened, and the girls and I went to the car. They were both very quiet and thoughtful, two characteristics uncommon in the last two years of melodramatic outbursts, egomania, and unfettered verbosity.

"What was Daryl saying when I came out of the house?" I asked Caron.

It took her a moment to concoct a lie worthy of her innate talents. "We were talking about putting up posters at the grocery store and the library."

"Oh, really? Colonel Culworthy seemed interested in what he was saying," I persisted. "I didn't understand his comment about the cages, though."

"I didn't notice," she muttered. She twisted around in the seat and said to Inez, "I'm spending the night with you tomorrow, right?"

"You are?" Inez said, startled.

"Yes. Remember how we're going to make missing dog posters so we can put them up Saturday? We were just talking about it, for pity's sake, Inez. What are you doing back there—giving yourself a lobotomy with your nail file?"

"I was worrying about Nick and Nora," she said with a trace of spirit.

"Which is why we have to make posters," Caron said with a lot of spirit. "Remember?"

They bickered until we dropped Inez off at her house, and then Caron turned surly, another talent, and refused to say anything beyond "I don't know" or "Beats me." When we arrived home, I found a postcard from Miss Emily. The lavender script informed me that she was having a wonderful time and was bringing me a small desertscape she'd painted herself. The front of the card depicted unsmiling Indians in expensive costumes that were probably made in Taiwan, as was the postcard.

The realization that she'd be home in two weeks did not warm my cockles, presuming I had cockles. The realization that the pet owners were up to something wasn't all that soothing, either, especially since they'd decided to exclude me from the plan. The plot, I amended. The harebrained scheme. Howitzers and tanks. I knew that Colonel Culworthy had not been listening to Daryl discuss posters at the grocery store; anything that kept the two from arguing had ominous significance.

I wished Peter was in town. I glanced at the unoccupied half of the sofa and sighed, then fixed myself a drink before I lapsed into perilous thoughts. He and I were oil and water, not oil and vinegar. But at that moment, I felt very much alone, and had he been there, might have explored the possibility of vinaigrette.

The following day was a Friday, and usually a fairly decent day at the Book Depot. Caron had taken an overnight bag with her to school and vowed that the Willow Street neighborhood would be plastered with posters by noon Saturday. I made an unrewarded run by Miss Emily's, then went to the store where I found my hippie waiting under the portico of the bookstore. He snuffled around like a bloodhound and left without buying anything. A woman with the scrunched-up face of a Pekingese and a gratingly shrill voice pawed through the counted cross-stitch pattern books and scolded me for the mess on her way out the door.

The sudden compulsion to categorize people as animals struck me as a symptom of mental degeneration, but I couldn't control myself. Not when a well-coiffed Siamese cat bought a cookbook, while her two pointy-chinned children whined the entire time and almost knocked over the nonfiction rack. The next customer, a squatty, rumpled wino with a runny nose, had to be a bulldog, I decided as I took a dollar from the cash register and gave it to him, that being the most expedient way to rid the store of the noxious redolence that accompanied him.

I was having such fun that it took me a moment to realize the next customer was neither canine nor feline in essence, but was Daryl Defoe in a trench coat.

"Hi," I said, feeling justifiably foolish.

"I saw you come by Miss Emily's house this morning," he said.

"I was nurturing a wild dream that Nick and Nora had come home during the night, wagging their tails behind them. They hadn't."

"Then you don't think they're at NewCo?"

I waited while a sheepdog in sunglasses bought a study guide and left. "I don't think there's any evidence to prove that," I said carefully. "We didn't see them. Churls could be telling the truth."

"Was I telling the truth when I said the plaster mold slipped out of my hands?" He came to the counter and grasped the edge of it. His lips were pinched together so tightly they quivered, and a thunderstorm seemed to be gathering in his eyes.

"I don't have any reason not to believe you," I said, concerned for his blood pressure.

"Culworthy as much as accused me of dropping it on purpose. The only motive for doing that is to destroy the evidence and protect the identity of the person who let the dogs go free."

"Was it your footprint?" I said bluntly.

"I don't know." His intensity evaporated, and he stared at his white knuckles as if they belonged to someone else. "I live there, and I use the stairs several times a day. Maybe I dropped something and went near the gate to pick it up. I like Miss Emily. I wouldn't put her dogs at risk—even if she kept them locked up."

"How about Colonel Culworthy's dog? I saw you go around the corner of the house, and minutes later Patton charged the car."

His mouth moved indecisively as he looked at me. At last he said, "There's something I'd like to explain to you. It'll take some time. Could we maybe have a beer tomorrow after you close the store?"

"How about tonight?" I said innocently, remembering his appointment at nineteen-hundred o'clock or whatever Culworthy called it.

"I can't tonight. Tomorrow at seven?" When I nodded, he left hurriedly.

I was very intrigued by his desire to explain anything at all to me. I understood the others' motives;

they were distraught about their pets. Petless Daryl, on the other hand, had insinuated himself into the group, despite his dislike of Culworthy, and was apparently involved in whatever scheme they had devised.

I pondered the matter the rest of the day, closed the store as the beer garden across the street began to draw customers like a magnet, and walked to my apartment. There was a postcard from Miss Emily that extolled the beauty of the Southwest and mentioned her growing fondness for tequila sunrises at sunset. There was a short note from Peter, mentioning how crazy his mother made him and how crazy I made him in an altogether different (and presumably preferable) way. He hoped to be back in Farberville Sunday.

I called Luanne Bradshaw to see if she wanted to see a movie, but there was no answer, and after a minute of thought, I remembered she'd gone out of town to visit her daughter. No one else I could think of sounded interesting, so I resigned myself to an uneventful evening of news, weather, and a cozy mystery novel. One of the joys of being single.

I was reading the newspaper when the telephone rang. Supposing it was for Caron. I picked up the receiver and in a desultory voice, said, "Hello."

"Mrs. Malloy, this is Lydia Horne. I'm sorry to have to call you this late in the day, but we had a teachers' meeting after school and Mr. Higginbotham rambled for hours about the shop budget. Then my car battery was dead, and I had to wait until my husband got off work to rescue me with jumper cables."

"Sorry to hear that," I said.

"It happens," she said. "In any case, Caron's situation was discussed at the meeting, and I'm afraid we'll have to follow the policy."

"Wait a minute," I said, paying more attention. "Are you one of Caron's teachers?"

"Her biology teacher. Didn't she consult you about her stand and the possibility of expulsion?"

I rubbed my face with my free hand, trying to recall the conversation in the car about biology. It hadn't gone anywhere beyond a vague reference to an impending telephone call. The receiver was in my hand, and it seemed the ball was in my court. "Expulsion?" I echoed cleverly.

"You mean she hasn't told you what I said in the middle of the week? I'm surprised to hear that, Mrs. Malloy, especially considering the severe consequences of her action. I assured her that I understood, and to some degree sympathized, but I had to warn her that the faculty disciplinary committee might vote to uphold the administrative guidelines."

"What are we talking about, Mrs. Horne?"

"Why, Caron's refusal to dissect a frog next week in lab."

"Did she offer a reason?"

"She spoke very eloquently about her position as an animal rights activist. I myself was impressed, and as I said, felt some sympathy. But Biology I is mandatory for all sophomores, and one requirement for a passing grade is full participation in all lab assignments. No exceptions are allowed, and failure to comply with a teacher's explicit instructions is grounds for expulsion."

I reminded myself of my earlier observation concerning the danger of an erumpent social conscience—or the convenience of a politically defensible posture when confronted with the pristine white belly of a dead frog.

"I'll talk to her," I said grimly.

"I wish this wasn't a problem. We encourage the students to take responsibility for themselves and their environment, and to develop a personal philosophy to guide them. Then we turn around and tell them to ignore their beliefs and follow the rules. I was rather surprised by Caron's vehemence, but none of us can predict what's going on inside a teenager's mind, can we?"

I assured her that I certainly couldn't, told her I would talk to Caron immediately, and agreed to come to the high school Monday morning for a conference with the principal. None of this left me in a good mood, and the more I thought about my daughter's transformation from oblivious to all creatures great and small to dedicated animal activist, the more I doubted the sincerity of her stand. Which was going to get her expelled from school. Conferences, tedious meetings, the expense of legal representation, the tuition at the nearest (or farthest) convent—all of it because she didn't want to examine a racine interior in the name of knowledge.

It was almost a rite of passage, I told myself. One could not make the transition to adulthood without the obligatory hell of pimples, neurotic teachers, dim-witted parents, back-stabbing best friends, and the opportunity to cut a frog into little bitty pieces in Biology I.

I decided to call and delicately inquire into her motives before I ripped out my hair or overindulged myself in scotch, both appealing possibilities. Inez's mother answered the phone, and I asked to speak to Caron.

"The girls are planning to spend the night at your home tonight," she said. "They told me they were going to make posters of some sort."

"I must have misunderstood," I said, not yet ready to alarm her. "I'll call Rhonda Maguire's house and see if they're painting in the garage."

Once I'd hung up, though, I didn't bother to look up Rhonda's number because I knew damn well they weren't there. Mentally vowing to ground Caron for the rest of her life, I picked up my purse and went to pay a little visit to Willow Street.

It was after eight o'clock. Miss Emily's house was dark, downstairs and in Daryl's apartment. Culworthy's house was dark, too, and no one answered my insistent knock on Vidalia's door. I wasn't sure where George and Helen lived, but I doubted it mattered since I had a strong theory as to their collective whereabouts.

They were being attacked by pit bulls or being blasted by a shotgun. Or both.

Vascillating between anger and fear, I sat in my car and tried to decide what to do. If Peter was in town (and I seemed be thinking that much too often recently), I could have called him, explained the situation, and elicited at least token police protection while storming NewCo. The sheriff, off duty by now, would not be happy to hear the group was trespassing and dodging vicious dogs and shotgun pellets.

The sheriff had sent Deputy Rory Amos with us because he lived near NewCo. I drove to a convenience store and found his name in the telephone book, although the address was of the route and box variety and therefore of no help. Crossing my fingers, I called the number.

Deputy Amos answered. I quickly explained the situation, then listened while he cursed under his breath for a long while. He finally exhaled loudly and said, "You're right to suspect they're in danger.

Churls won't hesitate to loose the dogs and the law's on his side." He described his house, one of those along the NewCo road, and told me to get there as quickly as possible.

The half hour it took to drive to his house seemed like an eon, having entertained myself with ghastly images of Caron, Inez, pit bulls, and reconstructive plastic surgery. Deputy Amos lived in a small, bleak box. Lights were on inside, as was the porchlight he'd told me to watch for. I hurried to the door and knocked.

A young woman in tight designer jeans and a translucent blouse opened the door. Her short, dark hair had been coached into an elaborate style that included wings and a frizzy cascade of bangs. Her makeup was equally artistic, if heavy-handed. "He went down the road apiece to listen for gunfire," she said in a high, breathless voice, her chest heaving slightly as if she were expecting a handsome encyclopedia salesman. "You're supposed to wait here."

In that she did not move, I assumed she meant on the porch. "Are you Mrs. Amos?" I said.

"It ain't legal, but we've been living together for three years, ever since I got out of school." Tapping her foot impatiently, she glanced at her watch, leaned forward to look at the darkness behind me, and scowled. "I'm already late to meet some friends at a bar in Farberville. Tell Rory I may decide to sleep over at Darla's tonight and I'll see him when I get back."

She went past me to a mud-splattered sports car parked beside Deputy Amos's less remarkable truck. Minutes later the taillights blinked a farewell as she drove toward the highway. I went to the edge of the road, displeased at the instructions to wait, and finally got in my car and drove in the opposite direction to the NewCo gate.

My headlights caught Deputy Amos standing in the ditch. He was in uniform, and to my relief, armed. I parked, then went over to him and said, "Did you hear anything?"

"The dogs sound pretty excited, but I haven't heard a shotgun," he said, trying to sound like a grown-up cop but not succeeding. "I ran down here soon as I got your call. Could be you're wrong about the folks coming back here at night. They didn't look completely crazy."

Declining to debate that issue, I went to the gate. A light atop a utility pole beside the house shone on the cars and truck parked in the weedy grass. The house was lit from inside, but drapes blocked the windows and there was no indication whether Churls was home or not. The dogs, however, were definitely there; I could hear a discordant symphony of wuffly barks, growls, and howls. The sound chilled me.

"We've got to go in there," I said frantically. "My daughter and her friend are there with the others. Is your gun loaded?"

"I don't know what Sheriff Dorfer's gonna say about this," he groaned. "I tried to get hold of him, but he didn't call me back, so I guess he's out of pocket. This is trespassing, sure as we're standing here."

I climbed over the gate, halted within reach of it in case I was to be attacked by pit bulls, and then went toward the house. I could hear Amos as he clattered over the gate. He was still panting as he caught up with me, but neither of us had anything to say.

The dogs in the corridors of cages reacted to our

arrival with varied degrees of interest. Some barked or leapt against the metal fencing; others did not move at all. A few were so engrossed by the noise from behind the house that their heads did not turn. The barking and howling came from these captives, I realized as I struggled for air; the pit bulls in the pen were growling like bulldozers on an uneven terrain.

We raced around the corner of the house and froze. The dogs were in the pen, attacking a figure sprawled on the concrete floor. Blood splattered as one swung its head up, a hunk of flesh in its mouth. Another was latched onto its victim's throat. Even with its jaws clamped shut, the dog managed to growl in a rhythmic drone. The third bounced frenetically from one end of the body to the other.

"My God," I said, clutching Amos's arm. "Stop them!"

His face was ghostly in the dim light, and his voice broke like an adolescent's as he said, "There's someone in there."

I shoved him forward. "You've got to stop them. Shoot them!"

He took his gun from the holster, grasped it with two shaking hands, and shoved the barrel through the fence. He hesitated so long I wanted to leap on him, screeching, but at last three rapid gunshots exploded in the night. The growls did not stop. He fired three more times.

The growls ceased. The dogs in the cages in the side yard were startled into silence.

My ears reverberating with the sound, I forced myself to approach the pen. What was left of Newton Churls did not move. No flicker of life could be seen in his eyes, widened in fear and pain, nor in his curled, bloodied hands. His clothing was shredded and stained with blood. The dogs were slumped on him; the one clamped on Churls's throat had not loosened its jaws even now. Blood seeped from the ragged blacks holes in their sides, dripping onto the floor to mingle with what was already there.

Deputy Amos sank down in the grass and placed his gun on the ground in front of him as if the pen were a shrine. "Oh, my God," he said in a stunned voice. "Oh, my God."

I was gulping back acid, and my voice was no more in control than his. "There's no question that he's dead." My knees buckled sharply, and I sat down beside Amos. The silence was as suffocating as a heavy blanket. I closed my eyes, but the red spatters were impossible to escape and I felt myself beginning to sway.

"Oh, my God," Amos repeated. He said it several more times before he began to cry silently.

5

I don't know how long Deputy Amos and I sat on the grass outside the pen, his gun in front of us and the only sound the screeches of a bird far away in the woods. We were still there when the dogs at the side of the house began to make their strange wuffly noises.

"Mother?" said a thin, terrified voice.

I didn't turn around. "Are you and the others unharmed?"

"Yeah, we're okay. What happened. . . ?"

Their feet shuffled as they came nearer. I recognized Culworthy's snort, Vidalia's gasp, and Daryl's stunned voice as he said, "Holy hell, there's someone in there."

A muffled cry was followed by a retching noise; whose, I did not know or care. The low babble expressed shock and horror. I patted Deputy Amos's shoulder and stood up. The commandos were dressed in dark clothes, and their faces were smeared with black makeup. In different circumstances, I would have found them comical. Now, in the shadowy light, they looked like ghouls. "Newton Churls is in there," I said. "His dogs attacked him, and Deputy Amos had to shoot them."

"Is he dead?" asked Inez faintly.

I nodded. "Very much so."

Helen was holding onto her husband's arm, and she propelled him along for support as she approached the pen. "This is terrible. We can't just leave him like that."

Vidalia was hanging onto Culworthy's arm, but rather than propelling him, she was dragged along as he came forward and said, "Damn indecent to leave him there. Accident, but his fault for having vicious animals, I should say. The breed's known to attack, have to expect it."

"This was no accident," I said. "It was murder."

Deputy Amos struggled to his feet. "Murder? These dogs are trained to attack. He baited them with puppies and cats so they'd develop a taste for blood. Even a trainer's not safe with them, and Churls damn well knew it."

"I'm going to throw up now," Caron announced calmly, then covered her mouth and ran to the back fence. Inez followed her at a prudent distance.

"Why murder?" Culworthy snapped.

"Surely it's an accident," said Vidalia, nodding.

I ignored them and looked at Amos. "There's a padlock on the cage door. Newton Churls may have gone in there for some reason, but he wouldn't lock himself inside the pen with the dogs."

Amos went over to the lock and grabbed it. "We've got to get this off," he said, yanking at it so frantically that the whole pen rattled.

I shook my head. "You'd better call the sheriff."

"He plays poker on Fridays, and he's not gonna like this."

"Neither, one assumes, did Newton Churls."

He went into the house through the back door. The commandos regrouped nervously, except for Caron, who was clinging to the fence while Inez patted her back. "Well, did you find any proof your animals are here or have ever been here?" I asked angrily.

Culworthy cleared his throat. "No proof, actually."

"What, actually?" I said.

Helen was still hanging onto her husband, but she had regained some of her composure. "We weren't here long enough to put the complete plan into action. George and I were to see if we could find any animals being kept in the woods, but he forgot to check the flashlight batteries before we set out. He returned to borrow a flashlight. After a few minutes, I became nervous and followed him. That's when we heard the gunshots."

Daryl Defoe said, "I took down license plate numbers and went around to the shed to see if there were any more animals there. All I found were some busted cages."

"Colonel Culworthy and I were making a list of those POW animals," Vidalia said, fluttering her hand toward the side yard. "We thought we might present it to the director of the animal shelter, in case she might recognize one from her reports of stolen animals."

"I didn't see either of you," I said. "Deputy Amos and I walked past the cages."

"I might have ducked into an empty pen for a moment."

Culworthy's face was black, but his ears were red. "Thought I heard a noise, like someone escaping into the brush. Went to the edge of the woods, stood there."

"With his back to me," Vidalia added graciously. "He was ever so polite."

I was not. "Who allowed Caron and Inez to accompany you on this idiotic mission?"

"I argued with them," Daryl said.

"They were most insistent," chirped Vidalia. "All of us did our best to dissuade them, but it did no good whatsoever. Caron said something about alerting you and the sheriff if they were left behind."

Blackmail while in her minority. By the time she was twenty-one, who could begin to imagine the depth and breadth of her felonious mind? Colonel Culworthy was bending over the padlock, grumbling to himself, and the others were moving closer to the pen. I suggested we wait for the sheriff in the front yard.

We were doing so on the porch when lights flashed in the road beyond the gate. Doors slammed, and the gate was rattled unsuccessfully. "Deputy Amos!" the sheriff shouted.

I stood up. "He's in the house."

"Tell him to find the key for this damn lock, and not to take all night about it!"

I went into Churls's house. The living room was furnished in Early Salvation Army. The couch was lumpy, its upholstery worn to nothing in some areas and splotched in others. The plastic cover on the recliner was peeling like sunburned skin. The coffee table was littered with beer cans, cigarette butts, and wads of paper. The television set, however, took up most of a wall and was clearly state-of-the-art, with a control panel that might have come off a 747. Even to those of us unenamored of technology, it looked very expensive.

"Deputy Amos?" I called.

He came through a doorway. "I was about to go out the back door. Is the sheriff here?"

"He wants you to find the key to the lock on the gate. There're several vehicles, and I suppose they need to have access to the . . . yard."

"There's a board with keys in the kitchen. What's more interesting is what I found on the kitchen table."

He retreated, and I followed him with a bemused look. Lieutenant Peter Rosen had his minions so well trained that they would swallow their tongues before they'd give me the time of day. Deputy Amos, a truly cooperative chap, wanted to share his newly discovered evidence with me.

There was a battered metal box on the table. It had been pried open and its contents removed. "This is interesting," I said as I bent down to study it. "If it belonged to Churls, he wouldn't have had to force the lock. It either belongs to someone else, or someone else did this to it."

"I checked the house," he said nervously, "and there's no one here. No one else living here, from the looks of the bedroom."

"It's hard to envision a Mrs. Churls," I murmured. I went to the board on the wall and squinted at the coarsely printed labels below each key. I plucked one and said, "Here's the one the sheriff needs. And while I'm thinking about it, your—ah, the woman at your house said to tell you she's spending the night with a girlfriend."

"I'll be here all night, anyway," he said with a grimace. He sat down at the table, looking very young and vulnerable in the yellowish light from above. "I've pulled a couple of bodies out of car wrecks," he said, almost apologetically, "but we practically walked into the middle of this one."

"Why would the dogs attack like that?" I said.

Before he could answer (if indeed he could answer), Culworthy came to the doorway and said, "Sheriff wants the key. Sounds agitated."

Amos made a face at me, took the key from my hand, and went out of the room. Culworthy pointed at the broken box. "What's this?"

"I don't know if it's anything of importance," I said as I started to leave. I took a second look at the keyboard as I passed it; as I'd thought, the key labeled "dg pin" was hanging in its place.

The sheriff had parked on the lawn and was getting out of his car as we came out the door. The blue light was still rotating, illuminating faces for a dizzying brief second. Sheriff Dorfer halted and gaped. "What's with the clown makeup?"

Culworthy, Vidalia, and the Maranonis had attempted to wipe the dark greasepaint off their faces, but Daryl still resembled a vaudevillian actor from a racist era. Caron and Inez hovered in the shadows near the porch, their eyes white in contrast to their skin.

"Standard procedure," Culworthy blustered.

"Standard procedure for what?"

"Covert action."

The sheriff issued orders to his men, then took a cigar butt from his pocket and lit it, all the while glancing at each of us. He settled on me and said, "Care to explain about these escapees from the funny farm, Mizz Malloy?"

I contemplated throwing them to the wolves, or in this case, the sheriff, who was clearly irritated by either the interruption of his Friday evening poker game or the probability of a time-consuming murder investigation. But my daughter and Inez were co-conspirators, and I couldn't quite bring myself to do the dirty deed. I gave the sheriff a terse explanation of the reason they'd all been skulking on Churls's property.

Smoke curled from the cigar as the sheriff listened impassively. One of the deputies snickered, but stopped abruptly when the sheriff glared at him and retreated around one of the cars. The fin almost brushed his chin.

"I've seen that car before," I said, blinking.

"It was here when we arrived about an hour ago," Deputy Amos said, "but it wasn't here when we came a few days ago."

It finally came to me. "That car was parked at the Farberville Animal Shelter earlier this week."

"Whose is it?" demanded Sheriff Dorfer.

"I don't know. The director was there, along with one employee, who sleeps in a back room at night." I had a good idea which of the two drove a disreputable, gawdy car and which drove a clean hatchback, but I shrugged and the sheriff ordered one of the deputies to get the license plate numbers of all the vehicles and deal with the state bureau in the morning.

The sheriff peppered us with questions, but no one admitted to having seen or heard anything that related to the fatal attack in the dog pen. As I listened to a repeat recital of their activities, it occurred to me that each one of them had been on his or her own for a few moments, except for Caron and Inez, who'd been clinging to each other like Velcro. And Arnie was somewhere around the area, too, although no one had seen him and the excitement had not lured him out of hiding.

The commandos and I gave our names and addresses to a deputy and were then assigned times to report to the sheriff's office the following morning to make statements. Once dismissed, we straggled down the road to the gate.

"Where are your cars?" I asked.

"We all came in mine. Color of camouflage and impossible to spot at night. Parked behind a barn," Culworthy said smugly. "Couldn't alert Churls to our arrival. The barn serves as headquarters. Cut across the pasture and scaled the fence."

"We each were issued a flashlight," Vidalia said. "The colonel and Daryl were ever so careful in the planning. We were told what to wear and given orders. I'm sorry about that horrible man's death, but the rest of it was quite thrilling."

"Quite thrilling," George began sarcastically, then caught a look from Helen and stopped.

I ordered Caron and Inez to get in my car and drove away without further comment to the group. Caron took a package of tissues from the glove compartment and shared them with Inez. I was too shocked and bewildered to lecture them, although I assumed I would recover in due time.

"What are we going to do about Miss Emily's dogs?" Caron asked timidly.

"We were really, really sure they would be there," Inez said even more timidly.

"I don't know," I said. "The first time we came, Churls had been alerted by a call from the sheriff. If he had any stolen animals on the property, he had ample time to move them to another location. But not this time. You didn't see him, did you?"

Caron swallowed several times. "No, but Inez and I were so scared we sort of hung around by the place in the fence the entire time, just in case the pit bulls were loose. We were supposed to help list the animals with that gypsy person and that army person. We couldn't see the back of the house from there."

"Did you see anybody at all?"

"Everybody had these incredibly explicit orders. Once we were over the fence, we split up. All of them but that Defoe person thrashed their way toward the house, but he kind of melted into the dark. Then Inez thought she saw a bear, which was stupid."

"There are bears in this area," protested Inez. "If you'd paid attention in English when we did the section on folklore, you'd know it, too."

Caron opted to be gracious. "Yeah, like I'm sure the woods are crowded with polar bears. I'm surprised we weren't attacked by penguins. Anyway, it was seriously spooky, so Inez and I decided to wait."

"What about that car from the animal shelter?" Inez asked. "It probably belongs to that nasty man who was drunk. Do you think he murdered that other nasty man?"

"I don't know," I said.

"Why was he there?" Caron asked.

"I don't know."

"Where'd he go?" Inez asked.

"I don't know."

"Will the sheriff find him?" Caron asked.

"I don't know."

"Will they arrest him?" Inez asked.

"I don't know."

As the experts are so fond of reminding us in their learned articles in magazines lying around doctors' waiting rooms, with teenagers it's extremely important to be frank about one's limitations.

The next morning we made the now customary trip to Miss Emily's house, then reported to the sheriff's office at the designated time. The receptionist finished typing a sentence one key at a time, worked her gum into a less obtrusive location, and agreed to let the sheriff know we were there.

While we waited, Helen and George came down the corridor to the front room. George looked as if he intended to continue out the door, but Helen halted and said, "They didn't find Juniper or the others. They said there were some pens out in the woods, but there weren't any animals being kept in them."

"I'm sorry," I said gently.

"If only George had taken the time to put on his glasses, we'd have a better idea about the man who took the litter," she said as she gave her husband a cold look.

"I said I was sorry," he retorted.

"Would you recognize the voice?" I asked, not at all sure I could produce or reproduce Arnie's voice anytime soon.

"Whose voice?"

Annoyance flashed across Helen's face, but she kept most of it out of her voice. "The man who took the puppies, George."

He shook his head. "Nothing special about it, and the television was on beside the door. Despite the fact it was a shutout, the announcers were bleating statistics and pretending it was exciting."

"George is so conscientious," Helen said, rolling her eyes and smiling grimly. She took his arm and they left.

The gum-chewing receptionist returned and told Caron to follow her. I picked up a magazine and engrossed myself in a lengthy article about latest technological advances in radar guns and how best to utilize said data in court. Inez studied a dusty plastic plant for signs of life. Thirty minutes later the receptionist brought Caron back and took Inez away. Caron ignored my whispered demands to find out what she'd been asked, and went across the room to ascertain which department employees had been memorialized on a bronze plaque. Thirty minutes later it was my turn.

Sheriff Dorfer's desk was a wasteland of folders, papers, manuals, gnawed Styrofoam cups, burned matches, and an ashtray piled high with the smoldering remains of cigars and fat gray ashes. He presided over it like a rednecked Buddha, while a woman with a notebook sat in the corner.

"Mizz Malloy," he said sadly, "it looks like we've got ourself a murder, just as you suggested to Deputy Amos. I was real impressed with your powers of observation—so impressed that I asked a colleague in law enforcement about this observant woman bookseller. It was enlightening, what I heard about you. Damn near blinding."

"How very kind of you," I said, graciously electing to misinterpret his remarks. "Did you find the key for the padlock on the dog pen?"

He leaned back in his chair, propped one foot on the corner of his desk, and clasped his hands together on his rounded stomach. "What I heard about you," he continued blithely, "was that you stick your nose into official police business because you seem to fancy yourself some kind of armchair amateur detective."

"Amateur, yes, but I don't think it's fair to accuse me of idling away my time in an armchair, Sheriff Dorfer. When I read, I do so on the sofa or in the warmth of my bed. When I assist the police, I rarely do it at home."

"They didn't call it 'assisting,' Mizz Malloy. They

accused you of interfering and of meddling. Of almost getting yourself killed on more than one occasion. Of keeping secrets and even telling lies to the good ol' boys at the CID."

I gave him a rueful look. "I never would have characterized you as a common gossip. I must say I'm disappointed and may express the sentiment at the polls next fall."

"I don't care if you write in Elvis for sheriff," he said, now sounding a bit annoyed. "What I do care is that you get it through your head that I, unlike your detective boyfriend, will not tolerate you snooping around and trying to butt into my investigation. If somebody calls you to confess, you can pass it along to me, but if I hear one little word about you asking questions or talking to the suspects, I'll lock you up so darn fast your head'll spin till Halloween."

"Then shall I presume my daughter is not a suspect? Although a taboo on conversation with her has some appeal, it's not realistic on a day-to-day basis when I must inquire about her preferences for breakfast."

He took a cigar stub from his shirt pocket and lit it with great ceremony. "I can't see those girls pushing Churls into the pen with pit bulls," he rumbled through the swirls of acrid smoke. "He was an old coot, but he was wiry and tough from dealing with the animals."

"And with the bunchers who brought him stolen animals?"

Ashes cascaded down his shirt as he shifted his weight and glowered at me. "We don't have any proof he dealt in stolen animals. I believe I said as much to you on more than one occasion, and your friends didn't find hide nor hair of their pets, did they?"

"Did you find hide or hair of Arnie?" I asked nicely.

Things about his face seemed to bulge as if it were being inflated, and his red neck turned a shade darker. The stenographer opened her mouth, then clamped it shut and looked down at her notebook. I was about to inquire about his health when he said, "Thought you didn't know whose car that was, Mizz Malloy. You and I are getting off on a real bad footing, like two bullies on the first day of school. Thing is, I am the sheriff and you are the bookseller. When this interview is over, I'm going to conduct an investigation and you're going to sell books."

"I wasn't positive it was Arnie's car," I protested. "I suspected as much, but I didn't want to give you misinformation. Did you find Arnie out in the woods?"

"Not yet, but he'll turn up." Sheriff Dorfer took the cigar stub from between his lips, studied it for a moment, then jabbed it out in the ashtray. "Darla, wake up and get ready to take the lady's statement. I already heard all about the animals missing and your first trip to NewCo. Just tell about last night, and do it without embellishments."

I took pleasure in relating not only each step I'd taken, but every thought that had crossed by mind, from the mindless fear for Caron and Inez to my conclusions about the battered box and the missing key. The woman scribbled furiously, stopping me often to ask how to spell the polysyllabic words I was throwing in for fun. The sheriff sat in silence, his arms locked and his small dark eyes boring into me as if he doubted a sense of altruism was motivating me into such detail.

I finally ran out of such details and listened politely while he reiterated his threats of incarceration should I meddle. I nodded to the stenographer, who was limp and pale, and sailed out of the office without further attempts to annoy him. One can only go so far with unknown opponents.

The chairs in the front room were uninhabited. The receptionist shifted her gum long enough to tell me the girls had gone (left to my own devices, I never would have suspected this), and began to peck on her typewriter with one hesitant finger.

I stopped in the parking lot, savoring the spring sunlight and mild breeze, and considered what to do. In my mind was a twenty-one-day calendar, and each day since Miss Emily's departure had a red *X* on it. There were eight *X*s, and a hand hovered nearby with the pen of doom.

I finally decided I'd best open the Book Depot and hope I sold enough books to finance Miss Emily's prolonged hospitalization after she heard the bad news and collapsed.

I was sitting behind the counter, toying with phrases to explain my despicable lack of responsibility, when the telephone rang.

Jan Gallager sounded perplexed as she said, "Claire, what's going on? A deputy was just here, looking for Arnie. He's not here, and from the looks of the back room, he didn't sleep here last night. The deputy said Newton Churls had been killed by his dogs."

I gave her a synopsis of the situation, not burdening her as I had the witless stenographer. "Did Arnie ever mention Churls?" I asked.

"Not in my presence. Does the sheriff think Arnie locked Churls in the pen?"

"He was not inclined to discuss his theories with me," I said. "I can't see Arnie doing it, though. He's a wastrel and a drunk, but he lacks the essential energy required to be evil. I wouldn't accuse him of possessing a lofty degree of morality; he just bumbles along doing whatever seems most convenient and expedient."

"I suppose," she said doubtfully. "The deputies told me to arrange to have all the animals at NewCo brought here. I have no idea where we can keep them, since we're presently at ninety percent capacity. Do you know how many dogs I'm to pick up?"

I tried to remember the prisoners in the side yard. "There were more than a hundred the first time," I said slowly. "But I don't think there were that many last night. I wasn't doing any tail counts at the time, of course. However, I did notice some empty pens. That's strange, isn't it?"

"Not it there's been a sale between the two visits," Jan said.

"You mean Churls sold some of the animals to a lab?"

"They end up at a lab, but I'm talking about a middleman sale. The dealers take their animals to a specified location and sell them to buyers who have contracts with the labs. That's one of the things that defeats us when we try to locate stolen animals— they're liable to be three states away within a matter of days."

I bit into my lip, trying not to envision Nick and Nora on a truck heading for either coast and a great deal of unpleasantness. "Has there been a sale since the animals disappeared?"

"Now that I think about it, no. The sales we're aware of take place on Sunday mornings at eight o'clock. Members of the local animal rights group have attended some of them and were not at all welcome. One of the women was knocked down, and a reporter was threatened with a shotgun. One of the men required extensive dental work. The dealers don't enjoy being observed."

I checked my omnipresent mental calendar. "Is there any possibility the stolen basset hounds might be sold tomorrow?"

"If they were taken by someone other than Churls, they might be there. The only sale he'll be trying to make is in hell, and I doubt the devil himself will be bidding on that soul."

"But if we could go to the sale, we might be able to intercept the dogs before they're taken out of the state. Do you know if there is one this week?"

After a moment of silence, Jan said, "I don't have the information. Call Brian Runnels and see if he knows anything. He's active in the group. But you need to realize that this could be dangerous; those men are not benevolent businessmen. Even the ones who deal with animals from legitimate sources can become uncomfortable if they think they're being monitored."

I assured her that I would be prudent, then found Runnels's telephone number and called him. His wife said he was in his greenhouse but agreed to fetch him. He sounded amiable as he told me there was a sale the following morning in a tiny town. I scribbled down directions, trying not to express dismay at the purported five-hour drive to Guttler, Missouri. He sounded less amiable as he echoed Jan's warnings about possible danger.

"I'd go with you if I could," he concluded, "but my daughter's in a pom-pom squad competition and the finals tomorrow afternoon. We're taking a gaggle of them out to dinner afterward."

I thanked him for the information and hung up. A litter of college boys came in, but I lacked enthusiasm to categorize them as anything but nuisances and was still slumped by the counter when they wandered away.

It seemed important to attend the sale and look for Nick and Nora. Assuming Jan Gallager and Brian Runnels had not been trying to frighten me for their own dark purposes, it was likely to be dangerous. A woman by herself would provoke speculation, if not outright suspicion. Furthermore, I thought as I slid deeper into gloom, if I found the dogs, I would then be obliged to take action in order to retrieve them, and I would be doing so in the face of hostility and shotguns.

So I needed a date, in a manner of speaking. Peter was not available, and I certainly couldn't call Sheriff Dorfer and demand an escort. Caron and Inez would be of no use, nor would flighty Vidalia. Colonel Culworthy was not a tactful sort (snort, snort), and would have the dealers snarling at us within minutes of our arrival. George Maranoni was not an impressive presence. The process of elimination having worked well, I was down to Daryl Defoe. He was not burly, but he'd mentioned a year in Vietnam.

I was about to telephone him when a customer came into the store. Several others followed, and I was kept occupied for the better part of the afternoon. The beer garden was again beginning to draw a happy hour crowd by the time I'd dealt with the final trickle, and I remembered Daryl was coming at seven in order to confide in me. All I had to do was stuff him in my car and allow him to confide all the way to Guttler, Missouri, and with any luck at all,

all the way back while Nick and Nora drooled on his shoulder.

I took the CLOSED sign to the front door and was putting it in place when I happened to glance at the railroad tracks that ran along the west side of the Book Depot and the east side of the beer garden. A man in a baggy raincoat was trudging down the middle of the tracks toward Thurber Street. Stumbling, I corrected myself. He had a bottle in one hand, and he paused every few steps to take a drink from it. As he passed the wooden fence that protected freight trains from long-necked glass projectiles, I could hear him whistling.

The sign slipped out of my hand as I continued to stare at this familiar figure in a familiar state of inebriation. When he reached the edge of the street, he peered cautiously in both directions, then nearly stepped into the path of a convertible. The driver cursed, but Arnie took a mouthful of whiskey, sprayed it on the hood of the car, lifted the bottle in salute, and ambled ahead.

"Yo, Senator!" he said as he approached me. "How's it going?"

"Fine, just fine. Where have you been, Arnie?"

"Taking a hike. I've been taking a nice hike so I can enjoy the wonder of nature on this fine spring afternoon. Say, Senator, do you think I could avail myself of the facilities inside this fine establishment? The wonder of nature has created the call of nature, to put it delicate-like."

I escorted him to the tiny rest room in my office, snatched the bottle from his hand, and shoved him inside. By the time he emerged, I'd started coffee and hidden the bottle behind the self-help rack.

"Tell me more about your hike," I commanded as pleasantly as I could.

He cocked his head and sucked noisily on his lips. "Well, I got to admit certain details are a little bit fuzzy," he said. "I don't recall starting out, but we both know I did because you have to start somewhere, doncha? I mean, if you don't start, then you're sitting at home watching television and having a beer instead of out taking a hike to enjoy the—"

"Stop, Arnie," I said before I strangled him. It occurred to me that Sheriff Dorfer might feel I ought to call and report Arnie's appearance—rather than question him at my leisure. However, I poured my suspect a cup of inky coffee and settled him in the chair behind my desk.

"I remember dogs," he offered.

"The dogs at the animal shelter?"

"Yeah, I suppose." He took a sip of coffee and recoiled. "Wowsy, Senator, this is strong stuff. Maybe I better dilute it with a shot of whiskey. Does my bottle happen to be handy?"

"No," I said sternly. "Do you remember driving to NewCo last night?" When he looked even blanker than usual, I said, "The property owned by Newton Churls, an unpleasant man who traded in animals."

"He's something, ain't he?" He craned his head as he looked around the office for his bottle. "Ol' Newton Churls, huh? Now that I think of it, I did drive out there last night. Then I decided to enjoy the wonder of nature by walking back to town."

"In the dark? Come on, Arnie, you didn't see much nature while you stumbled down the railroad tracks. Why did you go out there in the first place?"

"I don't recall," he said loftily, although his eyes had flickered before he hastily averted them.

"Let me guess, then." I went to the desk and put my fists on it so I could stare down at him. "My guess is that you went out in the shelter truck earlier in the week and picked up some roving dogs. Some of these you assigned a number and duly delivered to the shelter. Others received no number and were deposited somewhere. Last night you took them to NewCo to sell to Churls. How am I doing, Arnie?"

He gave me a patronizing grin. "Just like a politician to get things addled up. Wowsy, you boys can't enact a bill without cluttering it up so bad it comes out like corned-beef hash." The grin turned sly. "But I might see my way to clear it up for you—if I could have my bottle back, that is."

Entertaining dark thoughts about the prevalency of blackmail, I fetched his bottle and banged it down in front of him. "Clear it up for me, Arnie."

He took a lengthy pull on the bottle, wiped his mouth on his coat cuff, and after a few false moves, got his feet settled on the corner of the desk. "I have been known to sell a dog or cat to Churls. I figure they're strays, gonna get killed at the shelter anyways, might as well let one of us come out smelling like a rose."

His redolence in no way evoked images of roses, but I merely nodded, and in an encouraging voice, said, "So every now and then you took an animal to Churls. I assume he paid you handsomely for your endeavor?"

"That old fart?" Arnie cackled. "He paid like the miser he is, which means he moaned and groaned over every dollar and whined about how he wasn't making spit for profit. Last night he wouldn't even pay me. He claimed he was broker than one of your basic homeless derelicts and said I'd have to come back next week to get my money. Can you imagine the nerve of that guy?"

"What animals did you take him last night?"

He scratched his oily hair while he struggled out of the whiskey-induced haze. "Oh, yeah, it's coming back. Last week I picked up a whole bunch of real good animals. Churls pays better for heavier animals, so I always keep an eye out for 'em. Anyways, I had four stashed in an old trailer not too far from the shelter, and last night I said to myself, I said, Arnie, if you want to celebrate the weekend in the manner to which you're accustomed, you'd better get some—"

Feeling as though I were in a freezer, I said, "Describe the animals, Arnie. Now."

"Two of those squatty dogs with the sad eyes," he said obligingly, then stopped as footsteps thundered from the main room of the bookstore.

Sheriff Dorfer filled the doorway, his gun aimed squarely at Arnie. Other deputies, all armed, were behind him, struggling to see over his shoulder.

"Arnold Riggles, you are under arrest!" the sheriff thundered. He slowly turned his head to gaze at me, and lowered his voice to a growl. "And you, Claire Malloy, are under arrest, too."

6

Being arrested was exceedingly inconvenient at that moment. Arnie didn't seem to mind, but I had more important things to do if I was to find Nick and Nora and thus save Miss Emily from terminal distress.

Sheriff Dorfer grimly recited the Miranda warning. Arnie said that all made perfectly good sense to him, and what with me being a politician and all, why, I'd probably heard it a zillion times at all those senate investigations.

"Once or twice," I said with a charmingly wry smile. "But don't you think this is a bit extreme, Sheriff Dorfer? Arnie appeared on the railroad tracks only a short time ago. I offered him coffee and was reaching for the telephone to call you when you stormed the gates, so to speak." I poised my hand over the telephone to emphasize how close I'd been to making the call.

He was not impressed. "You're harboring a fugitive, Mizz Malloy."

"No one told me he was a fugitive, so I wasn't harboring him. I was doing my civic duty by sobering him up while we waited for you."

"And impeding an investigation."

"He hasn't been here more than ten or fifteen minutes. It was a very minor impediment." I stopped and frowned. "How did you know he was here?"

94

"The police took a report from some college professor who almost ran over a drunk out front. The driver was not happy about the encounter, and he noted the drunk stagger into the Book Depot. Some bright officer thought the description sounded like our missing suspect and passed it along to us."

"How very astute of the officer," I murmured while I desperately tried to think how to extricate myself from the mess and hit the road for Guttler. Sheriff Dorfer was not in a cooperative mood, based on the ferocity of the looks being sent in my direction and the tightness of his finger on the trigger. I spotted Deputy Amos behind him and waved, but he looked away.

For the most part, I am a law-abiding citizen. I have been known to jaywalk, and have received my fair share of parking citations (an oxymoronic phrase), but I have always stopped short of flagrant disregard for our boys in blue, or in this case, khaki. It is possible I'm not as conscientious with a certain plain-clothed detective, but at the moment that was irrelevant.

Thanks to Arnie, Miss Emily's dogs had been at NewCo. They were no longer there. If someone else took them to the animal sale to be held in a little more than twelve hours, they could be in another state by noon tomorrow, and in a cold, stainless steel lab by evening. Arnie had mentioned four animals; the unspecified pair could be from the trio of Patton, Juniper, and Astra.

I resolved this moral dilemma and gave the sheriff a meek look. "I don't think you have cause to take me into custody, but I will debate it at your office—after I've contacted my attorney. Come on, Arnie." I grasped his shoulder and jerked him to his feet, and

95

we followed the sheriff out of the office. Arnie, a murder suspect, was handcuffed; I, a modest meddler, was deemed unworthy of hardware. As we paraded past the counter, I surreptitiously grabbed the piece of paper with directions to Guttler.

But not as surreptitiously as I'd thought. From behind me, Deputy Amos said, "What's that?"

"My last chance to save the basset hounds," I said honestly, then shifted gears. "Oh, fiddlesticks, I left my purse in the office. Be back in a jiffy."

Before he or any of the others could react, I dashed back to the office, snatched up my purse, and continued out the rear door. I was scrambling through the brush along the steep slope adjacent to the railroad tracks before I heard voices bellowing at me, and a good three blocks down the street before I collapsed behind a forsythia and dared to catch my breath.

I wasn't sure if I'd committed a felony, a misdemeanor, or a breach of etiquette. Sheriff Dorfer might be in the throes of an apoplectic fit by now, but I could not take responsibility for that. I also could not stroll back to the bookstore and hop in my car, I realized as I removed a prickly twig from my hair, nor could I go home and try to arrange to borrow a car.

Headlights approached. I huddled in the dry leaves beneath the bush and made all kinds of wild resolutions to be kept if I was not apprehended. The car passed by, thus obligating me to radical alterations in my life-style and Caron's, no matter how averse the latter was to adoption of the basic rituals of civilization, such as making her bed every morning. At the moment, however, I needed to do something, and I couldn't decide what it was, having had no experience being on the lam.

Sitting under a bush was not productive, but walking down the sidewalk was downright perilous. Headlights approached from the opposite direction; I again burrowed into the leaves. The lights silhouetted a figure riding a bicycle in my direction. The car pulled alongside him, and I heard him being asked if he'd seen a red-haired woman acting suspiciously.

Although the response was inaudible, the cyclist shook his head and I caught a glimpse of a fuzzy ponytail. It was my customer, the science fiction hippie. I ducked my head as the car drove past, then waited until the hippie was in front of me and hissed at him.

"Yeah?" he said as he put his foot on the pavement, not sounding at all surprised at being addressed by a bush. For all I knew, it could have happened to him on a regular basis, and according to the official record, it was how Moses got his start.

"It's Claire Malloy," I whispered.

"Groovy. What are you doing in the bush?"

Fifteen minutes later I was perched on the back of his bicycle and we were wobbling up Thurber Street toward the perceived sanctuary of Miss Emily's house. My hair was hidden under a red bandana and I was wearing an army fatigue jacket and his pair of wire-rimmed glasses. I kept my head plastered against his back as though so overcome with lust that I was reduced to nuzzling his ponytail. He pedaled along blindly but contentedly, no doubt salivating at the prospect of a dozen free books.

A deputy sheriff's car passed us, but the occupants were scanning the pedestrians, and the cyclist and his lovesick girlfriend attracted no interest. Within five minutes we arrived at Willow Street. He assured me I could keep the outfit, and with a wave, pedaled down the street.

I stood at the curb. Both floors of the house were dark; Miss Emily was sipping tequila in Taos and Daryl Defoe was most likely at the Book Depot wondering why I wasn't. Wishing I'd watched more television detective shows and therefore learned the gentle art of evading the authorities, I took the key from the mailbox and let myself into the house.

I had a hideout and a disguise, but no transportation to Guttler, Missouri—a problem I'd never envisioned having to face in this lifetime. I closed the heavy drapes, enveloping myself in a cloud of dust that provoked half a dozen sneezes, and switched on a small lamp next to the telephone. I knew Miss Emily was a tippler, and after a brisk search of the cabinets, settled on the settee with a glass of sherry and called my apartment.

"Hello?" Caron said breathlessly.

"What's wrong?"

"Oh, it's you, Rhonda," she said. "Did you finish painting that really neat poster for the Mousse concert?"

"Shall I presume we have company?"

"Yes, I adore the drummer!" she gushed. "He's the baddest of them all, don't you think? Well, the lead singer's kinda cute if you like older guys. He's practically twenty, you know."

I could imagine the stony-faced deputy in the middle of the living room, getting stonier as he realized he might have to listen to a lengthy exposé of relative merits of each member of Mousse. I wasn't sure I could stand too much of it, myself.

"Listen," I said, "I'm going out of town until late tomorrow afternoon or so. If a true emergency comes up, the animal shelter director will know where I am. I'm not going to tell you because I don't want you to be tortured, nor do I want you to blurt it out at the mere mention of being momentarily inconvenienced."

"Let's not get bitchy, Rhonda. Sometimes you're worse than my mother, and that's not easy to be. She majored in it at college and did a graduate—"

"Spend the night at Inez's house, all right?" I banged down the receiver and took a long sip of the sweet sherry. Luanne was still out of town, so I couldn't beg the use of her car. I called the number of the animal shelter and listened to a dozen plaintive rings. Jan Gallager was not listed in the directory, and when I called information, I was told rather snootily that at the customer's request, the number could not be given out.

I wondered if Miss Emily might have a car parked in the garage beside the house. If she did, it was likely to be of antique vintage, but I went into the kitchen, flipped on the light, and began to hunt through junk-filled drawers for a car key (or a crank).

As I moved past the window above the sink, I saw a light flash in the yard. Gulping unattractively, I switched off the overhead light. Could the sheriff have remembered the addresses of the stolen animals and sent men to search for numero uno on his most-wanted list? And if so, were they armed with assault weapons and instructed to take no enemies? Should I prepare for tear gas and/or hand grenades? I went back to the window, but there was no flicker to be seen, much less the glint of moonlight on the barrel of an Uzi.

I'd never had much respect for the heady heroine

in a gossamer negligee who creeps up to the tower, fully aware that the murderer knows darn well she's got the sole proof of his guilt clutched in her sweet yet sweaty palm. A simple telephone call to the police would almost always suffice.

I, however, crept to the living room and peeked through the drapes, in that a simple telephone call to the police would result in an even less tolerable situation. Someone was behind the thick trunk of an ancient elm tree; a tiny light flickered twice and then went dead.

This was so exciting that I returned to the kitchen window and watched as a light flickered near the honeysuckle on the fence. I wasn't exactly frightened by all this fireflyish behavior. Whoever had murdered Newton Churls had no reason to stalk a mild-mannered bookseller. On the other hand, I did make sure the front door was locked as I went into the inky bedroom and stumbled through piles of magazines to the window.

I held back the sheer and watched yet another light. I returned to the living room and sat down near the telephone, just in case an ax crashed through the door or I heard howls. When a board creaked on the porch, I drained the sherry and tried to think of a reasonable explanation to smooth the sheriff's ruffled ego.

Nothing much came to mind, so I waited patiently for the deputies to pound on the door and demand entry. The board squeaked more loudly. The situation was becoming entirely too melodramatic for my taste. Caron would have reveled in it, threatening to swoon, fluttering her eyelashes, reeling about with her hands clasped in the traditional Gothic pose, making outlandish remarks, and having a lovely time.

The house seemed to be creaking from its floor-boards to its attic. It was a hundred years old, I told myself calmly, and the wind had picked up since the time I'd lost my mind and dashed out the back door of the bookstore. I wasn't trapped. I was safely in-stalled in the haven of my choice; the doors were locked, the drawbridge drawn, the drapes closed to thwart erstwhile Peeping Toms.

It was possible that my hand was trembling as I refilled my glass, but I managed to do so with only a small splash on the toe of my shoe and on the dull patina of the hardwood floor. There may have been a trickle of adrenaline in my blood, and a nascent lump in my throat. The hardy heroines did survive, I reminded myself as my eyes darted between the doorway to the kitchen and the nearby front door, with occasional detours to the ceiling when a partic-ularly loud creak caught my attention. The police or the hero or the mounties always showed up at the ultimate moment. I was safe. Perfectly, perfectly safe.

A stick cracked somewhere in the backyard. Had Nick, Nora, and Patton been there, the sneaky soul would have been announced with barks and snarls of indignation. As it was, they might be on their way to Guttler while I sat on the settee awaiting further de-velopments.

I was still reasonably composed when the back doorknob rattled. I was on the verge of hysterics when I forced myself to tiptoe to the doorway and peer around it. Two wide, white eyes stared through the glass at me from under a great mass of gray hair, and I could almost hear the beads rattling.

I turned on the light and curled my lip, expecting Vidalia to smile in return, but instead she gasped and ducked out of view as if she'd caught a glimpse of the bride of one of those silly B-grade movie monsters. I went to the front door, turned on the porch light, and stepped outside, more than a little irritated with the neighborhood loonies.

"Come out, come out, wherever you are," I said flatly.

George poked his head out from behind the elm tree. His voice was high and waspish as he said, "Identify yourself or I'll call the police."

"Name, rank, and serial number," snapped an unseen but familiar voice from around the corner of the house. "Armed, you know. Can't be held responsible if you're wounded."

"Colonel," Helen said uncertainly from her post, wherever it might have been, "I think that's—"

"Hold your positions!" he interrupted. "Keep her covered until we're satisfied."

Vidalia's face hovered above a shrub, as if it were a helium balloon on a string. "I do believe, Colonel, that we've made a teeny tiny mistake."

"No," I said, "you've made a great big mistake." I pulled off the bandana and glasses. "Would you like to come inside for tea and cookies, or would you prefer to play cops and robbers in the dark? It's a very nice night, and I really won't have my feelings hurt if you stay out a little longer. Just don't stay out past your bedtimes."

I went inside and sat down. There was a spurt of discussion in the yard, and then the group trudged inside with varying amounts of embarrassment and found places to sit.

"Care to explain?" I asked.

Colonel Culworthy harrumphed. "Neighborhood watch. Pet patrol sort of thing. Secure the streets in case someone tries to steal another animal."

Vidalia flashed her gold tooth at me and said, "Colonel Culworthy organized us, of course. I'm assigned to this block, and when I saw a light inside Emily's, I flashed my light three times. Three means possible intruder. Two means message acknowledged, and three—pause—two means"—she gave me a panicky look—"something else."

"Armed, woman," Culworthy said. "Means the enemy is armed and dangerous. Went over it with you for an hour."

"It's the cusp," she said with a sniffle. "I always find it difficult to retain things during the cusp."

George crossed his legs and settled back in his chair. "We haven't seen you since our encounter at the sheriff's office this morning. Did he wring every last drop out of you?"

Helen rumbled, but I gazed at him and said, "Every last drop, right down to my theories about the identity of the murderer."

"How fascinating," he said smoothly. Helen was now rumbling like a volcano, forcing him to raise his voice slightly. "And on whom did you cast your suspicion, Claire?"

There was something very peculiar about him, but I couldn't quite put my finger on it. "It could have been any of you," I said. "You left Helen in the woods when you went for another flashlight. The colonel and Vidalia were separated, and Daryl claimed he went to the far side of the house."

Helen erupted. "How dare you accuse any of us of murder! We are all responsible members of this community. I worked for thirty-seven years at the county clerk's office, and George for nearly that many years at the post office. Neither of us has had so much as a speeding ticket."

"I retired with full military honors," Culworthy sputtered. "Got the papers to prove it."

"I once received a stern letter from the library about overdue books," Vidalia said with a coy look.

While I, a veritable paragon of innocence, was wanted by the sheriff's department for harboring a fugitive, impeding an investigation, and escaping from custody. I saw no reason to enlighten them. "All I said was that each of you had the opportunity to come up to the pen while Churls was inside it and click the padlock. Perhaps pit bulls are unstable enough to attack anyone who invades their territory."

"Nonsense," Helen said uneasily. She jabbed her husband, who echoed her remark.

I glanced at my watch, calculated the amount of time before I had to be on the highway to Guttler, and said, "Not necessarily. The fact that he had the puppies enraged us all, and I've learned more recently that he indeed did purchase animals from a very dubious source. If one of you had encountered him behind the house, and he'd opened the pen to let the dogs loose, shoving him in and locking the padlock might be interpreted as an act of self-defense. What happened to Churls could not have been foreseen." If I thought I'd hear a confession, the expenditure of brain cells was in vain.

"Why in heaven's name were you dressed like that," Vidalia trilled, getting back to business. "It was most alarming to see a strange woman in Emily's kitchen."

The four of them waited expectantly for me to produce a rational explanation. Culworthy snorted several times, and George winked at me from behind his bifocals. Helen folded her hands in her laps. Vidalia gave me her most encouraging smile.

"Where's Daryl?" I asked in a weak attempt at diversion.

"Acted most peculiar," Culworthy said. "Talked to him at oh eighteen hundred, said he was busy but would be back later to patrol Olive Street."

"I was patrolling Olive," George said.

Culworthy shook his head. "Supposed to be on Walnut."

"I was supposed to be on Walnut," Helen said. She took a folded paper from her pocket and flapped it at him. "When you issued the assignments, I wrote it all down so none of us would be confused. Now it seems you're the one who's confused, Colonel."

"Never been confused a day in my life."

"Do you want to look at my notes?"

"Never needed notes, never will. Trained in military maneuvers, madam, and spent thirty years telling wet-eared privates where to go and when to be there. Furthermore, can't abide pushy women contradicting me. If we were on the battlefield, I'd have you flogged."

The ensuing exchange drove me to the porch, and when that was deemed insufficient, on out to the yard and around the corner of the house to the staircase that led to Daryl's apartment. The windows were dark, the door closed.

Time was slipping away rapidly. The directions I'd received from Runnels were meant to be followed during daylight, when highway signs were easily visible and landmarks unmissable. On the one hand, there was truth to the adage involving safety in numbers, and if I proposed a mission hinting of danger, those inside squabbling away like a flock of geese would be pushing and shoving to sit in the front seat.

But I'd eliminated each for good cause, and al-

105

though I'd proposed a scenario in which Churls's death was self-defense, I was still aware of the emptied box on the table. Daryl had the same motive and opportunity I'd assigned to the others, and I hadn't planned on being totally relaxed in his company. It seemed I wasn't to be afforded that minor tension.

For a person with no particular affinity for pets, I'd not only devoted the majority of my waking hours for most of a week to them, I'd also committed a rather impressive number of crimes on their behalf. One more wouldn't matter, I decided.

I returned to the porch, opened the door, and said, "Vidalia, could I please have a word with you?"

She came outside, her face puckered with excitement, and said, "Oh, yes, is there something you want to tell me?"

I slid my arm through hers and gently coerced her down the steps to the sidewalk. As we started for her apartment house, I said, "Do you own a car?"

"Why, yes," she said delightedly. "Do you?"

"Mine's out of commission at the moment." I glanced over my shoulder. Culworthy was in the doorway of the house, his arms akimbo and the porch light shining on his metal buttons. I hurried her along. "Do you think I could borrow your car? It would mean so much to me, since I'm without transportation."

She was enchanted with my conspiratorial facade. "I'll pop inside and fetch the key. The car's parked in the little alley out back."

I waited until she was inside, then strolled around the building, hoping the colonel had ceased his surveillance. In the alley was a boxy little car that looked like a child's toy. My desk at the Book Depot was slightly larger and a good fifty years younger than this museum piece, but I wasn't exactly flabbergasted. She was not the type to drive a mundane Chevrolet.

Vidalia came out the back door and handed me a leather key case. "Isn't this exciting?"

And aren't you a fruitcake, I thought. "Thanks very much, Vidalia," I said levelly. "I'll be back tomorrow."

She went to the far side of the motorized cigar box, put her hands on her cheeks, and with glittering eyes, said, "Tomorrow will be perfect."

I got in the car and slammed the door.

She got in the car and slammed the door.

There was a moment of silence. I finally moistened my lips, took a nice, clean breath, and said, "What are you doing, Vidalia?"

"This is so exciting. I'm quite beside myself, you see, although perhaps some of it is due to the cusp. I did Astra's chart again this morning—poor, dear Astra, who must be utterly heartbroken without her own bed and her little rubber mousie and her—"

"You can't go with me."

"Of course I can," she said brightly. "If Astra comes home during this brief absence, she'll wait right here by the back door, yowling until I let her inside. I have explained to her in detail how sometimes I might be at the grocery store or the library, and she knows she's to wait right here."

Harboring a fugitive, impeding, escaping, grand theft auto—those were all crimes I could commit without a problem. But I sensed it would take assault and a hefty dose of battery to remove her from her car, or several hours of argument involving cusps, cats, and whatever else she threw at me. Having noticed that the speedometer only went to sixty, I did not have time to dally in the alley.

"Okay," I muttered as I put the key in the switch and was rewarded with an asthmatic wheeze from the engine. "But I'm giving the orders and you're following them. This might be dangerous."

"I'm sure you're ever as good a field commander as Colonel Culworthy. Some are born to lead, and some to follow. I shall pay strict attention and do whatever you order me to do, without the slightest concern for my physical safety."

"Thank you." I tried the key once again, and this time the car coughed for a minute, then purred to life. As we pulled onto Willow Street, I saw that Culworthy was in the doorway and had been joined by George and Helen. All three were staring as Vidalia and I chugged into the night.

7

"Where is it that we're going?" Vidalia asked cheerfully.

"Guttler, Missouri," I said. We were on a shoulderless, winding highway, and we had not encountered a car for a long while. The moon had slid below the horizon, but without the interference of urban lights, a ghostly white glow illuminated the surface of the road and what scenery there was. Every now and then a car raced up from behind us, braked in astonishment at our plodding pace, and whipped around us with minimal effort. My palms were moist on the steering wheel; I realized we were in more danger from a rear-end collision than from a loss of control at the perilous speed of fifty miles per millennium.

"Guttler, Missouri?" echoed Vidalia. "How fascinating. What is it we're going to do when we get there?"

I knew what I was going to do, within reason, but I hadn't decided what she was going to do. Runnels had told me to expect fifty or so trucks with cages or enclosed beds and several hundred animals, without water or food. I would be greeted by a large group of surly, uncommunicative (if I was lucky), brutish dealers who would be angered by my presence at the parking lot outside a livestock auction barn. Runnels had also mentioned the prevalence of well-stocked gun racks on the rear windows of the trucks. Jan's comment about one of the activists requiring dental work had not been dismissed lightly.

"We'll find a motel when we get to Guttler," I said. "I have one errand in the morning, and then I'll pick you up at the motel and we'll drive back to Farberville."

Vidalia was flighty, but she wasn't a candidate for mind-numbing medication and cushioned wallpaper quite yet. "I shall assume this errand of your has something to do with the animals stolen from the neighborhood, including poor Astra."

It was time to add mendacity to my rap sheet. "No, I wish there were something I could do, but we'll have to let the sheriff handle the case. I'm going to pick up several boxes of mystery novels. They're from—ah, an estate. A collection of first editions, I was told when I purchased the lot."

She laughed gaily at my lie. "In a place called Guttler? How very quaint of you to tell me that. Oh well, we have several hours ahead of us and I do enjoy guessing games. I could start with the traditional question, 'Animal, vegetable, or mineral?' but there's no reason to waste a question on that because we both know the category is animal. Let me see . . ."

I sternly told her I had no intentions of participating in a guessing game and that my sole purpose was to pick up the books. I refused to answer her questions, but she was a keen observer of inadvertent body language and clapped her hands when I winced or blinked. Within an hour, she had arrived at a description of our mission that was pretty much accurate, and was proposing actions that required a side trip to an arsenal.

"You're going to wait at the motel," I said firmly. "It would be much too dangerous for you to go there alone," Vidalia said, dismissing my firmness with a toss of her chin. "I shall be your bodyguard." She weighed all of a hundred pounds, was gray-haired and frail, and could be easily toppled by a gust of wind. I said as much, then glanced at the fuel gauge and noted it was low. We continued the argument as we came to a small town. It was nearly midnight; the local citizens, from splotchy pink neonates to whiskery great-grandpas, were nestled all snug in their beds. The only indication of life were the streetlights, and they were few and far between.

I stopped in front of a dark gas station. "I hadn't thought about this," I said, sighing. "There are plenty of all-night service stations on the interstate. I'm not sure if we can find anything open on the back highways, though."

"Pull over to the pump," Vidalia said.

"It'll be locked."

"That remains to be seen, doesn't it?" She hopped out of the car before I could say anything, plucked the nozzle from the gas pump, and gestured imperiously at me to pull forward. Shortly thereafter, the pump began to hum and the odor of gasoline to sweeten the night air.

As we drove away, I made a mental note of the species of station and vowed to send a check, in an attempt to reassure myself I had not abandoned every last iota of respect for the law. Not yet, anyway.

"Who do you believe murdered Churls?" Vidalia asked once we were again chugging down the highway.

I glanced at headlights in the rearview mirror and

waited to be passed, but the distant vehicle seemed content to match our speed. I relaxed my grip on the steering wheel and said, "As I said earlier, any of you could have."

"Possibly, but none of us did. What about the driver of that ungainly car found in Churls's yard?" she asked, doing a much better imitation of Miss Jane Marple than I ever had. Had she pulled out her knitting, I wouldn't have raised an eyebrow. "You said at the time it belonged to one of the people at the animal shelter."

I told her what Arnie had admitted in the office of the Book Depot, eliding over my subsequent arrest and unladylike departure. "He went out there with four animals, and Churls refused to pay him. That gives him a shaky motive, but Arnie's got a shaky mind," I said pensively. "If Arnie decided to lock Churls in the pen and take his money from the cash box, that would explain the destruction of the lock. He must have still been there when the Willow Street commandos arrived, and realized he couldn't show himself by driving away."

Vidalia shook her head. "I'm afraid you haven't explained everything, Claire, although I must say your hypothesis is nice. If Arnie brought Nick, Nora, and two other animals to the property, left Churls in the cage, and decided to walk back to Farberville, why didn't we find the animals?"

I had no answer. "Let's just hope we find them in Guttler."

"Yes, indeed," she said. "Colonel Culworthy makes every effort to present a gruff facade, but he's a cream-filled cupcake when it comes to Patton. You may find this hard to believe, but he himself sewed a little khaki rain outfit and knitted an olive drab sweater for Patton. He was too embarrassed to purchase the yarn and pattern, so he asked me to do it for him. Now he claims he ordered the outfits from a pet catalog. Isn't that amazing?"

"Then there is no Mrs. Colonel Culworthy?"

Vidalia gazed out the window. "One evening some months ago, he and I enjoyed a few martinis and a spirited game of gin rummy in my sitting room. He told me how his wife had gone shopping in a town near the base and never returned. He discovered she'd taken most of her things, but not Patton. Patton was her last anniversary present."

I slowed down as we entered another slumbering town. "I suppose the dog has a great deal of emotional significance for him?"

"More than one would suspect."

"Helen Maranoni seems distressed about Juniper," I said as I glanced at her.

"Doesn't she? I think George is, too, although he hides it."

"What do you know about them?"

"Very little." She yawned broadly, her fingers fluttering in front of her mouth. "They bought their house only a month or so ago."

The highway grew darker, the curves sharper, and the towns sparser as we continued toward Guttler. Vidalia had nodded off, and I was fighting the same impulse as I drove past closed cafés that might have provided caffeine and protein. I attempted to rouse myself with a virulent mental lecture about the idiocy of this mission, even comparing it unfavorably with Culworthy's blundering maneuvers.

Periodically I noticed headlights behind me, but no cars loomed on my bumper. I cracked the window for fresh air and pondered Vidalia's question:

Why didn't they find the dogs? Drumming my fingers on the top of the wheel, I ran through my hypothetical schedule of events at NewCo. Arnie arrives with four animals. Churls accepts the animals but refuses to pay him. Arnie locks Churls in the pit bulls' pen and opens the metal box. The intrepid band arrives. Arnie takes the cash and a hike. Deputy Amos and I arrive.

"So why didn't they find the dogs?" I muttered repetitiously until it had a rollicky cadence. I'd given it a melody by the time I saw a battered, pockmarked sign that announced the outer limits of Guttler, population twenty-two hundred.

The eastern sky was noticeably lighter as I looked curiously at the town, wondering if a goodly percentage of the twenty-two hundred inhabitants had defected or died. The store windows were covered with mustard-colored newspapers and peeling tape. The gas station had been gutted by a fire, as had the house next door. No one had gotten around to removing the ebon skeletons. Apparently the zoning regulations did not preclude mobile homes, since the majority of visible housing was comprised of rusty oblong boxes ringed with weeds. A pickup truck stopped in front of one, and its driver, a pudgy dwarf, spat on the gravel as he went inside. If nothing else, his presence confirmed the existence of a population of sorts.

Guttler did not have a Hilton. It did not have a Holiday Inn, nor did it have a trashy establishment that rented by the hour. It did have a café, however, made of concrete blocks and surrounded by pickup trucks and a stray car or two. The neon sign blinked suggestively, and white light spilled out of the front window. It was not only open, it was clearly the local hot spot for grits, gravy, and early morning gossip.

I parked, frowned at myself in the mirror, and nudged Vidalia, who was snoring ever so discreetly. "We're here," I told her, trying to sound pleased. After more encouragement on my part, she finally awakened and gazed blankly at the exterior of the Red Bird Café. "Is this where we find the animals?" she asked querulously. "It doesn't look very clean."

"We have very few options," I said. "I'm in dire need of a rest room and a lot of coffee. My last meal was lunch yesterday. How bad can it be?"

It was bad. It was the worst I'd ever seen, or at least remained inside after a quick look—and I'd traveled in Algeria and Morocco. The glass-topped counter with a cash register and a toothpick dispenser was unattended, but beyond it was a low, wide counter packed shoulder-to-shoulder by men in denim overalls and caps. I didn't know about shoes and shirts, but clearly personal hygiene was not a requirement for service. There was loud, good-natured banter as we opened the door, but it stopped abruptly and they all stared at us, their expressions unfathomable. There were a few booths with red plastic seat covers and stained tabletops; those occupants seemed equally stunned by our audacity.

Vidalia gurgled and stepped back, but I caught her elbow and dragged her to the only unoccupied booth.

"Sit here and order coffee for me," I said quietly, although in the continued silence it was easily heard by the forty or so people watching us as if we were alien life-forms. I flashed a smile at the men along the counter and looked around for the rest rooms.

A waitress in a pink uniform bustled out of the kitchen, balancing plates up both arms. Her hair, piled in a lacquered beehive, had a subtle tint that matched the color of her uniform. She grasped the situation without hesitation. "It's out back, honey," she said in the sugary drawl common to the profession. "Can't miss it."

I went around to the back of the building and found it, but it was certainly something I'd have preferred to miss for all eternity. As I came back, a dirty white truck with a dozen cages in its bed pulled into the lot and parked. The cages contained dogs with the same resigned demeanor as those we'd seen at NewCo.

"Whacha staring at?"

I frowned at the driver, a pimply young man with stringy yellow hair, a receding chin line, and pale, porcine eyes. "The dogs look as though they need water and more room," I said tartly.

"So?"

I decided it would not be productive to be gunned down in the parking lot. "So I answered your question," I said as I went back into the café.

Vidalia was fanning herself with a plastic-encased menu and shooting frantic looks at those at nearby tables. When I sat down across from her, she clutched my hand and whispered, "Thank heavens you're back, Claire. I was so very worried about you. These people are not friendly, you know."

"They may be curious about your attire," I murmured, wishing I'd suggested she leave the scarlet scarf and her bead collection in the car. Her eye makeup was smudged, and she bore a disturbing resemblance to a raccoon who'd been in a brawl.

The waitress brought coffee for me and tea for Vidalia. "What y'all doing in town? Passing through on your way to St. Louis?"

Everyone seemed interested, so I spoke loudly. "That's right. My aunt's going to babysit for her sister's kids."

"I am?" said Vidalia, startled.

"The twins," I said brightly. "Little Nick and Nora, both cute as roly-poly puppies." I smiled at the waitress while aiming my toe at Vidalia's shin. "My aunt gets confused at times, but you know how that is."

"You can say that again, honey," the waitress said. She looked over her shoulder at the men along the counter. "This lady's going to baby-sit for her sister's twin babies in St. Louis. Ain't that nice?" Nobody seemed enthralled, but a few of them turned back to their food and coffee. The waitress poised a pencil over her pad, but before I could order, she said, "Where'd you say you and your aunt are from?"

"I didn't," I said.

"Farberville," Vidalia chirped. "We both live in Farberville. Claire has her very own bookstore, and I'm retired."

The yellow-haired boy flopped down in the next booth and stared sullenly at me. I kicked Vidalia once again, grimaced at the waitress, and said, "Auntie is a tiny bit confused; she must be thinking of my cousin Luanne in Wichita Falls. Luanne has a lovely store that specializes in religious books, records, and little knickknacks."

Giving me a mutinous look, Vidalia said, "Oh, that's right. Luanne in Wichita has the bookstore with the ceramic praying hands and the braille editions of the Bible."

The waitress winked at me. After she took our orders and left, I leaned over the table and whispered, "We don't want them to know who we are or why we're here. This is a covert operation."

"I know that," Vidalia whispered back. "Colonel Culworthy has trained us for the possibility of this form of warfare."

"Right," I said, then sank back and waited grimly until our breakfasts arrived. The food was limp, greasy, burned, and tepid, but I shoveled it down greedily, allowed the waitress to refill my coffee cup several times, and was beginning to feel better by seven-thirty. I looked at Vidalia, who was humming under her breath as she spread jelly on a piece of toast, and tried to figure out where I could stash her while I went to the dog sale.

My yellow-haired friend paused beside our table. "Have a nice day," he said in a gravelly voice. It was a threat.

"Why, thank you," Vidalia said absently.

Most of the other customers were checking their watches, joking with the waitress while they settled bills at the cash register, and slapping each other on the back as they crowded out the door.

By the time Vidalia and I came outside the café, the parking lot had been depleted. I took the page of directions from my purse to review the route to the livestock sale barn. Vidalia was drifting about like a dandelion seed in a breeze, toying with the beads around her neck and singing to herself. Taking her with me seemed as immoral as dropping a puppy in a pen with pit bulls, but the alternatives were extremely limited.

"Let's go," I said, resigned. While we drove down the narrow side road, I elicited promises that she

118

would wait in the car, ever vigilant and prepared to drive for help.

We encountered more and more pickup trucks until we were the sole civilians in the procession. All of the trucks had either enclosed beds or cages, and as Runnels had promised, gun racks. It was not the place to disparage the dogmatic policies of the NRA.

I parked at the far edge of a field, gave Vidalia a paperback mystery from the glove compartment, and made her swear to wait in the car while I made the rounds of the dealers. I then put the bandana on my head, settled the wire-rimmed glasses in place, and got out of the car, narrowly avoiding stepping on that which is indigenous to livestock barn environs.

The sale was what I'd envisioned. Those with animals to sell had parked in longs rows along the fences. Some dogs were tethered to stakes, others left in cages. Those with cats had grouped at one end. The odor was unmistakably organic; I made no attempt to isolate the elements that contributed to the miasma. The pathetic wuffly noises from the dogs competed with conversations and the nasal wails of country singers coming from radios.

There were a few women sitting together in aluminum chairs, sharing coffee from thermos bottles and doughnuts from a box. A group of children shrieked as they chased each other between the trucks. From inside a cab, a baby cried. A toddler with an unpleasant nose howled as its diaper slid down its legs. The dealers were already transacting business. Dogs were examined, occasionally hefted to judge weight, and cats were prodded through the wire mesh. Prices were tossed out for spirited negotiation. Pint bottles in brown sacks were passed back and forth, and spitting seemed obligatory.

In an eerie way, it had the ambiance of a local crafts fair or a family reunion. Had the ultimate goal not been to deliver animals to laboratories, it might have struck me as a festive rural scene.

I was not invisible. As in the café, voices broke off as I casually sauntered past the trucks and attempted to peer into the cages for the animals stolen from Willow Street. The majority of the dogs were hounds, but of the lean, hunting variety. I was the recipient of increasing narrow looks, but I continued on my way, my face as blank as possible and my fists hidden in the pockets of the fatigue jacket.

A bark caught my attention, since most of the dogs had been deprived of that ability. I turned around and tried to determine the direction of the barker, but the crowd pushed me forward and the noise seemed to swell until I couldn't even hear the wuffles. The yellow-haired boy gave me a sneering smile as I passed by his truck. I heard another bark from behind me. I stepped out of the tidal wave, but a fat, bearish man with a pink face blocked my way. His expression was childlike and genial, but I felt a flicker of alarm and moved back into the crowd.

The stench of unwashed bodies, mingled with animal excrement and exhaust fumes from the trucks still arriving, was making me queasy. I glanced back and saw Yellow Hair coming after me. The fat man was rubbing his hands together as he pushed through the bodies. I elbowed my way between two grizzled sorts.

Now I could hear cats yowling. A radio blared out the nasal lament of a discarded lover. A small boy

120

crashed into me, stuck out his tongue, and skittered away before I could reciprocate. Yellow Hair seemed closer. This was not the place to find a friendly cop— or even a friendly face.

I darted between two trucks, but a high fence blocked me from the field. I spun around. Yellow Hair and Baby Bear stood in the narrow space between the trucks, both looking pleased with themselves. The bumpers of trucks were against the fence; I was in a corridor with an entrance but no exit.

A face appeared between their shoulders. For a brief, paralytic moment, I met Daryl Defoe's startled look. The two men crowded me into the fence. I kicked at their legs, and as I opened my mouth to scream, Yellow Hair grabbed me around the neck with one arm and clamped his hand on my mouth. "Now, now, Mizz Malloy," he simpered in my ear, "we don't want to have to cut your vocal cords."

I caught a glimpse of a padded object coming down on me. The lights went out.

Writers, particularly those in the mystery genre, seem to take great pleasure in bopping people over the head and rendering them unconscious. It is not only gratuitous, but also selfish on the writer's part to use a trite device. Very little consideration is given to the victim, who returns to consciousness with a blinding headache, a severe sense of disorientation, overall shakiness, and a gnawing fear that his or her skill is battered beyond repair.

Groaning, I tentatively explored the back of my head. I found no blood, no brain seepage, no permanent indentation that would rival the Grand Canyon. It merely felt like it. I forced myself to open my eyes, and after a brief battle with nausea, tried to figure out where the hell I was.

The good news was that Yellow Hair and Baby Bear were not in the small room with rough wood walls and rafters decorated with cobwebs. The bad news was that I was, and I had a sneaking suspicion that the door would prove to be locked, presuming the assailants knew their business, whatever it was. There were no windows; sunlight wormed through cracks in the roof and walls. I leaned against a grain sack and pieced together what had happened from my arrival at the sale to my departure from consciousness.

Had I seen Daryl Defoe seconds before the attack, or had I simply seen someone who resembled him? My head throbbed so fiercely that I put that aside. Yellow Hair and Baby Bear had come after me as if they knew who I was and why I was there, I thought with a frown. I'd heard my name muttered. But that, of course, was impossible. Vidalia had blurted out my first name in the café, and Yellow Hair might have heard her. No one else, except for Jan Gallager and Brian Runnels, had any idea that I planned to attend the sale.

I stood up and kept my hand on the wall until the floor stopped undulating. The door was secured on the outside. Banging and rattling did not succeed, nor did pounding on it with my fists and screeching for help. I put my ear against it and listened. I heard nothing but ducks.

I was not in the immediate vicinity of the sale, which had been as noisy as a carnival. I had no way to judge how long I'd been unconscious, other than it was still daylight, nor did I want to consider another encounter with my attackers. I needed some sort of tool to break the hinges, I decided as I began to search the shabby yet effective cell. There were sacks of feed, pieces of rope and leather straps, a stack of flowerpots, and several plastic tubs with screws and nails. I dragged the remains of a rocking chair across the room, climbed on it, and felt around on a high shelf, willing myself not to think of spiders and other unappealing denizens of dirty storage sheds.

I found a metal object that proved to be a tent stake. As I carefully got down from the chair, the door behind me opened. Squeezing the stake and telling myself it was a dull dagger, I turned around.

With the glare behind her, Vidalia's hair was a halo of fog engulfing her face. "I think we ought to be going," she murmured.

I tossed down my weapon and hurried across the room. "Are those men nearby?"

"Which men would that be?"

I grabbed her arm as I went through the door. On our left was a labyrinth of dog pens, mostly empty, and beyond that a scummy pond. Two trucks were parked in front of a trailer on our right, one that I recognized and the other unremarkable. A dog came to the fence and wuffled at us, and near the pond two ducks argued. A robin hopped across the driveway. In other instances, it might have seemed bucolic.

"Where's your car?" I demanded.

"I felt it prudent to park down the road," Vidalia said. "I could almost hear Colonel Culworthy's lecture about—"

"Which way?"

She went around the corner of the shed, and I followed her, trying not to step on her heels. We passed the last of the dog pens, slipped down a muddy slope, and battled through a patch of stunted fir trees and tentacles of prickly branches.

Vidalia's car was parked at the edge of a rugged dirt road. I paused to listen for voices or engines from the hill above us, but it seemed my departure had not yet been noticed. I dove into the car and within seconds we were lurching down the road, splashing through puddles and bouncing madly. The sorry excuse for a road curved and dipped for what felt like miles, but at last we arrived at a paved road.

"Which way?" I asked curtly.

"If you wish to return to the sale, to the left. If you prefer to go back to Farberville, to the right," she said. "I was thinking it might be nice to have a cup of tea before we started the long drive home."

"Not in this state," I growled as I yanked the steering wheel to the right. We did not vanish over the hill in an instant, but we made it and the next several without a dirty white truck appearing in the rearview mirror.

Vidalia reached over and removed a cobweb from my hair. "I was terribly worried about you, Claire. This whole trip has been most unsettling."

"I tend to agree," I said, still glancing nervously in the mirror. "How did you find me at that place?"

"Well, I was reading the novel you kindly loaned me, and had reached a very exciting part in which the amateur sleuth, who happens to own a bookstore just like you do, although hers is on an island in North Carolina and specializes in mysteries—"

"Vidalia, do you mind!"

"Goodness, you sound grumpy. I have some aspirins in my purse; perhaps you might like to take one?" When I glowered, she sniffed and said, "Luckily, I looked up as that man from the café came by.

There was another man with him, and at first glance I thought they were escorting a girlfriend who was a tiny bit tipsy. Then I saw your bandana. I was quite confident you hadn't been drinking, especially at such an early hour, and watched carefully as they helped you into a truck and drove away. I wasn't at all sure what to do, but I heard Colonal Culworthy telling me that I must be brave and act quickly, so I tailed the truck."

As we drove though Guttler, I toyed with the idea of stopping at the Red Bird Café to call the state police and report the assault and kidnapping. My witness—a dotty gypsy—would back up my story, but Yellow Hair and Baby Bear would proffer an entirely different one. We drove on.

"I don't suppose you saw Astra?" Vidalia said sadly.

"No, but I think I saw someone familiar. Right before I was hit, I thought I saw Daryl Defoe in the crowd."

"Why was he there?"

I shook my head, then immediately regretted the movement. "I have no idea, and I can't swear it was he. I didn't tell anyone that I was going to the sale, and there's no way he could have known." I slowed down for a church bus that was going even slower than we were, and checked once again in the mirror. "Unless he followed us, of course. There was a car last night that stayed behind us most of the trip."

"Daryl doesn't own a car, or if he does, he never parks it at Emily's house. I always see him walking to and from school with that briefcase, except when he rides with his girlfriend."

"He has a girlfriend?" I said, having difficulty imagining him in the role of a suitor.

"I'm not sure. Astra is very demanding, so I hardly ever notice his comings and goings."

"But he does have access to a car, which means he could have followed us to Guttler. Why, I don't know. Maybe I didn't see him," I added. "Maybe it was a preconcussion hallucination."

"Oh, but you most likely did, because I saw him, too. I waved, but he didn't see me. It's very interesting, isn't it?"

"Very interesting," I said with a sigh.

8

It was late in the afternoon when Vidalia and I arrived back in Farberville. My shoulder and neck muscles were aching and my head was gripped by a cosmic vise. My stomach remained unhappily aware of the greasy breakfast at the Red Bird Café and the dubious hamburgers we'd eaten on the road. Before Vidalia started snoring, we'd discussed every permutation we could devise to explain why Daryl had been at the animal sale in Guttler. Nothing had made much sense, nor had we come up with an explanation for the attack and abduction by Yellow Hair and Baby Bear.

I drove past my apartment. I had no idea how seriously the sheriff was taking my unauthorized hiatus, although I supposed it fell somewhere between minor annoyance and a statewide "armed and dangerous" APB. There were no official vehicles lurking among the sorority girls' modest limousines, no snipers on the roof, no nondescript van parked within electronic surveillance range. The downstairs tenant, an elderly theater professor with a cane, shuffled slowly past the sorority house and went through our common front door with no more than his usual difficulties.

I disembarked at the corner, thanked Vidalia for the use of her car and for rescuing me, and trudged up the stairs to solitude and scotch.

Lieutenant Peter Rosen sat on the sofa, presumably in a civilian capacity since he wore slacks and a sweater rather than his customary detective garb of three-piece suits and Italian shirts. Caron and Inez, in identical sweatshirts, were sprawled on chairs. All three of them goggled at me as I went into the kitchen, poured myself a stiff drink, and tried to concoct a passable story.

"Welcome back," I said to Peter as I sat down beside him. "How's your mother?"

I might as well have spoken in tongues. The three continued to stare at me; their reaction was not any friendlier than what I'd encountered in the Red Bird Café. "How's your mother?" I repeated, emphasizing each syllable.

"Dotty as hell," he said. He was clearly perplexed and not in a wryly bemused, what-have-you-gotten-yourself-into fashion.

I smiled at the girls. "Did you have a pleasant weekend?"

"Yeah," Caron said numbly. Inez nodded with an equal lack of enthusiasm, although in her case it was not remarkably abnormal.

"How about Chinese for dinner? I'm starving," I continued brightly, pretending I wasn't surrounded by three end products of botched brain surgery.

Peter's eyes were narrowed, a bad sign. "There's an outstanding warrant for your arrest, Claire. Jorgeson heard about it and left a note on my desk."

"Where were you last night and today?" Caron demanded. "Why are you wearing that incredibly tacky army jacket?"

Inez blinked solemnly. "Your face is scratched."

"Why does the sheriff want you so badly?" Peter added in his officiously official cop voice that I detest. "According to highlights of the warrant, you harbored a fugitive, impeded an investigation, and escaped while you were in custody. Those are felonies, you know."

"I did wonder about that," I said.

Caron was still staring at me as if I were not the gentle soul who'd changed her diapers, force-fed her strained carrots, corrected her grammar, and held her hand all night when she decided she hated her hair. "And that Arnie person Called Here to speak to you. He said something bizarre about senators being buddy-buddy with lawyers, then said it was his only call and would I send a pizza to the county jail." She swallowed several times. "I didn't, of course, but why did he call you?"

Peter flinched. "Is this the same Arnie. . . ?"

"I'm afraid so," I said. "He came hiking down the railroad tracks yesterday afternoon, and one thing led to another, and I suppose he's been booked for murder by now." I had ample time to finish my drink in the ensuing silence, and I then sweetly suggested to the girls that they run along and allow me to talk to Peter.

After a few rounds of arguments, they sulkily retired to Caron's bedroom. I told Peter the entire story, beginning with Miss Emily's six pages of lavender prose and concluding with a vague mention of being knocked unconscious and locked in a storage shed.

He looked at me for a long while, no doubt expecting to see tiny lavender butterflies flutter out of my ears. "This is the craziest story I've heard since I left my mother's house this morning. You don't even like dogs. You claim you're allergic, but I've always assumed it was a deep-seated aversion, if not a phobia."

"And all I've been doing for the last week is looking at dogs, thinking about dogs, talking about dogs, and searching for dogs, not to mention watching dogs kill someone. I'm quite sure I'll dream about dogs tonight—unless I get lucky and dream about astrologically correct cats."

"You amaze me at times," he said. His perfect white teeth flashed at me, and his molasses-colored eyes lingered on my mouth. Something mellowed inside me; I discovered I was leaning toward him.

The sensation alarmed me. Firmly ignoring it, I said, "What puzzles me the most is how the two men knew my name. I can't imagine Runnels having any involvement, nor can I think of a reason why Jan Gallager would have told someone who subsequently called Yellow Hair and ordered him to prevent me from looking for the stolen animals."

Peter seemed more interested in the arrest warrant and kept harping on it until I was driven to another drink. I brought him a beer, sat down tangentially, and attempted to express my pleasure at his return. Rather than responding in an appropriately warm manner, he said, "You have to call Sheriff Dorfer's office—now. I'll go with you and do what I can to keep him from locking you up with Arnie and charging you with conspiracy."

"Don't be silly. I'll call him in a few minutes and we'll discuss it as adults. He was a bit huffy yesterday, but now that he's had a chance to think it over, I'm sure he's realized that he made an error."

"I've met him before," Peter said.

"So have I," I said, supremely confident of my assessment.

Three hours later I had begun to doubt myself. The sheriff's office was thick with smoke. I'd had no sleep the night before and was struggling to stay awake (and breathe). Sheriff Dorfer had had a long talk with Peter, and then questioned me relentlessly, demanding that I repeat conversations I'd repeated a dozen times, making tasteless remarks about the women's correction facility, and lacking the common courtesy to provide a smoke-free environment and decent coffee. The stenographer grunted from time to time, but laboriously recorded each and every word. This time, apparently, spelling didn't count.

Sheriff Dorfer dismissed the woman, who shot me a dirty look as she left the room, then leaned back in his chair. "What am I gonna do with you, Mizz Malloy?"

"Tell me to stop meddling?"

"I was thinking more along the lines of locking you up," he said, shaking his head morosely as he worked the cigar butt from one corner of his mouth to the other. "Thing is, we're overcrowded and understaffed, and you're not exactly a menace to society, although I won't put that in writing and I'll deny ever saying it." He inhaled deeply and blew a stream of blue smoke into the already polluted atmosphere of his office. "Is there any point in making you promise to mind your own business?"

"Finding those animals *is* my business," I said. "Has Arnie been arraigned for the murder of Newton Churls?"

"He's still in residence downstairs, if that's what you're asking."

"How much cash did he have on him?"

"Mizz Malloy, it's late and we're both tired. I

131

thought we agreed that you were going to butt out of the case."

"As soon as the basset hounds and the other missing animals are returned, I will gladly retire. I'm not interested in Newton Churls's murder, or whatever it was. If you're convinced Arnie's the guilty party, that's fine with me. He told me he argued with Churls. Presuming his pockets were stuffed with Churls's money, you've got a good case." All of this was delivered in a cool voice, but I was watching him closely.

"We think he hid the money in the woods when he walked back to town," the sheriff muttered. "I had three deputies start searching his route this morning, but it's damn near twenty miles of railroad track. Arnie was feeling no pain. Deputy Amos and the others are soaking their feet, counting blisters, and threatening to resign."

"Were Arnie's fingerprints on the box?"

"No prints except for Churls's, but anyone who's watched television knows to be careful." He sighed and wheezed, and finally told me to go away, which I did briskly. Peter was in the front room, and we drove back to my apartment. I related the gist of the interrogation, adding that although the sheriff had failed to appreciate the necessity of my departure from his custody, he had decided to forget about it.

"What'd he say about the attackers?" Peter asked.

I sank back on the sofa. "He implied they were just a couple of good ol' boys having fun with an outsider. I'm not positive, but I don't think the Willow Street animals were at the sale. I'd checked almost all the cages when the goons cornered me. If the animals weren't there, what was their motive?"

"Amorous intent?" he murmured, displaying some himself.

I closed my eyes and was feeling much better when the telephone rang. I squeezed my eyes more tightly and ignored it, aware that Caron would answer it in her bedroom. She sounded deeply offended as she yelled, "It's for you, Mother!"

I reluctantly extricated myself from Peter's embrace and picked up the receiver.

"Claire, dear, this is Emily Parchester," came a breathless voice. "How are you?"

"I'm fine, thank you," I said, startled. "Are you having a nice trip?"

"Everything's been absolutely lovely. Sandra, our tour escort, has become ever so careful to count noses, on account of Mr. Delmaro having been left behind twice. He's a bit of a maverick."

Her laugh was gay, mine shaky. "That's good to hear," I said. I crossed my fingers. "There haven't been any changes in the itinerary, I hope?"

"Only a small one. Several of us decided we'd seen enough of the desert, and we suggested a detour to Las Vegas. Sandra was appalled, but we took a vote and informed her in no uncertain terms that democracy would prevail. Mr. Delmaro was naughty and slipped the bus driver twenty dollars, so he assured Sandra that the charter bus went where its customers desired. She's so furious she hasn't spoken to any of us all day . . . unless that might have something to do with the whoopee cushion . . ."

"Don't lose your pension at the blackjack table," I said faintly.

"Mr. Delmaro has been teaching me how to play the card games," Miss Emily said. Her wicked little giggle made me wonder what else Mr. Delmaro had been teaching her. "Have you had any problems with Nick and Nora? I know they must miss me

133

dreadfully, and I do hope they're not too depressed to eat."

"Everything's fine," I said with what conviction I could muster. The truth would have alarmed her, and there was nothing she could do from Nevada, even with the devilish Mr. Delmaro at her side.

We exchanged good-byes. I told Peter I was exhausted, which was true, and he made me promise to cease any activities that would enrage the sheriff. I meekly agreed. Once I was in bed, however, I found myself wide-awake and damp with sweat as I considered how next to proceed in order to retrieve the dogs and live happily ever after.

The leading character was the recently deceased Newton Churls. The sheriff seemed content with Arnie as the murderer, but I wasn't comfortable with the scenario—and it did nothing to resolve the stolen animal problem. When I at last fell asleep, my nightmares were as rift with canines as I'd dourly predicted.

As I made coffee the next morning, I remembered the telephone call from Caron's biology teacher. My reluctant agreement to appear at the school for a conference had been lost in the jumble of the weekend. Now it came back like an ulcer. My daughter was going to get herself expelled from school unless she could be bullied into dissecting a frog.

I was definitely not in a good mood when she came into the kitchen. "I have an appointment at the high school later this morning," I said icily.

She buried her head in the refrigerator. "Then Mrs. Horne called?"

"Yes, Mrs. Horne called. She called Friday evening, which is why I called Inez's house and learned that the two of you had lied to me and to her mother.

Now that I think about it, you're grounded until you leave for the convent."

"Oh, Mother." She took out a carton of milk and ever-so casually filled a glass, all the while watching me narrowly. "You know I did it to save Miss Emily's dogs from torture and death at the hands of some yuppified Dr. Frankenstein in a med school." She paused, and then nonchalantly added, "How did Miss Emily take the news about poor Nick and Nora?"

I gave her a sour look that should have curdled her milk. "I didn't tell her. And I was serious when I said you're grounded. Since you won't be attending school the remainder of the semester, you can stay in your room twenty-four hours a day and write letters on behalf of the ASPCA. I'll get yarn and you can knit sweaters and booties for orphaned Alaskan puppies."

"Oh, Mother."

"Oh, Mother—what?" I snapped.

She sat down across from me and attempted to appear earnest. "It's morally wrong to kill frogs so that a bunch of kids can poke their livers and stuff. The kids don't care, but the frogs do. Someone has to take a stand and refuse to condone the senseless slaughter."

"Do you honestly believe this or are you squeamish about the dissection and looking for a way to avoid it?"

"I honestly believe it," she said promptly.

"You're not worried about all the local publicity this will generate?" I continued, still not sure if she was lying. She was so very adept at it that I had fallen for excuses that later were proven to have no validity whatsoever—and only the vaguest relationship to reality. "We'll have to attend a school board hearing to argue your expulsion. You'll have to swear you're sincere in your beliefs, and they'll question you at length."

"Will I have my picture in the newspaper? Do you think the local television station will interview me? What about state coverage?" She was turning pinker and squeakier with each proposed media opportunity. "The national news? 'The Tonight Show'?"

I shooed her out of the room before she demanded the services of a press agent, refilled my coffee cup, and wondered why I hadn't had a tubal ligation sixteen years ago and become a sports model. After she'd gone to school to tell everyone when to watch Caron on Carson, I drove to Willow Street and trudged through the house to the backyard.

The dogs were not there. As I stood on the sunny porch, Colonel Culworthy came out of his house and whistled rather plaintively.

I approached the honeysuckle fence. "No sign of Patton?"

He walked across the yard, moving slowly and without any of his usual militant rigidity. "I called the animal shelter this morning. The woman tried to sound sympathetic, but she was annoyed by my call. Guess I'll put up posters. Run an ad in the paper and offer a reward."

"Maybe we could all chip in and run a big ad," I said, noticing his bristly gray hair needed a trim and his trousers a crease. "Why don't you find out the rates and call everyone?"

"I'll do it today. Patton's like a child to me," he said gruffly. He looked over his shoulder at the doghouse, but not before I'd spotted a tear in the corner of his eye. "Hate to think of him lost or hungry."

"Did Vidalia tell you where we went yesterday?"

"Talked to her this morning about it. Damn fool thing to do, the two of you. Likely to get yourselves hurt—or worse. Told her she was too old for that sort of thing."

I suspected he was more concerned with Vidalia's health than mine. She had a naïveté that probably appealed to him, and she was attractive in her own strange way. He was also hurt that we hadn't included him in the madcap mission, I realized.

"I didn't intend for Vidalia to come with me," I said. "I was going to ask Daryl, but he wasn't available. Have you seen him since Saturday afternoon?"

He thought for a moment. "No, can't say I have."

I glanced at the second story window, which was covered with a curtain. "I'd like to ask him something. He's probably in class by now, but I guess I'll find out."

"Meet you at the bottom of the stairs." Colonel Culworthy marched back into his house, slamming the door.

I wasn't irritated enough to crawl under the forsythia in order to outrace him, so I went back through the house and met him as ordered. I was slightly annoyed when he preceded me up the stairs, however, and increasingly so when he pounded on the door.

"Defoe!" he barked. "Open up in there!"

There was no response. I shouldered Culworthy aside and knocked on the door, shouting, "It's Claire Malloy, Daryl!"

Again, nothing. I tried the knob and discovered it was unlocked. I considered offering a lame excuse to Culworthy, decided it wasn't worth the effort, added (breaking and) entering to my list, and opened the door.

"Daryl?" I called as I stepped inside. The room was sparsely furnished with the minimum: sofa, chair, coffee table. There had been no attempt to personalize it with pictures or posters, and not so much as a magazine indicated someone lived there. Its starkness was disturbing, especially to those of us who waded through chaos on a daily basis. "He's not much of an interior decorator," I murmured to Culworthy, who was snorting under his breath.

The kitchen was minute and equally bereft of clutter. I opened a cabinet and found one coffee mug, two chipped glasses, and a few plastic plates and bowls. The refrigerator held a carton of milk, a jar of mustard, and half a loaf of bluish bread.

"Not much of a gourmet cook, either," Culworthy said with a curt laugh.

I went into the third room, which proved to be a bedroom and a study. An elaborate computer system covered a desktop. Stacks of printer paper were aligned on a shelf, along with text books and computer magazines. The battered briefcase was in the corner. The bed was neatly made, and the surface of the dresser pristine except for a small photograph in a silver frame.

"Vidalia mentioned that Daryl has a girlfriend," I said as I picked up the frame. "What she didn't mention," I added slowly, "was that the girlfriend is Jan Gallager. This must have been taken ten years ago, but she hasn't changed all that much."

"Haven't ever met her," Culworthy said. "Talked to her on the telephone several times. She sounded pleasant, concerned about the stolen animals. Seemed to know her stuff."

I sat down on the corner of the bed, still holding the frame, and shook my head. "She's competent.

What's bothering me is that she didn't mention Daryl when I was reporting the stolen animals. She may not know the house number, but she didn't even flinch when I said Willow Street."

"She's sticking to business. Her personal life shouldn't interfere with what happens at the animal shelter."

"But why wouldn't she say something about Nick and Nora? She must have seen them from the window or noticed them when she visited." I chewed on my lower lip for a minute, then looked up at him. "Have you ever seen a slender, dark-haired woman on the stairs?"

"No, but my living quarters are on the far side of my house. Never saw any woman drive up or come in the yard."

"Vidalia has, though." I replaced the frame on the dresser, and began opening desk drawers. They contained the minimum paraphernalia needed for computer work and college classes, all arranged for maximum accessibility. The briefcase contained computer printouts, a legal pad with pages of figures that resembled bird tracks, a used textbook, and the remains of a sandwich in a plastic bag.

I turned my attention to the dresser, where I determined he was neat and ill-equipped for more than three or four days without a jaunt to a launderette. The closet confirmed it. "This is strange," I said as I closed the closet door and walked into the living room.

"Strange?" Culworthy snorted. "Shows he's organized."

"Oh, he's organized," I said. "But I failed to find a checkbook, a bill, a letter, a date book, a class schedule, or anything with his name on it. Everyone leaves a trail of paper. His life appears to be—well, generic. Anyone could move in and take over the impersonal living room, unused kitchen, and organized desk."

Culworthy pulled on the tip of his mustache as his eyes darted around the room. "You're right, Malloy. Poverty's a factor, but there should be something. Vidalia told me you saw him at that animal sale. Hard to explain."

"I know someone who can explain some things," I said, frowning through the doorway at the photograph on the dresser.

Culworthy stayed on my heels all the way to my car, and climbed in the passenger's side without comment. I toyed with a few arguments, discarded them with a shrug, and took my keys from my purse. Before I could get in the car, Vidalia came out of her door and called to me.

I waited as she hurried across the street. "Did you and the colonel hear good news?" she demanded. "Have you an inkling as to the whereabouts of poor Astra and the others?"

"No," I said. "Colonel Culworthy's going to look into running a large ad in the newspaper, though, and putting up posters."

"Wherever are you going?" she asked, waving sweetly at Culworthy in the passenger's seat.

Inevitability settled in, and shortly thereafter she was settled in the backseat and we were heading for the animal shelter. I asked her to describe Daryl's girlfriend, and her description was close enough to what I'd expected to hear.

"When did you see this woman?" I asked.

"One night last week, and it was really rather late for a lady to be seen entering a gentleman's apart-

140

ment," she said, winking coyly at me in the rearview mirror. "It must have been nearly midnight. There was a full moon, so naturally Astra insisted we take a nice walk. She becomes quite kittenish in the moonlight, attacking shadows and pouncing about playfully."

"You saw the woman one time?" I inserted.

"I thought you asked about the last time," she said. "I saw her one other time. It must have been— oh, let me think . . . why, several weeks ago, I believe. You might ask George Maranoni for a more precise date."

"Maranoni?" Culworthy said. "What was he doing there?"

Having opened my mouth to ask the same thing (although without the overtone of jealousy), I merely glanced quizzically at her in the mirror.

"Walking his dog," Vidalia said, sounding flustered.

The line across Culworthy's forehead deepened, as did his voice. "You and Maranoni at midnight? Arranged it, huh?"

"Of course not, Colonel Culworthy. I would hardly arrange to meet a gentleman on the street at midnight, much less a married gentleman! I must add that no true gentleman would accuse a lady of that kind of behavior."

"Asking, not accusing," he said brusquely.

It was not the time for a spat. I turned the corner hard enough to cause them to gasp, then said, "So you've seen her twice?"

"Oh, yes," Vidalia said. "And she acted curiously both times, I might say. She was being furtive, distinctly furtive. It was obvious; even George remarked on it at the time."

Culworthy snorted under his breath but kept his comments to himself, and we arrived at the animal shelter without further accusations. The shelter truck was in the parking lot; the hatchback was not.

A large woman in a uniform greeted us from behind the counter, as did wuffles and barks from behind the door that led to the pens. The door to the office was closed, and when I asked if Jan was there, the woman shook her head and said, "No, she came in an hour ago and said she was going out to NewCo to look for the USDA files for the animals we brought in from there."

"Why does she need the files?" Culworthy asked.

"I don't have any idea," the woman said, aggrieved. "All those pathetic animals will have to be put down. We don't have any use for the numbers in the file, and we sure as hell have enough papers and folders crammed in the cabinets to keep us busy. Jan said she wanted them, though, and that's where she is. Me, I'm going crazy. Arnie's gone, and one of the officers is sick. With Jan out of pocket, I might as well crawl into a cage and nibble the kibble."

Vidalia, Culworthy, and I returned to the car. "That's odd," I commented. "It's a long drive out there for a file she doesn't need."

"Damn suspicious," Culworthy said with a decisive nod. "Sounds like she's avoiding us."

Vidalia leaned over the top of the seat. "She didn't know we were coming, Colonel Culworthy, unless, of course, she had some sort of premonition. I was trying very hard to remember exactly what Daryl's visitor looked like, and she might have been seized by a psychic sensation. It does happen, you know."

"Not in the military," he said sharply.

"Ah, but the military was very closemouthed about the UFO investigation in the fifties, wasn't it?"

"I think," I interrupted, "that we'd better run out there. I'm having a premonition of my own."

Vidalia clapped her hands. "How very thrilling! I simply adore to be in the presence of inexplicable psychic phenomena. Don't you, Colonel Culworthy?"

He didn't, and they argued all the way out the highway east of Farberville and were still at it as we passed Deputy Amos's house. I stopped in the middle of the road, and said, "I wonder if I ought to see if he's home and able to accompany us?"

"Scene of a crime," said Culworthy. "May find tape on the gate or an order not to trespass."

Which reminded me of Sheriff Dorfer's threats, should I continue to investigate the purported murder or any other aspect of the crime. Visiting NewCo qualified. "His truck's not there," I said grimly, then drove away.

The gate was open and the blue hatchback was parked in front of Churls's porch. I pulled in next to it, cut off the engine, and got out of the car. This time there were no wuffly barks from imprisoned dogs. It was as quiet as it had been after Deputy Amos had fired his gun three nights ago.

Colonel Culworthy helped Vidalia out of the back-seat, then slammed the car door closed. The noise startled me, but I bit my lip and went up the porch steps to the door. It, like the gate, was open, and it seemed the sheriff's department had no funds for official seals and orange tape.

The boards creaked behind me as Vidalia and Culworthy came to the door. Vidalia's eyes were round and her hands clasped together tightly. The colonel looked as leery as I presumed I did, and his voice was muted as he said, "Suppose we ought to have a look inside, Malloy."

"Go right ahead," I said graciously. He was firmly

rooted to the porch, however, so I cautiously opened the door a few more inches and went into the front room. "Jan?" I called softly, frowning at the couch cushions now on the floor.

Vidalia and Culworthy were clinging to each other as we crept across the shabby room to the kitchen doorway. The metal cash box was gone from the table, and a chair lay on its side. The cabinet doors were open; cereal boxes and soup cans littered the countertop and floor. The refrigerator was open, too, and that which had been on shelves was swept out. Even the freezer had been emptied.

I continued into the bedroom, which was the antithesis of Daryl's. The unmade bed had dingy sheets and a decaying quilt, and dirty clothes were scattered on the floor. A mail-order landscape hung askew on the wall; I resisted the urge to straighten it as I went farther into the room. All the drawers in the dresser had been yanked out and their contents dumped on the floor—unless Newton Churls had been a remarkably untidy housekeeper. The mattress was misaligned on the frame.

"Been searched," Culworthy said.

"It certainly looks that way," I said as I headed for the kitchen. As I stepped into the room, the back door crashed open and Jan Gallager stumbled through the doorway. When she saw me, she froze, her mouth agape and her face contorted with surprise. Her forehead was beaded with sweat.

"Claire?" she croaked.

I nodded, keenly aware of the gun in her hand. Behind me, Culworthy sputtered wordlessly and Vidalia let out a gasp that heated my neck.

Jan rubbed her face with her free hand (thank goodness), and took a deep breath. "You scared me," she said shakily. "I didn't expect to find someone in—in here like this. Does the telephone work?"

"I have no idea," I said. The gun was pointed at the floor, but I was still keeping an eye on it. "Why do you ask?"

"We've got to call an ambulance," she said as she grabbed the receiver.

"Ambulance?" Culworthy barked.

She frantically punched buttons. "It's Daryl. He's been shot!"

9

I dashed out the back door. The door to the pit bull pen was ajar, and Daryl Defoe had collapsed in the center of the concrete floor. Blood seeped from a wound in his chest, but there was not nearly as much as there had been when we'd found Newton Churls's savaged body.

I dropped to my knees beside Daryl. His eyes flickered, and he let out an agonized groan. "Get me out of here," he said hoarsely. "I can't take it. Please get me out of here."

"Who shot you, Daryl?"

His eyes closed and his head flopped to one side. I looked up as Vidalia and Colonel Culworthy approached the pen. "He's alive," I said.

"An ambulance is coming," Vidalia said. "Is there anything we can do for him?"

Jan ran into the pen with a blanket and knelt beside Daryl to cover him. "They said they'd be here as quickly as possible," she said, stroking his forehead. "It's so damn far. I hope he can hang on."

"What happened out here?" I asked.

She rocked back and gave me a bewildered shrug. "I don't know. I came out to pick up a file and for some reason glanced out the kitchen window. He was lying here, just like this. I ran out to the pen, ascertained that he was alive, and was coming inside to call the ambulance when you and . . ." she gestured at Vidalia and the Colonel, who were hanging on the fence and her every word with equal intensity, "those two suddenly appeared. In that the house had been vacant one minute earlier, it gave me quite a start."

"What about the gun?" I said softly.

She looked even more bewildered. "It was lying in the grass. I didn't stop to think; I just grabbed it."

Vidalia had been studying Jan. She met my eyes and nodded, but before I could decide what to do, I heard a car come up the driveway on the opposite side of the house.

"The ambulance!" Jan scrambled to her feet. "I'd better show them the way."

"It's too soon for the ambulance," I said. I caught her arm and stopped her. "Let's wait and see who it is, Jan. If you didn't shoot Daryl, someone else did."

"If I didn't. . . ?" she said weakly.

"Smoking gun, you know," Culworthy said through the fence.

Jan jerked her arm free and stared at me. "But why would I shoot Daryl?"

Deputy Amos came around the corner of the house, dressed in jeans and a T-shirt, and limping slightly. He halted as he caught sight of our group and the motionless form beneath the blanket. "Oh, my God," he gurgled.

"We've called for an ambulance," I said. "He's been shot, but he's not dead."

Ignoring Vidalia's chipper greeting, Deputy Amos came inside the pen and squatted down. "This is the guy who was here with you before," he said in a shocked voice. "What happened? Who shot him?"

"We don't know," I said, hoping we weren't going to add to the body count on the concrete floor.

He gulped several times, but when he stood up, he seemed to have remembered at least some of his training. "I . . . I'd better call the sheriff. Don't touch anything. Maybe you ought to move away from the pen or something."

Jan was bent over Daryl, crooning to him and lightly stroking his face, but Vidalia and Culworthy obediently moved a few yards back. I followed Amos into the kitchen and waited while he called the sheriff's department and gave a garbled explanation of the situation. The mention of my name elicited a series of squawks from the receiver, which was less than comforting.

"They'll be here as fast as they can," he told me after he'd hung up. "What is going on, Mrs. Malloy? Every time you show up, someone gets . . . hurt." Sweat glistened on his face like a light frost, and he was gulping unsteadily.

I mentally revised my estimate of his age to less than twenty. "I don't know what happened," I said carefully, "but I'm not responsible. Vidalia, Colonel Culworthy, and I arrived a very few minutes ago. Jan Gallager's car was parked out front. We went inside to find her, and she came into the kitchen and announced that Daryl had been shot."

We both turned to stare at the gun on the table. Deputy Amos started to pick it up, then yanked his hand back as if it had hissed at him. "How'd it get here?"

"Jan was carrying it," I admitted.

"Did you hear a shot?" he asked. I shook my head. "Does she have a motive to shoot the victim?"

"I don't know," I said honestly, declining to go

into detail. Vidalia had confirmed that Jan had visited Daryl's apartment late at night, and her youthfulness in the photograph hinted that their relationship had been established a long time ago. I wanted to talk to her, but I wanted to do so privately, and this was not the time.

A siren whined in the distance. I told Deputy Amos I would go out front to direct the medics and escaped before he could ask further questions, such as why I was there when I'd been ordered not to set foot near the property.

The sheriff asked, of course. Because I could not rely on Culworthy's discretion concerning the photograph, I grudgingly related the entire story, stressing that I'd gone to Miss Emily's house on the purest of motives and had entered Daryl's apartment merely to determine that he wasn't incapacitated by illness.

The interrogation took place in the now-familiar confines of the sheriff's office. Jan had been driven away from NewCo in an official car, and she'd looked very small and wan through the window. Vidalia, Culworthy, and I had been ordered to drive to the sheriff's office; the presence of a tobacco-chewing deputy in the backseat had put a damper on conversation. Once there, we'd been deposited in separate rooms to ponder our sins in solitude.

Sheriff Dorfer was making unhappy noises as he lit the umpteenth cigar. I decided it would not be wise to comment on the lack of amenities or the uncomfortable chair seat, and waited politely until he completed the ritual.

"Arnie didn't have anything to do with the shooting," I pointed out. "He's in a cell in this building. The three of us have each other as alibis, and it's difficult to imagine Jan shooting her boyfriend. She was deeply upset."

"Mizz Malloy," he said, "you're something, aren't you?"

"I certainly am, and I'm delighted that you've finally noticed. What I don't understand is how Daryl fits into this," I continued. "He was eager to join the group and insisted on involving himself even though he hadn't lost a pet. I wonder what he was doing at NewCo?" I paused to visualize the scene. I'd parked next to Jan's car, and Churls's Lincoln was where it had been earlier. The truck with the cages was still there. Arnie's monstrosity was missing; I assumed it had been impounded by the sheriff. "Or how he got there," I added, frowning. "He doesn't have a car, and it's a long way from Farberville. He didn't ride with Jan; he was already there when she arrived."

Sheriff Dorfer was regarding me without expression. His eyes were flickering, however, and his hand seemed to tremble as he took the cigar from his mouth and stubbed it out in the ashtray. "So what's your theory?" he said in an ominously quiet voice. "I feel real sure you've got one, Mizz Malloy."

"Sarcasm does not become you." I crossed my legs and tried to make myself comfortable on the hard seat. "Well, somehow it goes back to the stolen pets. Arnie admitted he picked up four hefty animals and took them to NewCo Friday evening. Someone broke the cash box. Churls ended up locked in the pen and was being mauled when I arrived. The animals vanished, as did Arnie. Where are the four animals?"

"I'm sure those folks feel real bad about their pets, and in fact, Miss Lattis and Colonel Culworthy made it more than clear. But I don't have the manpower to launch a full-scale investigation into the theft of a pair of basset hounds, a retriever, and a cat. I've got one murderer downstairs, and a perfectly good attempted murderer in a detention room talking to her lawyer."

"But she doesn't have a motive."

The sheriff ran his hand across his gray hair. "I don't give a damn, Mizz Malloy. It looks like they went out there together, got into an argument, and she ended it with a bullet. Then she realized what she'd done, panicked, and ran into the house to call the ambulance. It happens all the time, lovers or married folks attacking each other and then regretting it."

"Where did she find the weapon? If they went there together, they must have been on amiable terms."

"Maybe it belongs to Defoe and he carries it in his pocket. Some of those Vietnam vets have been known to act a might odd."

I conceded that one, especially since Daryl had been known to act more than a might odd. "Who searched Churls's house?" I asked. "And why? What cash was there had been taken, possibly by Arnie. Churls didn't look like the type to have a Rolex stashed under his mattress or diamond cuff links in a drawer."

"The Gallager woman claimed she went out there to find some damn-fool file. Right now she's denying she trashed the house looking for it, but it doesn't matter. She and Defoe were the only two people at the scene, and her fingerprints are on the weapon."

We argued for a while longer, then the sheriff repeated all his tedious threats and told me to get out of his sight and stay out of it in the future. I sailed out of his office and down the corridor, wishing there

151

was a way I could speak to Jan. Vidalia and Culworthy sat on the plastic couch in the entryway; the former was twinkling merrily and the latter grumbling to himself.

"I'm beginning to feel at home here," Vidalia said as we went out to the parking lot. "That nice receptionist offered us coffee and showed me pictures of her sister's baby."

"Damn foolishness," muttered Culworthy.

"The baby was adorable."

"Not what I meant." He opened the car door for her, assuming correctly that I could handle my own. "The sheriff said to get another dog. Said after a week I wouldn't know the difference. The man's a fascist."

"He certainly is," Vidalia said tartly.

I wasn't paying much attention to the two, who tended to remind me of Caron and Inez on a bad day—or a good day, for that matter. Caron. "What time is it?" I yelped.

Culworthy consulted his watch, then squinted at the sky to confirm his information. I was about to leap across the seat at him when he said, "Twelve hundred hours. Noon."

"I had an appointment at the high school at eleven," I said.

"No excuse for tardiness," Culworthy said. "We don't tolerate that sort of thing in the service."

"When I was in school, they gave us pink slips," Vidalia contributed from the backseat.

I rested my forehead on the steering wheel, gazing bleakly at my bloodstained knees. Everything was unraveling at an alarming rate, I thought. Miss Emily's dogs were nowhere to be found. Arnie was in jail for murder, and in some obscure way, I felt responsible for him. Jan would soon be charged with attempted murder. My daughter faced expulsion, and missing the conference was not helping the situation. And unless I climbed in the clothes dryer and remained there (on permanently depressed), I would have to face Peter, who would have heard the latest tidbit on the cop vine.

It was only noon (a.k.a. twelve hundred hours). I had the remainder of the day to have a car wreck, start a fire in the Book Depot, learn I'd been cut out of some unknown relative's will, or receive a letter from the IRS.

Vidalia patted my shoulder. "There, there, I'm quite certain they'll give you a pink slip. After all, you have an excuse. You were detained by the authorities."

I reluctantly raised my head and saw a deputy walk past the car with a man clad in an orange jumpsuit, rubber sandals, and handcuffs. The two went down an exterior flight of stairs on their way, I guessed, to the jail in the basement.

Vidalia and Culworthy debated the validity of my excuse as I drove them home. A sheriff's car was parked in front of Miss Emily's house, and a deputy was headed for Daryl's apartment. I dropped the two off at the curb, refused Vidalia's offer of a tuna sandwich and a nice cup of tea, and drove to my apartment as quickly as I dared, although speeding was such a minor misdemeanor that it hardly would have made my rap sheet.

Thirty minutes later I was dressed in a stern blue suit and sensible heels. My hair was held back in a semblance of a bun, and my reading glasses were planted squarely on the bridge of my nose. In lieu of a briefcase, a large purse hung from my well-padded shoulder. I found a notebook in Caron's room. I practiced a few pinched smiles in the mirror, made a final adjustment to my panty hose, and drove back to the parking lot adjoining the sheriff's headquarters.

I went down the concrete steps into a small reception room. The two deputies in the office were protected by glass, and neither deigned to acknowledge my grand entrance. I sniffed once or twice to get into the role, then rapped on the glass with a well-educated knuckle.

One of the deputies opened a small window. "Yeah?"

"I am Ms. Malloy of the regional office of the ACLU," I said briskly. "I need to see Arnold Riggles. There is a possibility of the violation of his constitutional rights."

The deputy studied me while I did my best to look like a taloned legal eagle. He then conferred with his associate, who gave me the same appraisal, and after a few minutes activated a buzzer and gestured at me to go through a door. I followed him down a hallway lined with metal doors, each with a grill. I looked around curiously, never having been in a jail before and having reasonably decent expectations of being locked up in this particular one in the near future. The ambiance was not of repressed violence but of futility; too many small-time criminals had gazed blankly through the grills, wishing they'd paid their child support or bought drugs from a legitimate dealer.

The deputy unlocked the last door and held it open for me. "Holler when you're ready to go," he said. "Visitor, Arnie."

I entered the small room, trying not to wince as

154

the door banged closed behind me. The furnishings were basic, the walls cold and damp, the ceiling oppressive. The occupant, on the other hand, was rather cheerful, considering his situation. Effusive, one might say. Others might say drunk.

"Senator, Senator, how ya doin'?" Arnie said, struggling to lift himself off the narrow cot. "I been thinking about you. Thought you was goin' send a pizza?"

I let the purse strap slide off my shoulder. "How's it going, Arnie? Are they treating you decently?"

He sat down on the commode and graciously pointed at the cot. "Sit down, Senator, and rest your feet. Say, you're all slicked up today, aren't you? Going to the White House for lunch?"

"Perhaps later," I murmured as I sat on the edge of the cot. "I didn't realize they served cocktails in cells these days. I was expecting bread and water."

Arnie took a pint bottle from his pocket. "Wanna snort?"

"Where did you get that?"

He waggled his finger at me, saying, "Wowsy, Senator, that's highly confidential—top secret and for your eyes only and all that kinda stuff." He took a drink and screwed the cap back on. "So what happened to that pizza?"

"Do the deputies know you've got whiskey in here?" I persisted. "It's not against the regulations?"

"Might be," he said, scratching his ear. "Anyways, to what do I owe the honor of your majesty's presence?"

I decided to ask my questions before I was deified. "Can you describe the animals you took to Newton Churls a few nights ago?"

"Lemme think." He took another drink, sucked

155

noisily on his teeth, and finally said, "Those two fat, squatty hounds, a retriever, and the nastiest ol' black cat I've ever seen. I mean, this one could scratch the warts off a witch's rear."

"How did you manage to get them in the truck?"

Arnie smiled smugly. "I always carry some goodies in the glove compartment. The hounds came bounding up like they was too dumb to walk, and I tossed them some Doggie Woggies. The retriever was in the same spot the next day. As for—"

"Wait a minute," I said. "You did have to let them out of their fenced yards, didn't you?"

"Oh, Senator, I am disappointed in you. I wouldn't never do that. I just watch for strays, and when I see one, I say to myself, I say, Arnie, you—"

"The dogs were loose?"

"They were snuffling on the sidewalk when I saw 'em. The cat was prowling around an alley on the other side of the street. I opened a can of sardines, and it liked to knock me down."

"And you didn't pick up a large poodle?"

"Those fur balls come in different sizes?"

I had no reason not to believe him, if only because he was incapable of devising lies at the moment. "What exactly happened at NewCo?"

He scratched his neck, took another drink, and finally said, "It's on the murky side. My boss stayed around till almost dark, doing paperwork and playing with the puppies. As soon as she left, I took the truck over to the trailer and loaded the animals—in more ways than one, if you follow my drift."

"No, Arnie, I do not follow your drift."

"They've got these pills out at the shelter that calm the animals down. I borrowed some so we could have ourselves a peaceful drive. Once everybody was snoozing, I went by a tavern for a game of pool and a drink or two." His hand drifted to his arm pit for a lengthy indulgence. "Well, anyways, I drove out to ol' Newt's place about dark, unless it was later, and unloaded the animals."

"Yes," I said, leaning forward. "Then you and Churls had an argument about payment, right?"

"First we had another argument, then we had that one."

"You had another argument? What was it about, Arnie?"

His face was beginning to sag; either gravity or alcohol was taking control, and his voice was blurry. "Gambling, Senator. Now I'm as opposed to gambling as anyone, but every now and then I attend a sporting event and it adds to my interest if I wager a buck or two." Despite a hiccup, he managed to take yet another drink from the rapidly depleting bottle. "Speaking of interest, I keep meaning to ask you about the regulation of the prime lending rate, Senator. It seems to me—"

"Finish your story, and then we'll discuss the fiscal policy," I said quickly. I held out my hand. "On second thought, I'd love a snort."

He gave me the bottle. "To your continued health. Okay, Newt started griping about how I owed him money from the last fight, and I had to admit he had a point of sorts. He said he'd pay me a few bucks— just to tide me over the weekend—and I said I'd bring some more strays the next day. Then all of a sudden, Newt says he's got company and for me to get the hell down the hill and wait till he hollers to come back."

"Did you hear or see anyone?" I asked, clutching the bottle tightly.

Arnie screwed up his face, then sighed. "Nope, but I'd picked up a bottle of rotgut to amuse myself on the drive, and it is possible I wasn't at my keenest, sensorially speaking. I went down the hill a piece, like he said, and found a log to sit on. It was kinda peaceful for a long time, and I was drinking and looking at the stars when I heard shots and voices and I said to myself, I said, Arnie, there ain't no call to get yourself involved in what's going on, and I just went on down the hill till I came to the railroad tracks."

I tried to visualize the events. "So you never went inside Churls's house, right?" His head bobbled, and I interpreted it as a confirmation of sorts. "And when you left the backyard, Churls was there with the four animals you'd brought?"

"Front yard, Senator," he corrected me with a crooked smile. "Trying to trick ol' Arnie, were you?"

The cell door opened and Sheriff Dorfer filled the doorway. He looked at the bottle in my hand, then at Arnie, who was grinning dopily and swaying as if in a hurricane. I hurriedly handed the bottle to Arnie, stood up, and resettled my glasses on my nose.

"I was just leaving," I said with measured dignity. "How thoughtful of you to unlock the door for me. If you'll excuse me now, Sheriff Dorfer, I must run along to the Book Depot to sell some books. That is, after all, my primary calling."

He stepped back, as did the deputy behind him. I nodded at Arnie, and went out of the cell and down the corridor, my head held high and my knees no steadier than Arnie's smile. No bellow stopped me, nor did a bullet between my nicely contoured shoulder blades, and I made it to my car safely. A yellow envelope informed me that I'd parked in a reserved space and would be twenty-five dollars poorer because of it. I told myself that the sentence was mild.

When I arrived at the Book Depot, I called the high school and told the secretary I'd been detained unavoidably, although I did not elaborate. The conference was rescheduled for the following morning at eleven, when Mrs. Horne had her planning period. I called the hospital and inquired about Daryl, and was told he was critical.

I thought about all the paperwork I'd left undone, the cartons of books I had not unpacked, the invoices I had not checked, the orders I had not placed, the dusting I had neglected. I then opened Caron's notebook, found a clean sheet, and did my best to construct a chronology of everything that had occurred since Miss Emily rode into the sunset. I lacked specific times, but I was fairly certain I'd jotted down all the pertinent events, and I was frowning at the list when my aged hippie came into the store.

"I have your jacket, bandana, and glasses at my apartment," I said. "I'll bring them here in the morning."

He came to the counter. "That was kinda neat, wasn't it? Like, I'd never realized what an intense woman you are. Your hands like seared my body. Any chance you'd like to ride out to the lake this evening? I'll pedal and you can hold me all the way."

His leer was so unfocused that I wondered about the depth of his hallucinogenic experimentation twenty years ago. "I don't think so, but it was very kind of you to give me a ride. Why don't you pick out your free books?"

"Groovy." He was not overwhelmed with disappointment as he wandered around the science fiction rack, and every now and then he read aloud a title and giggled.

I returned to my chronology, not sure what good it was doing but aware that it was de rigueur in mystery novels—the source of my training and enlightenment. The bell above the door jangled. Lieutenant Peter Rosen was back in uniform, and in a snit, if his scowl was to be considered an omen. I closed the notebook as he came across the room.

I was going to greet him politely, but he said, "I just got a call from Sheriff Harvey Dorfer. Damn it, Claire, less than twelve hours ago you promised to—"

"And how are you?"

"I'm dandy. You, on the other hand, are within inches of being locked up in the county jail, and I'm not going to be able to prevent it."

"Will you bring Caron to visit me on Sunday afternoons?"

He was not in the mood for agreeable repartee, it seemed. "The sheriff was so angry he was almost impossible to understand. He sputtered for five minutes before I realized what he was talking about. Contraband was mentioned, as was—"

"I did not take that whiskey bottle to Arnie," I said, seizing what I suspected was my only area of innocence. "In fact, I asked him several times where it came from, but he wouldn't tell me." Peter bristled, but before he could speak, I said, "Where do you think it did come from? He's been in jail for two days, and I would think he would have been searched when he was booked."

"He was," Peter said levelly. "That's why the sheriff assumed you smuggled in the bottle in a large shoulder bag."

"The sheriff assumes incorrectly. Instead of hurling accusations at innocent parties, he ought to review his security measures. Did Arnie have any other visitors?"

Peter crossed his arms and let out a sigh that hinted (or reeked) of frustration. "The only visitor Arnie's had is an attorney from the legal clinic, and she swore he was drunk when she arrived, and still drunk when she slammed out three minutes later."

"Martian sex slaves," said a disembodied voice laden with awe.

"A customer," I explained. "I did get some answers from Arnie before we were interrupted. He found Nick, Nora, and Patton on the sidewalk, and lured them into the truck with something called Doggie Woggies. If we believe his story, then we still don't know how the three dogs got out of their fenced yards."

He was seething, but the corner of his mouth twitched and I could tell he was intrigued professionally. "So what did our boy do with the animals?"

"He kept them in a trailer until he had a chance to drive out to NewCo to sell them to Churls. He said something about owing Churls money for a gambling debt, too."

"Pit bull fights across the state line," Peter said. "I asked the sheriff, and he was willing to share the information with a fellow law enforcement agent. He is not quite so pleased to be cooperating with an amateur who keeps popping up like a dandelion in an otherwise well-manicured lawn."

"He is a classic example of anal retention," I said as I resisted the urge to pull out my notebook and make a notation about Churls's bookmaking activities.

"The sultry sirens of Venus," drifted the voice from behind the rack. "Swept into a whirlpool of sexual slime . . ."

Peter wiggled his eyebrows at me. "How about I come by tonight to sweep you into a whirlpool? I haven't had a chance to properly make amends for my absence, during which you managed to enrage a sheriff and attend a murder and a shooting."

We agreed on a time, although I admitted reservations about being swept into any variety of slime, and he wandered away to investigate whatever crimes were being committed on the superficially peaceful streets of Farberville.

The hippie appeared with an armful of books, repeated his invitation for a moonlit ride, and left. My first customer of the day had cost me about forty dollars, I estimated. If business picked up, I could be bankrupt by the end of the day.

I was thinking about George Maranoni when Caron and Inez trudged into the store. Caron dropped her books on the counter and said, "Well?"

"Well, there's something slightly wrong with George's story," I said, drawing a circle around his name. "I can't quite bring it into focus, though."

"That's Not What I Meant," Caron snapped. "Am I expelled or not?"

"I missed the appointment; it's rescheduled for tomorrow."

"You might hear from Mrs. Horne before then," Inez said timidly. She was going to continue, but Caron's elbow bouncing off her ribs may have deterred her.

I put down the pencil. "Why am I going to hear from Mrs. Horne before then?" I inquired coolly.

Caron crossed her arms as Peter had done, and her noisy sigh was as frustrated. "It's not my fault, you know. I merely explained my position to Louis Wilderberry, who talked to all the sophomore football players, who asked me questions. Then Rhonda Maguire decided she wasn't getting any attention, so she announced she was making a petition for everybody to sign, and pretty soon the entire class was huffing and puffing and Mrs. Horne said I was an instigator. I had to look it up in the dictionary, for pete's sake!"

"Rhonda claims she's the instigator, but she just wants Louis to invite her to the school dance," Inez said.

Caron stuck out her lower lip. "She thinks she's some kind of flab fatale. Louis happened to appreciate the maturity of my reasoning, and now Rhonda's trying to butt in by telling everybody I'm just too squeamish to touch a dead frog."

"Are you?" I asked.

"Of course not! If I wanted to touch a dead frog, I would. I happen to think it's morally wrong, that's all." The lower lip reached its limit.

I realized I had, too.

10

I looked up George Maranoni's address in the telephone book, told the girls to mind the store, and drove to Walnut Street. The Maranonis lived in a yellow Victorian house that, like Miss Emily's, had seen better days, although theirs appeared not to be subdivided into apartments. The paint had flaked off on the woodwork, and several windows on the third floor were covered with cardboard. The grass was shaggy, leaves clotted the untended flower beds, and weeds lined the unpaved driveway.

I parked at the curb and went up creaking steps to the porch. The antique doorbell required a twist, but I heard nothing inside and resorted to the less exotic technique of knocking. I was about to leave when George opened the door a few inches.

"Yes?" he said blankly.

"I came by to talk to you."

"About what?" he said in the same voice.

Wondering if he'd been drinking, I hesitated for a moment, then said, "About Juniper's theft and the puppies."

"Juniper? I don't know about Juniper, but I gave the puppies away last week. Sorry."

He closed the door. I lifted my hand to knock, but thought better of it and was heading for my car when Helen Maranoni drove into the driveway. As she got out of her car, she gave me an odd look, and I realized I was still wearing some vestiges of my ACLU disguise.

"Can I help you?" she asked.

"I wanted to ask your husband a few questions about the man who took the puppies. He wasn't . . . cooperative."

"He's ill," she said, holding up a sack from a pharmacy. "I don't like to leave him, but I had to get his prescription refilled. It seems to cost more every time."

"I hope he feels better," I said, somewhat guilty about my earlier suspicion.

"Thank you. He has a recurring problem with arthritis, and these damp spring days make it worse. Do you have any new information concerning Juniper's whereabouts?"

I told her about the animal sale in Guttler and then related what had happened that morning at NewCo. She was appropriately shocked to hear Daryl had been shot.

"The woman at the animal shelter is under arrest?" she said, frowning. "If she's a criminal, might she not have lied about the stolen pets, too?"

"An employee at the shelter admitted that he picked up Nick, Nora, Patton, and Astra last week and attempted to sell them to Newton Churls. He denies any knowledge of Juniper, I'm afraid. Is it possible she escaped somehow and went looking for her puppies?"

Helen glanced at the house. "No, the gate is secure and the fence is more than high enough to keep her from jumping over it. Furthermore, Juniper's quite devoted to me and would never go off for this long. Even when she engaged in the illicit liaison with

165

some neighborhood mongrel, she was barking to be let in that same morning."

"How did she get out?"

"It's hard to say," Helen said, glancing again at the house. "I wasn't aware she was out until I heard her at the front door, and had no idea that she'd . . . done what she did until the vet examined her for an unrelated problem. I was astonished, as was George, and we agreed to have her neutered as soon as she'd recovered from having the puppies." Her face sagged, and she wiped at the corner of her eye. "The puppies are just darling. We want to keep them, but we're on a strict budget and the food and vet bills would have been too much for us."

"Maybe if you advertise again, they can go to a legitimate good home," I said soothingly.

"And the shelter employee says he wasn't the one who came to the door and took them?"

I mentally replayed the key conversations. "We keep being interrupted when we talk, but I don't think he did. He claims he picks up strays, and I can't see him following up on an ad in a newspaper. It would require more concentration than he's got."

"I keep having nightmares about the animals at that horrible man's house," Helen said. "I must say he deserved his fate. You agree, don't you? He was going to put a helpless puppy in a pen with vicious animals that have been trained to kill."

"He wasn't a very nice person," I said.

She regarded me coolly. "He certainly wasn't. We're much better off without that sort in our community. Anyone who raises pit bulls ought to be forced to take responsibility for whatever the animals do."

"I suppose so," I said uneasily. "Churls would have been charged with murder if his animals had killed someone."

"They make an effective weapon, don't they?" With a sharp nod, she went inside the house and closed the door.

I drove around the corner and parked in front of Miss Emily's. Praying for a miracle, I cut through the side yard, grabbed the gate so tightly the wire cut into my fingers, and called for Nick and Nora. It was not my day for divine intervention, alas, and I was heading for my car when a sheriff's department car drove up.

"Deputy Amos," I said without enthusiasm, "are you in the process of serving an arrest warrant?"

He limped across the sidewalk. "No, the sheriff wanted me to take another look at Defoe's apartment. We're having a helluva time figuring out why he and the Gallager woman went back to NewCo this morning. She insisted she needed a file, but we found it in her office and now she's clammed up."

"How's Daryl?"

"Critical. We've got a deputy at the hospital, and we're hoping Defoe'll sing when he regains consciousness." Deputy Amos gave me a faint smile as he continued past me to the stairs.

In that he seemed to be in a garrulous mood, I followed him. "Did you find the spot where Arnie buried the money?" I asked as we went upstairs.

He was startled, either by my presence or my question. "How did you know about that, Mrs. Malloy? Did Arnie tell you anything that might indicate where he buried it?"

"Oh, no, Sheriff Dorfer mentioned something to me. Did you find anything?"

"Yeah, a four-foot copperhead in a bad mood, enough aluminum cans to fill a garbage bag, and a patch of brush covered with seed ticks. I had to strip buck-naked and let Bethanna pick 'em off me with tweezers half the night."

We were on the landing. He seemed unsure about the situation, but I wasn't through with him and he was no match for a quick-witted amateur sleuth. I resolved his dilemma by going inside the apartment. "I noticed something peculiar when I was here this morning," I said over my shoulder. "I couldn't find a single piece of paper with Daryl's name on it."

"That is kinda peculiar. What do you think it means?"

"I don't know if it means anything." I went into the bedroom and noticed the photograph on the dresser was gone. "Did Jan admit she and Daryl are . . . close friends?"

"She squirmed around until Sheriff Dorfer showed her the picture. She said they'd known each other for some time, but she says he didn't go out there to NewCo with her and she didn't hear the gunshot, much less shoot him herself." Deputy Amos looked uncomfortable as he came in the room. "I'm not sure you ought to be in here, Mrs. Malloy. It's not a crime scene or anything, but there may be evidence."

I obligingly went into the kitchen. "I've already told you I was here this morning," I said, adding a lack of logic (surely a misdemeanor) to my list. "Did you or your girlfriend see a car going toward NewCo this morning?"

"I asked Bethanna, but she was doing her hair and it takes her forever and a day. She said she heard a car, maybe two, but she wasn't paying any attention to anything but her curling iron and didn't check the time. I was way down at the barn, doing some chores. I can't see the road from there and I wouldn't hear a tank drive past the house."

"What about the other people who live along the road?"

"We'll ask them," he said from the doorway. "Listen, Mrs. Malloy, the sheriff is likely to be real pissed if he finds out you were here and asking me questions." His Adam's apple rippled as he swallowed nervously. "I think you'd better run along."

"It's been lovely," I said. I gave him a polite smile, and then went to my car and considered what, if anything, I'd learned. Not much, I told myself. Jan had admitted she knew Daryl, but she hadn't explained why she had been secretive, unless Deputy Amos had developed a sudden reticence.

I drove back to the Book Depot, where Caron and Inez were amusing each other (and alarming customers) with a vitriolic condemnation of Rhonda Maguire's most recent act of treachery. I sent them away. I made a few notes, then picked up the feather duster and drifted around the racks, relocating dust and trying to come up with a motive for keeping their relationship, or any relationship, a secret. Infidelity headed the list, of course. Jan didn't wear a wedding ring; it seemed probable that she was single, and I presumed Daryl was, too. Jan didn't seem the sort to cheat on a male friend, either. Her job did not preclude a relationship, and she was certainly old enough to engage in one. I needed to talk to her, but I doubted Sheriff Dorfer would settle for an irate call to Peter if Ms. Malloy of the ACLU appeared at the women's detention facility. And the cells were damp enough to frizz my hair.

After an internal debate between the two increasingly divergent sides of my conscience, I called the animal shelter. The officer sounded distraught, which made me feel all the more wicked as I identified myself and said, "Jan wanted me to pick up a few things at her place and take them to the jail. Does she still live in that duplex across from the campus?" I held my breath, because if the officer said yes, I had put the noose around my own neck and kicked over the stool.

"I didn't know she'd ever lived by the campus," the woman said, puzzled. "She has a house out this way." She then proceded to give me the address in a small subdivision, and graciously informed me that the key was where it always was, which was under the flowerpot by the door.

I graciously thanked her. The Book Depot was supposed to stay open until seven, but I stuck the CLOSED sign on the door and drove to Jan's house. It was small and nondescript, indicative of her salary, and wedged among others that differed only in color and degree of maintenance. Hers was neat, as I would have guessed.

I circled the block, looking for unmarked police cars, and parked in front of the house next door. The key was under the flowerpot. Once I was inside, I realized my muscles were tensed and my heart pounding too fiercely for one so practiced in crime.

The living room was pleasantly normal, with well-used furniture and a few houseplants. A knitting bag lay on the sofa. The magazines ran the gamut from *Vogue* to *Field and Stream,* including several unfamiliar ones with dogs and cats on the covers.

The kitchen and bathroom were unremarkable, both clean and equipped with the usual things. The first bedroom seemed to be uninhabited on a regular basis. The second was Jan's, I decided, as I went in and looked around curiously, although for what I had no theories. The bed was made and there were no clothes scattered about. I picked up a small frame and was not surprised to see Daryl's face. His hair was much shorter, almost as short as Colonel Culworthy's, and he was wearing an olive drab fatigue jacket. His T-shirt displayed the peace symbol, however, and he was grinning mischievously. In the background was a lush tangle of tropical plants.

All this told me nothing of interest, since he'd mentioned a year in Vietnam. I replaced the picture and eased open the drawer of the bedside table. Unlike her consort, Jan saved letters. Reminding myself that I was trying to help her rather than indict her, I took a yellowed envelope from the stack and squinted at the faded printing. It was addressed to her, and the postmark was of the old-fashioned variety that offered a date. The date was more than twenty years ago.

I pulled out the letter written on notebook paper, but before I could unfold it, I heard the front door open. A kaleidoscope of faces flashed through my mind, including Yellow Hair and Baby Bear, Sheriff Dorfer, and a whole slew of people who would be annoyed at my presence. I managed to stuff the envelope in the drawer and was edging toward the closet when Jan came into the room.

"Fancy finding you here," she said wearily. "I went by the shelter on my way home, and Linda mentioned that you were being so kind as to bring me a few things." She sank down on the bed and pulled off her shoes, letting each one fall to the floor with a thud. The lines on her face seemed deeper, harsher.

I did my best to look contrite. "I'm sorry about this, but I was trying to help you—and Daryl. I don't believe that you shot him. Has the sheriff changed his mind?"

"I was released on my own recognizance, with orders not to go out of town for any reason. They won't charge me until they see how Daryl does."

I held up the frame. "Look, Jan, I know about you and Daryl. What I don't understand is why you've been keeping it a secret."

She went to the closet and took out a plaid bathrobe. "It seemed easier."

"What seemed easier—skulking up the stairs to his apartment late at night? You're single and old enough to be involved with someone. Why go to all that trouble?"

"I have to deal with people in the community. Some of the shelter funding comes from the city, and the rest from the Humane Society," she said as she began to change into the robe. "I feel more comfortable without any gossip drifting about or speculation concerning my private life."

I resisted the urge to push her into the closet, lock the door, and make her talk. "That's utter baloney," I said, allowing my irritation to be heard. "You're on a major ego trip if you think the city board directors or the members of the Humane Society have the slightest interest in your private life. They might not care to read about your involvement in a drug bust or some dreary crime. Do you honestly think they care if you date a single man who's about your own age?"

Jan gazed impassively at me. "I'm old-fashioned about it, I suppose."

"No, you're lying about it," I said.

She averted her eyes as she went past me and into the hall. The bathroom door closed. I toyed with the idea of sneaking a look at the letter in the drawer, then went into the kitchen, put on the teakettle, and was preparing a tray when she came down the hall.

"You're still here," she said flatly.

"That's right, and I'm staying until you tell me the truth about Daryl Defoe. The guest room will do fine." I took the tray into the living room and set it on the coffee table. "I do have a date later," I added, "with a man. We're both single, you see, and even though he's a detective at the Farberville CID, no one thinks anything about it. I'll admit he doesn't stumble out of my house at six in the morning, singing loudly while he zips up his trousers, but we have no qualms about going to dinner or a movie."

She accepted a cup of tea and sat in the armchair. I waited, feigning patience, while she stared at the amber liquid and sighed several times. "If I tell you the truth, will you promise to keep it a secret?" she asked quietly.

"If you convince me that I ought to," I said.

"I'm married. It happened a long time ago, and I realized almost immediately that it was a mistake. He didn't have what it took to get through college, and when he finally dropped out, he found a factory job, started drinking heavily, and pounded out his frustrations on me."

"When was this?"

The cup rattled in the saucer, and her head remained down. "Fifteen years ago. We were living in Missouri, and one morning while he was benumbed

173

with a hangover, I threw some things in a suitcase and caught a bus back home."

I took off my shoes and curled up on the sofa. "What was his name, and why haven't you gotten a divorce?" I asked in a deceptively mild voice.

"Uh . . . Gary," she stammered. "Gary Gallager. I don't know where he is now, but I've always been afraid that if I filed for a divorce, he'd learn where I was and come after me. It's like being in the federal witness protection program, I suppose."

"Is Daryl in it?"

She gave me a quick frown. "No, and I'm not either. Look, I've told you the truth—I'm a married woman, so I can't date anyone without committing adultery. My reputation is vital to the welfare of the animal shelter."

"But no one knows you're married," I pointed out.

"Some day Gary may show up, looking for me. He could use the adultery as grounds, and then it would be public knowledge."

"Oh," I said with a sober nod. "Why did you go to NewCo this morning?"

"To pick up the USDA file."

I waggled my finger at her. "No, no, no. One of the sheriff's deputies told me they found that file in your office. What were you searching for, Jan?"

"I don't have to answer your questions."

"I'll borrow a nightgown and have the drugstore deliver a toothbrush."

She stood up and went to the window. Her back turned to me, she said, "Newton Churls raised pit bulls for fighting, and he attended fights across the state line. He also made book with locals, and I thought I might find a ledger with names and transactions. He's dead, but we can still nail the jerks that support the inhumanity of dogfighting. I was going to take what I found to the newspaper and try to get them interested in an exposé."

Sipping tea, I tried to decide if she was lying. The story about Gary Gallager wouldn't withstand scrutiny through cracked sunglasses, and I wasn't sure about the alleged ledger, either. "Why didn't you say that in the first place?" I asked.

"Because," she said, still facing the window, "I think there are some newsworthy names in it, and I want the proof in my possession before I mention its existence. I don't want to be beaten by some hulk in a pickup truck, have the shelter burned down, or even alert certain people who could make sure I never left NewCo."

"Whose names?"

When she turned around, the light from the window silhouetted her and her face was difficult to see. "I will not mention a single name until I have the proof. You can order a toothbrush, but let me warn you that my three dogs sleep on the bed in the guest room, and the mousetrap in the corner is there for a reason."

"Did you tell the sheriff that you're married?" I asked, changing gears.

"No, and I don't want anyone to tell him. It's my private business and it doesn't have anything to do with the pet thefts or Newton Churls's death. I didn't shoot Daryl, and I didn't hear anything or see anyone. If you don't mind, I've had an unpleasant day, and tomorrow will be worse because we're going to be forced to put down the animals from NewCo. It has to be done, but it upsets the entire staff." She put the teacup on the tray. "I'm going to call the

175

hospital, take a bath, and knit several miles of muffler to relax myself."

I suggested aspirin, and left. As I drove in the general direction of my apartment, I thought about her story and decided at least some of it was pure fabrication. Since having me as a houseguest was not the most appalling thing imaginable (I'm tidy and well-behaved), I further decided her motive was unknown but important.

There was no way to verify the existence of Gary Gallager, who might or might not be a real person, and therefore might or might not reside anywhere in the country. She claimed she'd fled from him in Missouri, but why would she return home and continue to use her married name if she was frightened that he would track her down? Even if that was true, she was confused about her dates, because, according to the envelope in her bedside table, she'd been Jan Gallager twenty years ago. All in all, it was not a very adept lie; I surely could have produced one worthy of a thick romance novel, if not a miniseries or trilogy.

When I arrived home, Caron was on the telephone in her bedroom, shrieking about Rhonda Maguire. I made a drink, tried to distract myself with the newspaper, and was lost in roiling thoughts when Peter knocked perfunctorily and came into the living room.

I fetched him a beer and we settled down on the sofa like an ancient married couple.

"Committed any more crimes this afternoon?" he asked.

I considered his question. "Do you enjoy my company?"

He nuzzled my neck and assured my earlobes that

he did, and very much indeed, thus allowing me to rule out what Jan might have deemed blackmail. I wanted to ask his opinion about the latest developments, but timing is everything when dealing with a man who thinks himself sensitive.

"Tell me about your mother," I commanded. The nuzzles grew more intense, and I was barely listening as he said, "She wants to meet you."

"What?" I croaked. I flung myself to the far end of the sofa. "Why?"

"She's just curious, and you of all people ought to understand how that operates," Peter said, glumly eyeing the space between us. "I told her a little bit about you. I'm always convinced what I say never registers, but all of a sudden she'll regurgitate some tidbit and demand more information."

"What did you tell her?"

He held up his hands. "That you were an attractive and intelligent widow, a terrible cook, a mystery novel reader, a martyred mother, and a meddlesome snoop."

"Well, I'm not," I sniffed, "and I don't like the idea of you talking about me to anyone, including your mother."

"She's institutionalized, Claire. She's not going to demand you appear for an inquisition. She wasn't all that fascinated, for that matter. She sent me away because she was expecting a message from Ulf, a twelfth-century Norse sorcerer." He paused, then frowned and said, "Not what?"

"Meddlesome."

"And why was the Book Depot closed at five o'clock this afternoon? Aerobics class? A séance?"

Tricky. "I was running an errand for a friend," I said with a vague gesture. "What am I going to do about Miss Emily's dogs, Peter? She'll be home in less than two weeks. The dogs may have been dissected by then. I'm not meddling this time—I have a responsibility to find Nick and Nora, and Sheriff Dorfer's not even interested. He's got Arnie, and that satisfies him. Colonel Culworthy, Vidalia, and the Maranonis are visibly aging from the worry. I wish I could dismiss the thefts with a kind yet condescending smile, but I can't!"

He seemed a little startled by my outburst. "The thefts took place within the city limits, so we can consider them within our jurisdiction. However, the chief's going to say pretty much what the sheriff did—there are too many other crimes requiring our attention. I'm on a homicide now. Nothing mysterious, but something that demands my time and creates stacks of paperwork. Homicides come before dognappings."

"The theft of the basset hounds will cause Miss Emily to have a heart attack," I said.

"My hands are tied." He looked at them, then leered at me. "Actually, they're not. And if you'll meet me in the middle of that cushion, I'll prove it to you."

"Whatever will your mother say?" I murmured, accepting the invitation. He tended toward tedium in certain matters, but he did other things with great charm.

After he'd left, I carried glasses into the kitchen, checked the locks, and turned off the light in the living room. I'd intended to go to bed, but I found myself at the front window, looking at the shadowy trees, the branches of which were beginning to take substance as buds neared opening. The sidewalk was vacant; the lawn in front of Farber Hall a rolling expanse of mottled camouflage . . . like Daryl's jacket in the photograph at Jan's house.

A pickup truck with one headlight drove by. I couldn't remember the current term, but in my high school days we'd called them cockeyes, and kept a tally. One hundred cockeyes and one was granted a wish, at least in theory (I didn't find a red Jaguar parked out front the next morning, nor, one hundred cockeyes later, was I asked on a date by the president of the Latin club, a *damnum sine injuria* if ever there was one). I doubted I could spot ninety-nine more before Miss Emily stepped off the carbon monoxide–belching bus and called for Nick and Nora.

The sheriff wasn't going to do anything, and Peter couldn't. Meddlesome or not, that left only amateurs, and we were a sorry bunch. Vidalia, faithfully doing Astra's chart. Colonel Culworthy, leading commando raids. The Maranonis, one vague and the other vitriolic. And Daryl Defoe, unconscious from a bullet wound to his chest.

Which put me back where I'd been a few hours earlier, when I was trying to figure out Jan's need to lie. As I ran through the story, something occurred to me. If she'd come home to Farberville, it was reasonable to assume she'd grown up here. I had a wispy memory of something in a previous conversation about recognizing Churls . . . who'd acted as if he'd recognized one of the commandos on our first visit.

But Jan hadn't been with us.

I couldn't ask Churls (unless Ulf could be persuaded to intercede), but I could find out about Jan's past, if she had been reared in Farberville. The high school had been on the hill in the south part of town for a long time; I didn't know when it was built, but I'd roamed the dim corridors at one time, due to un-

179

timely demise in the teachers' lounge, and it was obvious the first seniors by now had attended their offsprings' graduation ceremonies.

I didn't need to prowl for graffiti in the rest rooms in the basement, however. There was a record of everyone who'd attended, complete with organizations, awards, and snippety predictions, and it was accessible without the necessity of yet another felony. Since primeval times, each year there had been a copy of the Farberville High School *Falconnaire*—and I knew where to find them.

I tiptoed down the hall. Caron's room was dark and the only sound was a snuffly snore. I grabbed a jacket, my purse, and the car keys, made sure the front door was locked securely, and went around the back of the house to my car.

As I drove to Willow Street, I spotted a cockeye in the rearview mirror. That left only ninety-eight, should I have misjudged Miss Emily's penchant for hanging on to every last scrap of anything that came into her hands and had printed words. Her house was dark, as was Culworthy's next door. One light was on in the second floor of Vidalia's apartment house; as I watched, a woman carrying a baby paced past the window, neither happy.

The key was in the mailbox. I went inside, made sure the curtains were closed, and snapped on a lamp. Although what I was doing was perfectly legal, it didn't particularly feel that way and I wasn't certain the sheriff hadn't assigned someone to watch Daryl's apartment upstairs.

The yearbooks were in a bookcase in the bedroom, and went back forty years. Jan was somewhere around forty, I decided, as I did a bit of mental subtraction, took volumes from 1965 to 1973 from the shelf, and settled down on the living room sofa.

To my regret (and Miss Emily's, I was sure), the high school journalism budget precluded indexes. I blew the dust off 1965 and waded through the faculty and administration, teams, cheerleaders teetering on shoulders and prominently displaying their pompoms, and finally found the section of individual pictures grouped by class.

The freshmen were aptly named. Their faces were dewy, some with the lingering remains of childhood puffiness. There was still a hint of terror in their eyes, as if waiting for an upperclassman to harass them or to lose their way to the library. Smiles were tentative, and Peter Pan collars abounded. No Gallagers, no Defoes.

The sophomores had survived the tribulations of ninth grade and gazed back coolly, despite a higher incidence of acne. No Gallagers, no Defoes. The juniors were smug, and the seniors made it clear they'd assumed their adulthood and learned how to engage in all the vices befitting this new status. No Gallagers, no Defoes.

Jan might have transferred to the school after 1965, I told myself with more optimism than the theory warranted. I poured myself a glass of Miss Emily's sherry, stretched, and reached for 1966.

In 1969, I began to doze. Nixon was president, Armstrong had taken one giant step, Yasir Arafat was getting ready to cause grief to the newly elected Golda Meir, we'd learned how to pronounce Chappaquiddick, and several of my friends had driven to a farm outside Woodstock. We'd met Big Bird and Doonesbury for the first time.

And Jan Gallager was a junior at Farberville High School.

I rubbed my eyes for a minute, banishing ghosts, and peered at the picture. Her hair was long enough to be pulled back in a severe ponytail, but the smile was as friendly, the eyes as wide, the forehead as broad. Jan was in the band, belonged to the French Club and Mu Alpha Theta, and worked as a monitor in the office.

And next to her, his hair flopping in his eyes and his mouth curled in a mocking smile, was a photograph of Daryl Gallager, a.k.a. Daryl Defoe.

11

It was not a case of pregraduation nuptials, or even a case of serendipitous alphabetization. Daryl had the same forehead, the same wide-set eyes, the same dark hair. He also had the same last name; clearly it was a case of sibling-hood, as in fraternal twins or damn close to it.

I drained the glass of sherry as I continued to blink at the two photographs. Unlike his sister (sister!), Daryl had not belonged to any organizations or participated in any extracurricular activities. Considering his dearth of socialization skills, this was not surprising.

But what did it mean? I let my head sink back against the top of the settee and tried to think. Jan had given me a ridiculous story about being married, meant to explain why her visits to Daryl's apartment were clandestine. She might have been married somewhere along the line, but she was now using her maiden name and it was hardly scandalous to spend time with one's brother.

Who was using another name. Another poser, indeed. He could hardly claim to have been married and changed his name to suit his bride. He was using an alias, and he and Jan were determined to hide his true identity. That explained why there were no papers in his apartment, I supposed, although it didn't explain much of anything else.

I opened the 1970 yearbook and ascertained they were seniors. Jan had been initiated in the high school chapter of the Humane Society; Daryl had not. The caption beside her photograph predicted she would save wildlife; Daryl's caption predicted he would have one.

I returned the other volumes to the shelf, switched off the lights, and took the two relevant yearbooks to my car. I battled the impulse to drive to Jan's house and confront her with my discovery, reminding myself that I could do so in the morning.

The second thing I wanted to do would require two of my innate talents: delicacy and tact. Daryl had been in the army, and they were notorious for keeping records (at the taxpayers' expense). If I could persuade Peter to make inquiries, I might find out why Daryl Gallager preferred to be Daryl Defoe.

As I drove toward my apartment, I passed in front of the Maranonis' house. A light shone in an upstairs room, which was neither here nor there, but it made me think of my earlier conversation with Helen concerning George's peculiar behavior. She had mentioned arthritis. I was not a graduate of Johns Hopkins, but I doubted arthritis could produce that which I, in a burst of perspicacity, had diagnosed as mental confusion. And Vidalia had implied that George was behaving oddly when she'd encountered him on the sidewalk at midnight—while her explanation for being there sounded perfectly reasonable.

I still had no idea who killed Newton Churls, what happened to the contents of the cash box, why I was attacked at the animal sale in Guttler, who shot Daryl, and most importantly, where Nick and Nora and the others were. All I knew was that I needed answers.

The next morning Caron was subdued as she came into the kitchen. "Guess you're going to the high school?" she said as she poured a glass of orange juice. "The Hornet's kind of mad about all this."

"I would imagine so," I said, dressed primly for the impending conference and all the more resentful because of it.

"Well, it's not my fault."

"Is Rhonda Maguire's mother going to be there—in a dark dress and panty hose?"

Caron put the glass in the sink. "I doubt it. Rhonda Maguire's merely a self-serving bitch." She paused for maximum effect. "I, on the other hand, am An Instigator." Sniffling loudly, she went into her bedroom and slammed the door. She was still sniffling when she left for school.

When I arrived at the Book Depot, I pretended to do paperwork until I had stirred up the courage to call Peter at the police department. I let him reminisce about the previous evening, which had been lovely, then told him I'd had a teeny thought that might be significant.

"Does it have anything to do with a honeymoon?" he drawled, adding a few suggestions involving steamy tropical nights, champagne, and a potentially fascinating variation of that which we had perfected over the last few months.

Although I found his remarks intriguing, I refused to blush and coolly said, "In a way." I told him what Jan had said, ignored his sputters, and then told him what I'd discovered in Miss Emily's library of yearbooks. The sputters stopped. "Therefore," I added, "we need to send an inquiry to the military and find out if there's a reason why he's using an alias—twenty years after he served in Vietnam. I thought about passing this information to Sheriff Dorfer, but I was afraid he might misinterpret my motives."

"Very possibly," Peter said. "The sheriff won't have bothered with the victim's prints. I'll suggest it and do my best not to implicate you."

He made more lewd remarks, but I ignored them and told him I had a customer, which was true if one categorized the wino as such. I gave the wino a dollar from the cash register, watched him shuffle away, and pulled out my notebook once more to stare at the pages of disconnected notes.

I called the animal shelter, but there was no answer. I couldn't call Jan's house, in that I didn't have the unlisted number, and I wasn't sure of the warmth of the welcome should I appear on her front porch. I moved on to the masculine half of the Gallager twins. The hospital reported that he was stable, which was encouraging in that Jan would be charged only with assault with a deadly weapon or attempted murder—if Daryl identified her as the assailant.

Something snapped, and I couldn't tolerate the inertia any longer. Once again I closed the Book Depot (the frequency of said action was beginning to have a noticeably detrimental effect on sales), and drove to the hospital.

To my profound regret, there was a guard stationed in front of Daryl Gallager-Defoe's door, and to make things worse, the guard was Deputy Amos, who by now could recognize me in his sleep. Any idea of donning a white coat, stealing a clipboard, and bullying my way into the room evaporated, and I was reduced to a more mundane approach.

"Hi," I said as I came down the hall. "How's the patient?"

Deputy Amos tugged on his collar and stared over my head. "He's in protective custody, ma'am. No visitors allowed." It would have been more impressive had his voice not cracked, but I could tell he was trying.

"I wouldn't presume to disturb him," I murmured, lying through my lovely white incisors. "I was visiting an old friend in another wing and thought I'd pop by for a minute to see how poor Daryl Defoe's doing." I emphasized the last name, and noted with interest that the deputy did not flinch. "Has he identified the person who shot him?"

"Mrs. Malloy," he began plaintively. "the sheriff—"

"I was just asking," I said with a sniff. "I wanted to speak to Jan Gallager, and I didn't know whether to try the animal shelter or the county jail. If you're under orders to shoot me on the spot simply because I asked a perfectly reasonable question, I understand."

Red blotches appeared on his neck like the onset of hives, and he took a handkerchief from his back pocket to wipe his wet forehead. "I'm not supposed to shoot anybody. Defoe claims he doesn't remember what happened, and he's acting so weird the doctors are keeping him sedated. He keeps rambling about gooks and cages and stuff like that, and he almost strangled an orderly. I don't know what the sheriff's doing about charging the Gallager lady. I'm on duty, ma'am, so if you don't mind. . . ?"

Lapsing into a Columboish role, I nodded demurely and took a step, then spun back. "Did you find the ledger?"

"Ledger?"

"Never mind," I said with a polite smile, and left the hospital before he could shoot me on the spot, since I suspected he did have orders to that effect and was waiting until the corridor was free of witnesses.

I had more than an hour before the showdown at the high school. Plenty of time, I assured myself giddily as I headed for the animal shelter. It was closed, and the sign beside the door informed me that it would not open until eleven.

I continued to Jan's house, but her car was not parked in the driveway and no one responded to my knock. Feeling increasingly frustrated with my morning's limited allotment of snooping, I started back to the Book Depot and the piles of files that awaited me. However, at the fateful moment (more commonly known as the intersection with the highway that went east), I took a hard right, set my sights on NewCo and my speedometer needle on the illicit side of fifty-five.

As I bounced down the dirt road, I looked at each house for signs of life, and parked in front of the first one that had a truck in the yard. The woman who came out on the porch was short, squat, and convinced I was a missionary sent to lure her from the path of righteousness found only at her own church down the highway a piece. After I'd denied it several times and agreed to attend the next prayer meeting, I asked her if she seen any unfamiliar cars on the road the morning of the shooting. We determined that she'd seen Jan's and mine, and then a whole darn parade of sheriff's vehicles all screaming like wild injuns.

At the next inhabited house, I had a door slammed within inches of my elegant nose. There was no truck at Deputy Amos's house, which wasn't astounding in that I knew where he was . . . which was not in a position to see me continue past his house to the NewCo gate and park.

Without the slightest idea what I was doing, I walked up the rutted driveway and stopped to ponder the house and the kennel in the side yard. Arnie had driven into the front yard, and if I was to believe him, with three dogs and a cat in cages, all drugged. Newton Churls had come outside and watched him unload the animals, agreed to buy them, and then brought up the delicate issue of outstanding gambling debts. In the midst of the debate, Churls had noticed company and told Arnie to wait in the woods behind the house.

So Churls was there with the cages, and shortly thereafter the cages were gone and Churls was locked in the pen with his dear little doggies that he'd so meticulously trained to kill.

To some extent, I believed Arnie, but it occurred to me he might have detoured through the house on his way to the woods, if only long enough to break open the cash box and take what he felt was his. Unless, I thought grimly, he'd chanced upon a ledger and stolen it instead. If the ledger existed.

I was drawn to the house like guzzlers were drawn to the beer garden. The living room was still in disarray, and I gazed about blankly as I attempted to surmise where Churls would have hidden either of the two items of interest. After a moment, I went into the bedroom and moved aside the tacky landscape. I didn't find a safe, but the hole in the plaster wall was the ideal size for a metal cash box. Having no idea about the size of the ledger, I had no reason to think it wouldn't have slid in quite nicely.

If it existed, I repeated to myself as I warily explored the dark corners of the hole and ascertained that only dust and bits of plaster remained.

All this led to other ill-defined questions, and I wandered into the kitchen to frown at the table where the box had been. Arnie could have taken both the box and the ledger from the hole. Any one of the commandos, except for Caron and Inez, could have slipped in the house—if there had been adequate time. And assuming Churls had been occupied moving the cages to a very effective hiding place somewhere on or near his property.

Warning myself that I was imploding brains cells to no avail, I went into the living room and was about to go through the front door when I heard a car engine. I ducked back and moved to a window in time to see a truck come slowly up the driveway. It was a truck I'd seen before, although not at the animal shelter or in Churls's yard or in front of Deputy Amos's house. No such luck. I'd seen this truck outside the Red Bird Café in Guttler, and had had an unpleasant conversation with its driver—although not as unpleasant as the one we'd had at the animal sale later that morning. To make it all the more exciting, he'd brought his oversize, fuzzy friend along for the ride.

My comment was not ladylike, nor was my dash through the kitchen and out the back door. I yanked myself to a halt and looked for cover. Yellow Hair was somewhere between my car and me. Behind me was the pit bull pen, the fence, and the sloping hillside covered with scruffy, uninviting woods. I had no idea if the two would go into the house or around either side, which made all three possible routes unattractive, to say the very least.

I hurried past the pen. When I reached the fence, I

discovered there was no conveniently situated gate, and was again making unladylike comments as I clambered over the top. I heard not only an ominous ripping sound, but also a shout from behind me, and I neither halted to inspect the damage nor turned around to wave, but instead sprinted into the woods. The next ten minutes could have taken place on the bottom rung of Dante's Inferno, if not in the basement below it. Things grabbed at me, slapped at me, scratched at me, squawked at me, leapt at me, and in general did little to enhance the encounter with nature. Every now and then I thought I heard a shout, but I was listening with equal intensity to my curses, some of which I'd never before allowed to escape from my lips. I was amazed that I knew them; it was not, however, the time to revel at how my graduate studies in Anglo-Saxon literature had remained in the darker corners of my mind.

I sloshed through a creek, clawed my way up the muddy bank, and was congratulating myself when I took an imprudent step, tumbled down a small ravine, and banged my head on the railroad tracks. A crow squawked at me, abandoned the distastefully pink remains of breakfast, and flapped away. A second took its place.

Peter might be curious about the origin of the oozing red welts on my arms, legs, neck, and face, but I was fairly certain everything was functional. I was no longer terrified out of my wits, but I was not in the mood to chuckle about the situation, either. The third problem was as thorny as the brambles in the woods had been. I was on foot in the middle of nowhere, and I seemed to recall Sheriff Dorfer mentioning a twenty-mile hike to Farberville. There were no pay telephones on the nearby trees, and in any case my purse was tucked under the front seat of my car and I had nary a dime on my person. I still had my watch—and it was half-past eleven. I'd missed two conferences in as many days, and I doubted Mrs. Horne would be impressed by my maternal concern.

With the exception of my uneven breathing, everything was peaceful. The goons had given up their pursuit, assuming I hadn't imagined it. Their arrival shortly after my own was a coincidence of epic size, and as difficult to swallow as Caron's daily lapses into martyrdom. I was no fonder of coincidences than I was of conferences. There had been way too many of both of them lately.

After a quarter of an hour of throwing rocks at crows and watching scratches ooze, I headed back to Churls's house. I was unhappily aware of the heat as I climbed the muddy slope.

My aversion to sweat rivals my aversion to animals; my own experience in an aerobics class nearly resulted in therapy. Now my blouse was a second skin and I was licking salt off my lips and wiping it out of my eyes with each step. All in all, I was not a happy camper.

I approached the fence, although with more decorum and prudence than I'd displayed earlier. The backyard was deserted. I moved along the fence until I had a partial view of the front yard and noted with relief that Yellow Hair's truck was gone. There remained only one obstacle, but my dress was already unworthy of the Salvation Army Thrift Shop, so I hiked it up and climbed the fence with only a few expletives.

Minutes later, however, I once again loosed a lengthy string of them as I gazed at my tires . . . my four slashed tires. A small legacy from the guys, I realized bleakly. One flat tire was a nuisance, but not an insurmountable problem, in that anyone who can read a manual (and loosen the lug nuts) can change a tire and be on her way within the hour. I myself had done so upon occasion, although I had been known to procede very slowly and put aside my feminist sensibilities should a gentleman stop and offer to help.

In this situation, the manual would not help, nor would a good samaritan in a sedate sedan. I was at a dead end, in more ways than one. I sat down in the front seat and twisted the mirror to examine my face, which was hardly the winsome oval that met my eyes above the bathroom sink. The package of tissues in the glove compartment was empty, but I felt under the passenger's seat and found a tissue Caron had discarded when she'd played Rambo.

I did what I could, then reached under my seat for my purse. I found a sticky cup, more wadded tissues, rubber bands, and an old magazine. Another legacy from the guys, I supposed, trying to think what treasures they'd stolen. They were likely to be disappointed with the smattering of change, and more so if they attempted to purchase anything with the lone credit card that had seen its limit in mid-December. My driver's license would do them no more good than it would do me; the checkbook might make them privy to a balance of a few hundred dollars. My car keys were still in the ignition, but I wasn't overwhelmed with gratitude for the favor.

It was certainly a nuisance, but in the overall scheme of the day, almost a minor one. I went up the driveway to the house, trying to decide whom to call, and was relieved of the necessity of a decision when I determined the telephone was dead. The water had not been disconnected, and I splashed my face and used a stained towel to clean off my arms and legs as best I could. I left the remains of the panty hose on the bathroom floor.

I sat down on the steps of the porch. It was well past noon, and there was no point in bemoaning the missed conference. It was rather pleasant. Birds were making noises, and bees and other mysterious insects were drifting around the high grass. A dogwood tree bloomed at the edge of the brush, and I wryly recognized a clump of dogtooth violets.

Propping my elbows on the step, I leaned back and surveyed my domain. It was not the worst place to be stranded, I told myself lazily, and for once I was not in imminent danger of being scolded by anything more articulate than a blue jay. Caron was no doubt storming the halls of the high school, wailing about my nonappearance. Peter was being a detective. Arnie was sipping booze behind bars and fretting over social security reforms. Daryl was ranting in the hospital, Jan was at work, and the Willow Street gangsters were putting up posters and debating the wording of a classified ad. Miss Emily was fleecing a casino under the kindly guidance of Mr. Delmaro.

And I was sitting on a porch doing nothing to alleviate the immediate problem—or solve the mystery of Churls's death or find the missing pets or much of anything. The porch was not far from the spot where Arnie's car had been parked, I thought as I mentally recreated the scene. What had Churls done with the cages in such a short amount of time? It was a good ways to the labyrinth of cages, and Vidalia and Colonel Culworthy had searched there. The shed on the opposite side of the house was no closer, and Daryl Defoe-Gallager had been inside it. Churls hadn't taken them into the house, and he hadn't taken them down the driveway. This pretty much ruled out all points on the compass.

The wood of the step pressed into my elbows, slyly reminding me of its presence. I stirred myself into action and went down to the yard. The crawl space under the porch was nearly four feet high. In midday it was still dim; at night it would have made a lovely hiding place for, cages. I bent down and studied the dust.

The one clear footprint was familiar. I measured it against my own, and although I wasn't positive that it was identical to the one by Miss Emily's gate, it seemed to be of the same size and proportion.

I forced myself to crawl a short way under the porch, where I found three wooden boxes with meshed windows. They were empty, but still heavy enough to require tugging and extensive grumbling to extricate them from the hiding place.

I brushed the dust off my hands and gazed down with a proprietorial air at my discoveries. They provided one very small piece of the puzzle, but it was one more than I'd had a few minutes earlier. Churls had shoved the cages under the porch; the dogs and cat were sedated and unable to make themselves known to those of us who'd tromped up and down the steps, banged doors, shouted, and withstood the sheriff's questions. After everyone had departed, someone had returned to remove the animals. And left a footprint in the dust.

I had no idea who this was, mind you, or the new location of Nick, Nora, Patton, and Astra, but it confirmed Arnie's story (to some extent) and erased any lingering hints of metaphysical explanations.

As tempting as it was, I couldn't sit back down on the steps and contemplate the butterflies. I left the cages where they were and walked to the road. There was no reason to lock my car, but I did so, pocketed the keys, and headed for the fringes of civilization. There was no truck in Deputy Amos's yard, but the sports car was parked in the shade. The young woman with the fanciful hair came to the door and said, "Yeah?"

"I've had some car trouble," I said. "I was hoping I could use your telephone."

"Haven't I seen you before?"

"I was here a few days ago, when there was the . . . problem at NewCo," I said, uncomfortably aware of my disreputable condition. "If I could just use the telephone, I won't disturb you further."

"Yeah, it's okay with me." She stepped back and opened the door. "You a friend of Rory's or something?"

"Only in a professional capacity."

"Is that so?" she said without interest. She stopped at the impressively large television to turn it off, then went through a doorway.

I followed her to the kitchen, which would not have earned approval from the health department. "I'm going to call Farberville, but I'll pay the long-distance charge," I said as I spotted the telephone on a fly-speckled wall.

She folded her arms and leaned back against the edge of the counter. "How're you going to do that?"

"Your name's Bethanna, isn't it?" I said. She nodded impassively. "Well, Bethanna, whoever comes to pick me up will pay whatever you think is fair."

"Don't bother. You want some coffee?"

The aluminum coffeepot on the stove was black,

and the mug nearby was being explored by several flies. The dishes in the sink were encrusted with unspecified matter. A cockroach darted out of sight under an open box of cereal. Then again, I had a possible witness.

"I'd love some," I said with a bright smile. I sat down at the table. "There's certainly been a lot of activity at NewCo, hasn't there."

"You're telling me," she said. She set a cup of coffee on the table, took a bottle of beer from the refrigerator, and sat down across from me. "Now I remember you. You were here the night ol' Newt got mauled by his dogs, right? He was a cussed bastard, but nobody ought to exit like that. Rory was sick to his stomach half the night, and still wakes up in the middle of the night all sweaty and scared." She took a drink, belched softly, and gave me a puzzled look. "What were you doing down there this morning? Rory said nobody was supposed to go there after that other fellow got shot yesterday."

"Did you notice when I drove past your house?" I asked, ignoring her rather reasonable question.

"Yeah, it was during a commercial, and I happened to see a car while I was putting the laundry out on the line. About three hours ago, wasn't it? What were you doing all that time?"

I wasn't sure she would appreciate a detailed account. "Looking for clues. Did you see a white truck drive past a few minutes after I did?"

"I think so, but 'Name That Tune' was back on and I was watching it. I'm real good at guessing the song titles. Darla says I ought to apply to be a contestant."

"Have you ever seen that truck before?" I asked.

"Every now and then, or one that looked like it.

Employees of Newt's, maybe." Bethanna took a long drink, still watching me with a faintly suspicious frown. "Thought you needed to make a call?"

"I do," I said earnestly. "I guess you were too busy doing your hair yesterday to have noticed any cars or trucks going past your house?"

She patted her hair. "It takes me a good while, but everybody says it's striking, so it's worth it. I always leave the television on so I can listen to my game shows while I'm using the curling iron."

"Did you happen to see any cars or trucks?"

"Most likely I did," she murmured. "Say, don't you like the coffee? I made it fresh this morning."

I took a sip and managed a smile as the oily, bitter brew dribbled down my throat. "Delicious. Can you describe whatever you saw?"

"Lemme think here for a minute." She screwed up her face and stared at the ceiling. "First I saw some guy walking down the road. 'Wheel of Fortune' had just come on when a little blue car went by. The category was titles, not one of my best unless it's music or a movie. Turned out to be one of those tragic plays by Shakespeare. I'd heard of it, of course, but I couldn't have guessed it in a hundred years. I would have had to buy all the vowels." She held out her hand to allow me to admire a ring with a large diamond. "This is sweet, but they give away jewelry that cost ten thousand dollars or more. I get dizzy just imagining myself spinning the wheel and winning prizes like that."

I tightened my fingers around the handle of the mug. "Did you see any other cars?"

"I didn't pay that much attention. I was working on the title, and one of my rollers was coming loose. Rory came up from the barn and started shouting at me to find him a clean shirt."

"What about the white truck?"

"Like I said, I wasn't interested. You ever watch 'Celebrity Charades?' You know, the one where they get these television stars that haven't been in a show for ten years and have 'em act out funny jokes?"

I admitted that I'd missed that one. "Let me ask you one more thing and then I'll make my call," I said, trying to align things in my mind. "Do you remember the night Newton Churls was attacked by his dogs?"

"Oh, yes. You showed up at the door just as I was going into town to meet Darla and another girl what works with her," Bethanna said promptly. "There was all kinds of traffic that night, let me tell you."

"By all means."

"Well, first ol' Newt goes by, probably coming back from one of those dogfights, 'cause he had his pit bulls in the back of the truck and they were yammering. Then comes this ancient car that looked like it was trying to get its tail feathers up so it could fly. Then comes this jeep with all these people of a different ethnic persuasion, if you get my drift. I thought that was pretty damn funny, in that Newt ain't the most tolerant person I've met."

I leaned forward. "And. . . ?"

"You showed up and I left." She stood up. "I got chores to do, and I want to be done by the time my soaps come on. I like to do my nails then. Help yourself to the telephone, and feel free to wait on the porch."

"You didn't see the white truck that night?" I asked.

"I already told you what I saw." Bethanna went out the back door, and through the smudgy window I could see her begin to take stiff white sheets from the clothesline. She looked incongruous in her designer jeans and jewelry; her neighbors no doubt wore housecoats and aprons.

I needed to buy all the vowels and the consonants, too. Instead, I gritted my teeth and called Lieutenant Peter Rosen of the Farberbille CID. It turned out he knew as many expletives as I did, if not more.

12

I wandered down the road to my injured car and sat on the fender. If I smoked, it would have been the ideal time to light a cigarette and gaze pensively at Newton Churls's house at the top of the driveway, and at last achieve a burst of insight that would explain everything. I merely sat and swatted at an occasional mosquito.

An hour later, a surly simian arrived in a tow truck. He replaced one rear tire with the spare from my trunk, replaced the other with a spare from his truck, hooked the bumper of my car, and suggested I ride with him. As we drove toward the highway, he asked what had happened; I told him I didn't know, and after that scintillating exchange, we rode to Farberville in silence.

An hour after that, my tires had been repaired and my promise to send a check received with an unhappy grunt. I drove home. The day had been a total disaster, and had it not been for the cheery postcard from Miss Emily in the mailbox, I might have admitted defeat and found a nice, dark closet in which to reside. It seemed Miss Emily had found a casino with a trapeze act, and Mr. Delmaro had taught her an incredibly clever system to win at the two-dollar blackjack table. She sent her love to Nick and Nora.

I changed into jeans and a T-shirt, dabbed cream on all visible scratches, untangled my hair, then stood in the kitchen and gulped down a scotch and water for medicinal purposes. I didn't want to stay at home, where Peter could track me down. I didn't want to go to the Book Depot, where Caron could (and surely would) do the same.

Besides, I was beginning to have a glimmer of an idea that might explain at least part of the muddle. I drove to the animal shelter, parked beside Jan's car, and marched inside. The woman behind the counter gave me an unenthusiastic nod.

"I need to speak to Jan," I said.

"She's in her office, but she doesn't want to be disturbed. We've had a difficult day."

"So have I." I pushed open the door and went into the office. Jan was slouched in a chair, smoking a thin, black cigarette and thumbing through a stack of papers. Her khaki pants were wrinkled, her shirt stained with sweat and dusted with dog hairs. "I want to talk to you," I said as I sat down on a wooden chair.

She looked dully at me. "I had to euthanatize thirty dogs today, Claire. It's the most humane thing we can do, and we do everything we can to comfort them. I talk to them, stroke them, and sing softly until they're relaxed, but afterward I want to curl up and cry. Daryl's still in serious condition and the sheriff wants my lawyer and me to come to his office after work. All in all, I'm not in the mood for a chat."

"I'm sorry about the dogs," I said. "But this has to do with dogs that can be saved and returned to their owners, and your lies are making it harder. Let's talk about Daryl Gallager, shall we?"

"Gallager?" Her hand trembled as she put out her cigarette and carefully closed the folder in her lap.

"As in your brother, Daryl Gallager," I persisted. "I found the old yearbooks. You two were in the same class at Farberville High School. Daryl was drafted and served a year in Vietnam. Now he's back here, attending the college, and the both of you are hiding his identity. I would hypothesize he's wanted by a law enforcement agency of some kind. How about the U.S. Army?"

"That was twenty years ago," she said with an unconvincing laugh.

"The only thing that might keep them interested all this time is if Daryl went AWOL, so let's try that. It might explain his animosity toward Colonel Culworthy." If I could have paced, I would have, but the office was smaller than my own and I had no desire to stub my toe every three steps. I settled for crossing my legs and flicking my foot impatiently. "It's rather tricky to go AWOL when one is surrounded by rice paddies on the far side of the globe, so let's assume he was in the States at the time. In a hospital because of his leg wound?"

Jan rocked back in her chair and sighed. "He developed some severe psychological problems while he was in 'Nam. He and another private in his platoon were captured and held prisoner for more than three months before they were rescued. The conditions were barbaric. They were brought back to a mental hospital for evaluation, but Daryl panicked, attacked an orderly, and escaped. He's afraid he inadvertently killed the orderly, and for that reason, he's convinced they're still after him."

"Held prisoner," I repeated, recalling the horror

stories that had emerged as the vets had returned home to ambivalent welcomes. Carlton had avoided the draft by dieting to an unhealthy weight, but I had several old college buddies who'd come home enveloped in an impenetrable aura. "His apartment is completely devoid of personal effects and clutter. Does he have a problem with claustrophobia?"

"And cages," she said.

"So he did let Nick and Nora out of the pen, and Patton, too." I stopped for a minute as I remembered the painful clash of emotions in his eyes when I'd so bluntly asked him about it. "He let them out, but then he realized he'd endangered rather than liberated them. That's why he's been so determined to help us find them."

"He was devastated when I told him what he'd done."

"Especially when he recognized Newton Churls," I said, staring at her until she flinched. "You told me you recognized him, and you and your brother grew up together in that part of the county. When Daryl went with us to NewCo, he and Churls recognized each other, didn't they? Then Daryl had two things to worry about—the fate of the animals and exposure by Churls. We even had a deputy sheriff with us."

Jan began to pace, but apparently she'd had practice. "I haven't discussed it with him, Claire," she said nervously. "I haven't talked to him since . . . since you filed the report."

"That's not true. He must have been here when I called Saturday afternoon. You told me about the dog sale in Guttler. How else would he have known about it?"

Her flight plan included a circumnavigation of the

desk, an about-face at the door, and a final turn behind my chair. She executed all this successfully while saying, "Yes, he was here when you and I discussed the sale, and he borrowed my car that afternoon. He came out here to ask me if I thought he could trust you." She halted and met my eyes. "I told him he could."

"You should have trusted me," I said, then told her that I'd asked Peter to make inquiries about Daryl's military service. "The Pentagon has other things to worry about, and I cannot believe they'll prosecute a POW for what was likely to have been a psychotic episode. On the other hand, Sheriff Dorfer can't—and won't—overlook a homicide. When the commandos arrived at NewCo, Daryl slipped around one side of the house to investigate a shed. Did he continue to the back, find Churls about to loose the pit bulls, and shove him into the pen?"

Jan sank down in her chair and lit a cigarette with what now resembled palsied hands. "I don't know. He swore he didn't."

"What happened at NewCo yesterday morning?"

"I did go there to look for the ledger. Dogfighting is big business, and so is the sale of animals to laboratories. Newton Churls did some major financial transactions—and I want those names. I'm afraid Sheriff Dorfer may be involved. If his name's in the ledger, then the ledger's history, as in ashes."

The animal control officer opened the door. "Jan, there's a call from the regional office of the USDA."

"I'll have to take it," she said to me.

I nodded briskly at the officer as I went through the reception room. Once in my car, however, I gnawed on my lip and tried to fit this latest information into the scenario, which, in a contorted way, was beginning to make some sense. Daryl let the dogs out of the yards. Arnie picked them up (along with Astra), kept them a few days, and took them to NewCo. Churls hid them under the porch. Someone removed them.

I found myself driving to Miss Emily's house, as good a destination as any. There were a few bills in the mailbox; I dropped them in a basket in the entry. The African violets were in need of water and a pep talk. Once I'd sprinkled and encouraged them, I went out to the back porch and glumly watched the last of the late afternoon sun splash over the honeysuckle vine. I would have welcomed a dorsal assault from the basset hounds from Hell, or even a splatter of slobber on my shoes.

I went back through the house, locked the front door, and was on the way to my car when Vidalia called to me from across the street. I waited, trying to hide my reluctance, as she scurried up, beads clattering and a chartreuse scarf rippling in her wake.

"Oh, my goodness, dearie," she gasped, "you look dreadful, simply dreadful."

"Thank you. It's been one of those days."

She blinked at me, then clasped her hands together. One final ray of sunshine glinted on her gold tooth. "Yes, hasn't it? I did Astra's chart, and something very significant is about to happen. I was so overcome with elation that I had to make myself a cup of chamomile tea and lie down with a damp washcloth on my forehead."

"Is pesky old Pisces nearing the cusp?" I asked drily.

"What an odd thing to say," she murmured. She looked over my shoulder and began to wave wildly. "Colonel, oh, Colonel! You must tell me Patton's date of birth! We're on the verge of a major revelation. It's in the air, and so intense I can almost see it!"

"Balderdash," grumbled Culworthy as he joined us. "What happened to you, Malloy? Wouldn't pass muster like that."

"She had one of those days," Vidalia confided with a giggle. She put her hand on his arm and drifted into him. "Now, you really must tell me the date and time of Patton's birth, Colonel. I'm sure there'll be a conjunction of some sort."

"Balderdash, woman !"

"Oh, but, Colonel," she trilled, "I know something's going to happen. Look, you do, too. Your mustache is twitching like a dear little caterpillar."

He harrumphed a response, but I was too busy staring along the sidewalk to note it for posterity. Helen and George Maranoni were approaching us. In Helen's hand was a leash, and at the end of the leash was an enormous brown poodle with a bow on the top of its head. Its curly hair and soft brown eyes reminded me of Peter, although I was quite sure he would never be caught with a pink ribbon dangling down his neck . . . or a matching one around his tail.

George shuffled beside her, his head bent as if he were studying the cracks in the pavement, and his hands flopping at his sides. Helen saw us and smiled smugly.

"See?" Vidalia said, shaking Culworthy's arm. "Strange and wonderful things have already begun to happen. Juniper's back. It's only a matter of time before my dear Astra is nibbling salmon and your Patton is romping in the backyard."

"Look who's back," Helen announced.

"When did Juniper return?" I asked.

George had not yet acknowledged us, but Helen

smiled more broadly and said, "Only an hour ago. Isn't it a miracle?"

Vidalia was hopping up and down hard enough to rattle Culworthy's dentures. "And Astra shall be home, too! Helen, George, I am so very, very thrilled for you! And so is Colonel Culworthy!"

"What happened?" I asked Helen, ignoring the thrills and harrumphs from the two behind me. "Did she just come to the door?"

Helen bent down and stroked the fuzzy brown head. "It's a little bit complicated, but it seems Juniper wasn't stolen after all. George took her to the vet's to have"—she gave me a pinched look—"an operation, then forgot to mention it to me. I became aware of it when the nurse called and told me to pick Juniper up."

"George is still having a problem with arthritis?" I inquired delicately.

"That's not what it's called," George said, startling all of us. "Just a spot of forgetfulness every now and then. It comes with age, along with aches and pains and social security." He wiggled his bushy white eyebrows and leered at me, then took the leash from Helen's hand and led Juniper down the sidewalk. She watched him for a moment, her expression pained yet tender, then hurried to catch up with him. As they went around the corner, she slipped her arm through his.

"She really mustn't let him wander around late at night," Vidalia said sadly. "He might lose his way."

"Already has," Culworthy said, although without a trace of gruffness.

Vidalia finally convinced Culworthy to come to her apartment to provide the necessary information for Patton's chart. Martinis were mentioned. I drove back in the deepening twilight, thinking morosely about the Maranonis and the inevitabilities that would beset them as George's condition deteriorated. He hadn't forgotten to put on his glasses when he gave away the puppies. He had no memory of it whatsoever, but he and his wife were too proud to admit it.

As I headed down Thurber Street, I noticed there was a light on in the main room of the Book Depot. Perplexed, I parked in my lot, hurried across the gravel, and discovered the door was unlocked. It was unnerving, but not all that frightening with the flow of traffic on the street, the raucous music from the beer garden, and the pedestrians ambling along the sidewalk. I eased open the door, wincing at the squeaks, and called, "Caron? Inez?"

There was no answer, and no mop of red hair popped through the doorway of the office. I hesitated for a minute, unsure if this warranted an hysterical call to the police or simply more methodical attention to security whenever I left. The telephone rang. I threw caution to the wind and went to answer it.

"Mrs. Malloy," said an icy voice.

I recognized it. "Mrs. Horne, I am so very sorry about missing the conference this morning, but the most amazing—"

"Where are the frogs?"

"Where are the . . . frogs?" I echoed. I'd dedicated a week of my life to stolen dogs, and for a moment I wondered if I'd misunderstood her.

"That's right—where are the frogs?"

"I don't know," I said, rubbing my eyes. "Where are they supposed to be?"

"They are supposed to be in the cold storage room in the high school cafeteria, Mrs. Malloy."

"And I gather they're not there any longer? Is there any chance they hopped away?"

"This is hardly the time for humor," Mrs. Horne said, although I wouldn't have had too much trouble determining that from her tone of voice. "I have been calling your home and the store since school was dismissed five hours ago. May I add that it is now nine hours since your second scheduled conference with myself, the principal, a representative from the school board, and the chairperson of the faculty disciplinary committee?"

"I think you just did," I said weakly. I dragged the stool over and sat down. "Why do you think I know where the . . . frogs are?"

"They have been stolen."

"And you think I'm involved?"

"I *know* Caron is involved, Mrs. Malloy. I've taught sophomore biology for eleven years, and never before has this situation arisen. I've had girls who were squeamish, but not one of them had the audacity to not only defy the policy but to also steal school property. I teach biology, not politics. Caron has instigated a rebellion among—"

"Wait a minute," I said before she worked herself into an incomprehensible dither. "The frogs that were scheduled for dissection have disappeared, and you're accusing my daughter of theft. Is that right?"

"She was the one who stood up in the middle of—"

"Do you have any proof?"

The ensuing silence was somewhat satisfying. I had no idea if Caron had followed in her mother's felonious footsteps; she was more than capable of it, but she deserved a trial before she was imprisoned for racine robbery.

"Do you have any proof?" I repeated.

Mrs. Horne sniffed. "Well, Caron and some of her friends stayed after seventh period to make some sort of mouse banner in the art room. The art teacher, a flighty woman if ever I met one, told them to lock the door when they were finished, then simply left them there and went to meet her boyfriend." She sniffed more loudly at such irresponsibility. "I like to remove the specimens the day before lab so they'll have time to thaw nicely. I went down to the storage room. The five cartons, each containing one dozen specimens, were not where I'd placed them several weeks ago." The final sniff barely missed being an exclamation mark.

"Have there been any undersize drumsticks on the school lunch menu?" I know, I know, but it really had been, as Caron would put it, One of Those Days.

"May I please speak to Caron?"

"She's not here, and to be candid, I don't know where she is at the moment. I promise that as soon as I find her, I will determine if she and her friends took the cartons of frogs from the storage room in order to . . ." I searched my mind for the proper phrase to complete the sentence, but there didn't seem to be one. "Just why would they take them, Mrs. Horne? If they need to be thawed, they'll hardly be in any condition to be set free in the nearest pond." I struggled to keep a straight face—or at least a serious tone of voice—as I envisioned Caron and Inez kneeling on the bank, reverently watching frozen frogs float away in a bizarre version of a Viking funerary ceremony.

"I fail to appreciate your attitude. Tomorrow I will face five classes of sophomore biology students, all prepared to broaden their knowledge of basic biological systems by taking scalpel in hand and following my directions. What shall I say to them, Mrs. Malloy?'

I bit my lip, but I couldn't sop myself. "Froggie went a-courtin'?" I suggested, humming the next few bars.

She hung up, which was fine with me.

One of the plagues of Egypt was frogs, and said plague had been casteth upon me. Would Caron, Inez, and even the notoriously treacherous Rhonda Maguire, go so far as to steal five dozen frozen frogs in the name of animal rights? More disturbingly, where would they hide them? I resisted the urge to peek in my office, because if they were there, ignorance was vastly superior to bliss.

I decided I'd better go home and check the bathtub, then call Inez's mother and suggest she do the same. I opened the cash register drawer and was gaping at the empty compartments as the bell jangled above the door.

"Did you get your flat tires fixed?" Peter asked.

I continued to gape. There certainly hadn't been a fortune in the drawer, but I always kept some money for change and put the excess in a drawer in the office. "I don't understand this."

"I don't understand why you went to NewCo this morning, were chased through the woods, and found all four of your tires slashed," Peter said mildly.

"That's not what I'm talking about. All the money is missing from the cash register."

"The down payment on the BMW? I'll put out an APB. Roadblocks at every intersection. Alert the Swiss banks not to take any deposits until we get this cleared up." He flashed his teeth, perhaps because he noticed I was flashing my eyes. "Okay, how much is missing and when did you notice?"

"They stole my purse, but they didn't take my keys."

"Did they take your mind? What are we talking about?"

"Yellow Hair and his friend stole my purse when they vandalized the car, but the keys were in the ignition. In fact, I had the store key in my hand when I discovered the light was on and the door unlocked."

"If the door was unlocked, anyone could have come in from the street and emptied the cash register," he pointed out so reasonably that I wanted to throttle him.

"But who unlocked the door? Caron has the only spare."

Peter gave me a smile that oozed pity for my obvious dementia. "There you have it. Caron came by after school and unlocked the store. When she got bored, she wandered off without remembering to lock it."

"She didn't come by after school. She was"—I switched to a dramatic whisper—"stealing frogs."

"Stealing what?"

"Frogs. You know, those green speckled things that sit on lily pads and barrumph. Not these frogs, though; they're frozen. All sixty of them." I wrinkled my nose. "They were taken several hours ago, so they ought to be melting by now."

"Do you think," he said in a strangled voice that bore an eerie resemblance to a croak, "that you might elaborate?"

I did so, but the image of the frog cubes melting and Mrs. Horne's outrage and Caron's sacrifice to be politically correct was all too much for me. A few chuckles intruded into my attempted sober exposition, and shortly thereafter I was howling helplessly. I collapsed into Peter's arms, and we were both making cracks about frog-sicles and hop-along casseroles and such nonsense when the bell jangled.

I wiped the tears off my cheeks and looked around Peter's chest. My hippie gave me a twinkly smile.

"Hi," I said weakly.

"Don't let me interrupt anything," he said. "Now that you're here, I'll just get my backpack and be on my way."

Peter shot a copish look at him, and out of the corner of his mouth, said, "Do you think he took the money?"

"I don't know," I said out of the corner of my mouth.

The hippie ambled past us, went into the office, and emerged with a bulging denim backpack. With another twinkly smile, he hung it over his shoulder and started for the door.

"Wait," I said. "Why was your backpack in the office?"

"Your daughter and that spooky friend of hers asked me to keep an eye on the store until you got back. I saw a chick I used to know, so I went outside to talk to her for a minute about scoring some . . . thing." He wiggled his fingers at us and once again attempted to leave.

I caught him by one arm, and Peter caught him by the other. We politely escorted him back to the counter. "Where is Caron now?" I asked.

"Like, wow, I dunno."

"Like, take a guess," Peter said.

Squirming, he tugged on his beard and finally said, "Well, I was browsing in the SF, and the two of them were over here, acting real nervous and whispering about something. Then the telephone rang, and after a long argument, Caron answered it in a funny voice, like she was pretending to be someone else. I dunno what was said on the other end, but she started chirping like a cricket and getting all excited."

I glanced at Peter, then squeezed the hippie's arm and said, "Did you hear the word *frog* mentioned?"

"No, but she said something about dogs." He pulled his arm free and gave me a wounded look. "So she and the other girl took all the money out of the cash register, asked me to keep an eye on things, and went out by the curb. After about ten minutes, this truck pulled up and they got in. It was maybe an hour ago, and that's the last I saw of them. There was another call after that, but I didn't answer it on account of seeing the chick on the street. If you like don't mind, I've got an appointment with her."

"What color was the truck?" Peter said as he released the hippie's arm to put his hand on my shoulder.

"It was real splattered with mud," the hippie said, easing away from us, "but I'd say it was white or light gray." He bolted for the door, the backpack bouncing wildly.

I went to my office and sat down behind the desk. Peter sat down across from me, his expression carefully composed despite the tightness of his jaw and the deepened lines around his eyes.

Determined to remain equally composed, I moistened my lips and calmly said, "It's not all that difficult to figure out what happened, is it? Yellow Hair found something in my purse that indicated I owned the bookstore. He called and talked to Caron, who was pretending to be me in case Mrs. Horne was on the line. Yellow Hair demanded a ransom payoff for the dogs. Caron and Inez took whatever cash they found in the register and went tripping out to the curb." Somewhat less calmly, I ran my fingers through my hair, gulped back a sob, and said, "I think it's very important that we find Caron and Inez before something happens to them. In that Yellow Hair and Baby Bear were at NewCo this morning, it seems a logical place to start."

"I'd better alert the sheriff," Peter said, reaching for the telephone.

"No!" I grabbed his wrist. "Jan Gallager told me she thought he might be involved. We can't tip him off that we're going there. If he's in this with those goons, he might tell them to take the girls to Guttler or someplace else."

Peter pried my fingers from around his wrist, then came around the desk and put both hands on my shoulders. "They'll be okay, Claire," he said, bending down to kiss my damp forehead. "Caron and Inez aren't exactly mindless Barbie dolls. Those guys won't know what they've gotten themselves into, or how to get out of it."

"It's all my fault, Peter," I said, lapsing and then collapsing into misery. "I lectured Caron over and over again about her irresponsibility that resulted in Nick and Nora's disappearance. But it wasn't her doing. Daryl let the dogs out of the pen and good ol' Arnie picked them up. Caron may have ignored her duty to feed them, but it wouldn't have mattered either way. All my accusations made her feel guilty, and now she's in that truck with that awful man and I don't know—"

"It happens," he said firmly and in time to avert what was promising to be a display of hysterics that would have rivaled Caron's best efforts. He propelled me to my feet and out of the office. Ignoring my gurgle of guilt as we passed the cash register, he got me to his car and in the passenger's seat without further degeneration of my sensibilities.

"Do you have a gun?" I asked timidly as we pulled onto Thurber Street.

"I'm a cop."

"Then why don't you turn on the siren and lights?"

"I'm not a dumb cop."

I sank back in the seat and stared blankly through the windshield. "This is all peculiar," I commented, biting back a yelp as he ran a yellow light. "Jan's brother is the most likely suspect, but I don't—"

"Who?" Peter said, yanking the wheel so sharply my shoulder hit the door handle.

"Daryl Defoe is Jan Gallager's brother. He went AWOL twenty years ago and is still rather looney about cages. What we don't know is if he had the opportunity to lock Churls in the pen with the pit bulls, break into the cash box, steal the ledger, and appear with the other commandos when Deputy Amos and I arrived in the backyard."

Peter stopped for a red light, and when he looked at me, his teeth were positively blinding. "Goodness gracious, you're a regular encyclopedia of information. Is there any way you might be induced to share any of it?"

"If you or Sheriff Dorfer had been the least bit concerned about the stolen animals, you would have found all this out for yourselves," I said tartly. The mention of the animals reminded me of the present situation, however, and my irritation faded. "I know, people are more important than animals and homicides are more important than pet thefts, but as the

217

dominant species, we have an obligation to treat the lesser species with compassion."

"Shall I give you a puppy for your birthday?"

"No. I am more than capable of treating them with compassion from a civilized distance. I am talking about a moral obligation—not a daily one." I rolled down the window, took a deep breath, and began to tell him everything I knew.

13

We reached the turnoff as I finished my accounting of everything I knew. As it was a thirty-minute drive, I was rather impressed with the extent of my investigations, and was mentally patting myself on the back as we started down the dirt road to NewCo.

"It's a long way out here," Peter remarked as our headlights flashed on the dusty brush and deep ditches along the road.

"I've made the trip so many times I can do it with my eyes crossed," I said, sighing. "What will we do if Caron and Inez aren't there?"

"We'll have to notify the sheriff. Jan Gallager may think he's been gambling on pit bulls fights, or even taking money not to follow up on stolen animals, but that's not cold, hard evidence. He did send Deputy Amos with you the first time you and the others came to search for the pets."

"He was under a certain amount of pressure," I admitted. I scowled at the road, wishing we could make better time, then realized something was nibbling at my mind. "It is a long way out here, isn't it?"

"I'm going as fast as I dare. There are no shoulders, and the ditch is—"

"I wasn't criticizing your driving," I said, still trying to piece together my thoughts. "There's one question I never asked the commandos the night they staged their raid on NewCo."

"You missed a question? Good heavens, you must be worried sick about the basset hounds. Now that you've become so concerned about animals, I think I will get you that puppy. How about an English sheepdog? Then, on cold winter nights when I'm not available, he can curl up on your feet and keep you cozy while you read all those mysteries set on the windswept moors. Of course, when I am available, I'll curl up on your feet—if you promise to keep your toenails clipped."

Although I knew his banter was meant to divert me, I was formulating an acerbic response when a motorcycle headlight appeared down the road. "Who could that be?"

"I have no idea," Peter said, his eyes narrowed, "but I hope he doesn't slide onto the ditch when we pass each other."

As the light approached, I realized it was not a motorcycle, but a cockeye. That made three I'd seen in the last twenty-four hours. Unless it made one I'd seen three times. I grabbed Peter's arm and said, "That's Yellow Hair's truck. He's been following me since last night. That's why he showed up this morning before the dust had settled on the road. Do something, Peter—make him stop! We've got to find Caron and Inez."

"Are you sure that's who it is?"

"No, I'm not sure, damn it! But we can't risk allowing him to take the girls back to Guttler or some other sordid place. You've got to make him stop!"

Peter gave me a hooded look, but obediently swung the wheel and braked, effectively blocking the road. We waited silently as the light came closer and illuminated our car. In that I was on the nearer side, I was aware that if it didn't stop, I would have a bumper in my lap and broken glass between my teeth. Not too long ago I'd had broken glass embedded elsewhere in my body, and I did not look forward to a rerun.

At the last moment, the truck stopped, its one headlight blinding me; I froze as if I were a possum caught in the glare. A horn blared noisily, the sound loud and coarse in the darkness that surrounded us like a wool blanket. I let out a breath and meekly said, "You mentioned a gun?"

"A thirty-eight special, to be precise." He leaned across me and took an intimidating weapon from the glove compartment. "I hope I'm not about to give some elderly farmer's wife a heart attack," he muttered as he opened his car door. "Stay here."

Squinting, I watched him move around the front of the car and cut across the swath of light to the side of the truck. I rolled down my window and strained to hear what was being said, but the truck's engine was rumbling and all I could hear was a low exchange of male voices. When that became intolerable (approximately five seconds later), I got out of the car and went to Peter's side.

Yellow Hair smirked at me, and behind him Baby Bear blinked solemnly.

"I told you to wait in the car," Peter said.

"I did," I retorted. "These are the men, Lieutenant Rosen. They not only assaulted me, they vandalized my car and kidnapped two girls. Kidnapping is a federal offense, isn't it?"

"She's been smoking loco weed," Yellow Hair said, winking at Peter as if to establish a macho bond between them. "She might be a decent-looking lady if she wasn't all scratched up, but I'd sure keep her away from the loco weed." Baby Bear guffawed, but stopped when he caught my glower.

"Please explain what you're doing on this road," Peter said.

"Last I heard it wasn't a federal offense to drive down a road. But my buddy here and me went to visit a friend who lives down this way."

"Who?" I snapped.

"Fellow by the name of Newton Churls," he continued in the infuriating drawl. He paused to scratch a pimple on his chin. "Came by once already today, but he wasn't home. Thought we saw a burglar, but we weren't sure and neither one of us saw any reason to break our necks running around in the woods. Churls wasn't home this evening, either."

Peter's face was stony. "Newton Churls was murdered Friday night."

"Well, I guess that's why he wasn't home today," Yellow Hair said. He poked his companion. "Do you think that's why ol' Newt wasn't home, Bo?"

"I think that explains it, Joe Fred," Bo answered with facetious seriousness. "Bad timing on our part, wouldn't you say?"

"That's what I'd say. How about you?"

The redneck version of Abbott and Costello did not amuse me. "Where are the two girls you picked up at the Book Depot in Farberville?" I demanded, interrupting their and-whatta-you-think-bubba nonsense.

"Now, just exactly where would Farberville be?" Yellow Hair said. "You heard of this place called Farberville, Bo?"

"Shoot them," I said to Peter. "I'll testify that they threatened to attack us, and you were forced to shoot them to save our lives. Go ahead."

"We'll get to that in a minute," he said grimly. He asked the two for identification, and they reluctantly produced their wallets. Baby Bear (a.k.a. Bo) resided on a route in Guttler; Yellow Hair (a.k.a. Joe Fred) lived in another town, but I doubted it was an exclusive suburb of a city renowned for its cultural and artistic opportunities.

"We've got to find the girls," I muttered at Peter as he handed the wallets back to the men.

"Wish we had us some girls," Yellow Hair said, resuming his smirk. "Ol' Bo and me get tired of each other after a time. You got any pretty young friends, ma'am? We'd treat 'em real nice."

"And not cut their vocal cords?" I said.

Bo leaned forward and gave me an insulted look. "Now why would you go and say a thing like that? Joe Fred and me ain't ever been in trouble with the law. He has a nice little farm, and I work for my cousin at a body shop. Why, we go to the same church Sundays and say our prayers every night."

"Ain't it the truth?" Yellow Hair contributed. "Why, we're just a couple of good ol' choirboys."

I considered snatching Peter's gun from his hand and permanently erasing the smirk from the man's face. Peter looked indecisively at them, then took my arm and drew me away from the truck.

"I don't know if I can detain them, much less charge them," he told me in a low voice. "We're out of my jurisdiction, and the only thing we've got is your identification of them as the two men who assaulted you—in another state."

"Then don't detain them," I growled. "Shoot them." I pulled my arm free. "They know where Caron and Inez are. Those girls are fifteen years old, and they're probably scared out of their minds—if

223

they haven't been knocked unconscious or drugged." My voice rose an octave. "Or worse."

Peter looked over my shoulder at the truck. "Doesn't one of the sheriff's deputies live along here? He can make the arrest, and once they're in the county jail in Farberville, we can see what the department can do."

"Deputy Amos lives half a mile farther," I said, "but we can't wait while these kidnappers are taken to the jail and questioned by that fat jerk of a sheriff. For all we know, these men may be acting under his orders."

"One step at a time," Peter said. He put his fingers on my cheek for a moment, then went back to the truck, where the two were passing a jar of clear liquid back and forth. "Park your vehicle as close to the ditch as you can. I'm placing you under arrest and transporting you to a deputy's house until a squad car comes from Farberville."

"Under arrest for what?" Yellow Hair said, wiping his mouth on his wrist and giving Peter a surly look.

"I'll think of something. Now, move it."

Once they were in the backseat of Peter's car, they both refused to talk and I was too angry to do anything except glower. We drove the short way to Deputy Amos's house. The truck and the muddy sports car were parked in the front yard, and light shone from several windows. Peter told me to go to the door, and I did so nervously, unsure what we'd do if Amos wasn't there.

He opened the door. He was dressed in jeans and a faded blue work shirt, and his feet were bare. He had a beer in one hand and a half-eaten sandwich in the other. His eyes bulged like tiny balloons as he stared through the screen at me. "Mrs. Malloy? What are you—"

"It's a bit complicated. I'm with Lieutenant Rosen of the Farberville CID, and we need your assistance. That, and your handcuffs."

"Yeah, I'll just—put on my shoes," he said. As he went through the living room, he put down the beer and said something to Bethanna, who was so engrossed in a television show that she didn't look up.

Peter got out of the car. Deputy Amos came outside, tucking in his shirt and mumbling apologies for not being in his uniform. Peter met him at the front of the car to explain the situation; I could tell from Deputy Amos's expression that he was awed by Peter but exceedingly leery about taking the two men in custody.

"I'd better call Sheriff Dorfer," the deputy said, shaking his head.

Peter nodded as he took the handcuffs from Amos's limp hand. "Good idea. In the meantime, let's cuff these clowns to your truck. Mrs. Malloy and I are going to NewCo to search for the missing girls." Before Amos could offer an argument (and clearly he wanted to), Peter ordered Yellow Hair and Baby Bear to get out of his car, hustled them to the side of the truck, slipped the cuffs through the door handle, and then clicked the metal bracelets around the men's wrists.

It impressed all of us, including the recipients of his attention. Bethanna watched from the doorway, and Deputy Amos was still gaping as Peter and I drove out of the yard.

I leaned forward in the seat, my hands gripping the dashboard. "What if they're not here?"

Peter shrugged. "Then we'll find them someplace else." He parked in front of the gate and cut off the engine. The driveway was black, and beyond it the faint outline of the house was dimly lit by the utility pole beside it. Peter took a flashlight from what obviously was a well-equipped glove compartment. As we started up the driveway, hanging on each other like children on Halloween, I heard a noise that caused me to stumble on a rudely protruding root.

"That's a dog barking," I said excitedly.

"Don't fall and break your neck," Peter said, tightening his grip on me. "This is a rural area, and I imagine most of the people out here have several dogs. Maybe it's one of Deputy Amos's; his property is closer than it seems from the road."

I stumbled again, although for a different reason. I was not yet ready to offer it for a critique, though, so I nodded vaguely and willed myself to maintain a prudent pace. The three cages were in the front yard where I'd left them earlier in the day. We went past them and around the corner of the house. I eyed the metal structure, but another bark came from behind the house, and I hurried in that direction.

Peter caught up with me and flashed his light at the pen that, in the previous week, had contained three vicious pit bulls, Newton Churls's bloodied corpse, and most recently, Daryl Defoe's prone body. We both stopped abruptly. I was speechless, a condition that rarely befalls me. Peter's hand shook so hard the beam of light danced on the metal fencing.

Caron and Inez sat on the concrete floor, each of them being licked by a fat basset hound with a floppy pink tongue and a stubby, unrestrained tail. An enormous black fur ball with glittering yellow eyes clung to the fence above their heads, hissing at a golden retriever that pranced about like a Ping-Pong ball and let out an occasional bark that was either an invitation to play or a menu order.

It was quite a spectacle.

"Caron?" I said faintly. "Inez?"

Caron shielded her eyes and looked at us. "Mother, stop behaving like a dying trout and Do Something."

Inez shoved ineffectually at Nick (or Nora), straightened her glasses, and said, "This is very unpleasant, Mrs. Malloy."

"Are you okay?"

"Other than being drowned in slobber, we're dandy," Caron said. "Will you please do something before we go under for the third time?"

Peter nudged me into motion, and we approached the pen. Astra sent a hiss at us, provoking Patton into further frenzy of undisciplined barks. "Why are you sitting in there?" he asked.

Caron rolled her eyes. "Because we were tired of standing in here." One of the bassets floundered into her lap and tried to lick her extended lower lip. "Ugh! Stop it, you beast! Mother, Do Something!"

I went to the door of the pen and without surprise, noted the padlock firmly set in place. "Did those men take the key?"

Inez let out a shriek as dog spittle splattered her cheek. "Yes, they did. Is there any way. . . ?"

Peter tugged at the padlock, then looked at me and shook his head. "I'd try to shoot it off, but I can't predict where the bullet might ricochet and the girls might be hurt."

Nick and Nora had deserted the girls and were snuffling at me through the fence. I knelt to pat their noses, actually pleased to be doing so. Patton flung himself at me, and I gave him a wary smile. "We know where the men are. If they still have the key, I'll get it and bring it back. If they opted to throw it into the woods, I suppose all I can do is use Deputy

Amos's telephone and try to find a locksmith willing to make a house call at this hour."

"But that could take hours," Caron wailed. Nick and Nora rushed over to comfort her, which resulted in more wails and an impressive amount of blubbering.

Peter gave me the flashlight and was attempting to lure the dogs away from her as I hurried around the house and down the driveway. I could still hear wails as I hesitated at Peter's car, then decided I could walk more quickly than I could maneuver the car around in the narrow road.

I was breathing heavily as I turned into Deputy Amos's yard and started toward the truck. The handcuffs lay on the ground; Yellow Hair and Baby Bear were no longer sharing a metal bracelet. Clenching my teeth, I went to the front door and pounded on it.

Bethanna opened it cautiously. "Yeah?"

"Where's Deputy Amos—and where are the two prisoners we left here less than fifteen minutes ago?"

"I dunno," she said. "After you and that other fellow left, I went back to watching my show. A little later Rory said he was going down to the barn for a minute."

"Did he call the sheriff?"

She scratched her head and gave me a bewildered, bovine look. "I didn't pay any attention. I was watching—"

"Your show," I interrupted. I brushed past her and went into the kitchen, found a telephone book on the counter, and dialed the number of the sheriff's department. I tersely related the situation to a bored dispatcher, who wearily promised to hunt up Sheriff Dorfer and tell him what was happening.

Bethanna came into the kitchen and took a beer

from the refrigerator. "I heard that last part about the padlock. Rory has some tools in the barn. Maybe he's got some kind of saw that'll cut the lock."

Doubting I could find a compliant locksmith, I thanked her and went out the back door, ducked under the clothesline, and walked down a muddy road to a large, dilapidated barn. Light shone through the cracks and knotholes. I pushed open the door, calling, "Deputy Amos?"

He came out from behind a partition and goggled at me. "Mrs. Malloy, what are you doing here?"

It occurred to me that he should have been less startled to see me, in that we'd seen each other several hundred times in the last week, including twice that day. However, I let it go and told him what Peter and I had discovered in the pit bull pen at NewCo. Ignoring his stuttery spate of questions, I asked if he might have a saw capable of cutting through the lock.

"Uh, yeah, I think so." He went to a worktable and began to search through the jumble of tools.

"What happened to Yellow Hair and Baby Bear?" I said to his back.

His neck turned red. "It was my fault, really dumb. The big guy said his gut was killing him and doubled up, groaning something awful. The other one started yelling for me to unlock the guy before he barfed all over him. I went over to see if the guy was faking it, and they jumped me and got the key. Next thing I know, I'm lying on the ground with a lump on my head and they're long gone. The sheriff'll get 'em, though."

I studied him as he continued to hunt through the scattered tools. "I suppose so, and Lieutenant Rosen has their names and addresses." My gaze wandered to the partition, and I moved as quietly as I could to the edge of it to see what Deputy Amos had been doing.

There was a hole in the dirt floor, about eight-foot square and a yard deep. The hole had been there for some time; the earth was packed as tightly as a concrete surface. Surrounding this shallow yet interesting excavation were primitive benches.

"Here's a hacksaw," Deputy Amos said from behind me. "It ought to do the trick. If not, I know a welder who lives near the highway. We can get him to melt the darn lock so your daughter and her friend can get out."

I took the saw. "You know, there was a question I meant to ask Caron, but I forgot."

"Like how those guys talked them into going into the pen?"

"No, although that's a good one and I will inquire at a later time. I have a feeling she won't be in the mood to discuss it in the immediate future. I've been meaning to ask her at what time the commandos left Farberville the night Newton Churls was killed."

He blinked at me. "You called me about nine, didn't you?"

"No, it was earlier than that. I arrived here at nine, and it took more than twenty minutes to make the drive. I assumed the commandos had come much earlier, but there's no basis for the assumption. They might have been on their way here when I called you." I sat down on the nearest bench, and with a grimmace, plucked a tick off my ankle and flicked it into the pit. Ah, nature."

"I guess so," he said uneasily.

"We know it was dark when they got here. According to Helen Maranoni, she and George started down the path, realized the flashlight battery was dead, and he came back to borrow another light. I don't think Helen would have waited very long in the woods. And Vidalia was still searching those rows of cages when you and I arrived—she couldn't have been there more than five minutes."

"I guess I thought the same thing you did," he said. He shot a quick look at the hole. "Hope the saw works."

"So you didn't see their car on the road," I said slowly. "After I called, you told me you walked down to the gate. They were either already there, or arrived after my call. I tend to think the latter makes more sense."

He sat down on the opposite end of the bench. "But they had to be there before I went to the gate, or I'd have seen them coming down the road."

"If you stayed by the gate," I corrected him.

"I told you what I did. I heard the dogs all excited, but I was afraid to go onto the property 'cause Churls wouldn't have thought twice about setting the dogs loose if he thought there were trespassers."

"Trespassers, yes. But he thought he had a visitor, and he told Arnie, one of his bunchers, to wait down behind the back fence."

Deputy Amos's throat rippled as he glanced at me. "He told the guy to wait behind the fence so he could turn the dogs loose. It makes real good sense."

"No," I said regretfully. "He could have told Arnie to wait in the house. I think he didn't want his two guests to meet each other."

"Why not?"

"I'll have to work on that, but all parties were engaged in felonies. What's really been bothering me is that Churls hid the animals Arnie brought. Why would he do that, unless he knew someone might be coming that could identify them as stolen pets?" I paused for a minute, allowing him time to absorb my logic, which, as usual, was piercingly sharp. "I knew the group was coming, and I told you—and I didn't tell Newton Churls. I wouldn't have, even if I'd had the opportunity. That leaves you, Deputy Amos."

"Why would I do that, Mrs. Malloy?" he said in a stiff, adolescent voice.

I gestured at the hole. "You're not going to tell me you fill this with water in the winter and have the neighbors over to ice-skate, are you?" He mutely shook his head. "I don't know how he did it, but Churls got you involved in pit bull fights. Maybe you knowingly sold him some stolen animals and helped take animals to the sales, or perhaps you bet too much and found yourself in debt. In any case, you and he were partners, so you needed to protect him from accusations that might result in an inquiry."

He stepped into the pit, although not with the arrogance of a ringmaster in a top hat and a tuxedo. "There wasn't anything illegal going on here. Some of the boys may have brought their dogs to train them, but we didn't have any bloodshed or gambling."

"The forensics lab will run tests," I said.

"What's this?" Bethanna said from the edge of the partition. "It's not deep enough for a swimming pool, and a silly place for a garden. And why are you standing in there, Rory?"

He gave her a helpless look from the middle of the pit. "I told you to stay out of the barn, Bethanna."

"I just came to tell you all that Sheriff Dorfer's out in front," she said irritably. "I would have preferred to catch the last part of my show, when they tell you who the murderer is, but I thought I'd better tell you about the sheriff."

"This may be more exciting," I murmured. "Here's how I think the first and second acts went. Arnie took the animals to NewCo. He was arguing about money when you came to the gate to warn Churls that militant pet owners were on their way. Churls sent Arnie away, heard your story, and put the cages under the house."

"I told him it was too dangerous to keep them," Deputy Amos said under his breath.

"What are we talking about?" Bethanna demanded.

"My question exactly," said Sheriff Dorfer as he appeared from the main part of the barn. He snorted as he saw the pit, but sat down on the bench and pulled a stubby cigar from his pocket. "You go right ahead, Mizz Malloy. It's fascinating."

"It's supposed to be better than television," Bethanna said to him. She did so without conviction.

I realized I'd been clutching the saw as a potential weapon, and put it down on the ground. "So you and Churls argued," I said to the deputy in the pit. "Perhaps you followed him around the house, still arguing, and he said he was going to turn the pit bulls loose on several elderly people and two teenage girls. He unlocked the pen. You pushed him in, clicked the padlock, and took the key back to the kitchen."

"I didn't think they'd attack him. He was their trainer," Amos said with a groan. He covered his face with his hands, and his voice was barely audible as he said, "God knows I wouldn't have done it if I could have seen what would happen."

I was about to respond when Sheriff Dorfer

cleared his throat. "Well, Rory, that sounds pretty damn good, but the thing is, we just got back the autopsy report on the pit bulls. I wondered if someone had given them a drug, but it turns out they had a trace of raw meat in 'em. Tossing a hunk of meat in the pen would rile them. Once those dogs are riled, there's no way to stop them short of a bullet."

"I didn't do that," Amos said tearfully. He came over to me, and for a moment I was seriously worried he was going to fall on his knees in front of me. "When I left Churls, he was cussing a blue streak and making all kinds of threats. I didn't know what I was going to do. I owed him over five thousand dollars, and I only bring home twelve hundred and eighty a month. All along he's been saying not to fret about it, that he'd give me a cut from the fights, but somehow I seemed to owe him more every month."

I frowned at the sheriff. "That's a pitiful salary."

He busied himself with yet another cigar stub. "You think I'd smoke leftovers if the county paid decent salaries? My wife buys her winter coats at garage sales, and both my kids work after school."

"I'm sure it's a burden on everyone's family," I said, then sent a sympathetic smile at Bethanna. "I suppose you grew tired of watching Churls drive by in that Lincoln every day, didn't you? You must have guessed what was going on down here and realized a lot of cash changed hands—and most of it ended up in Churls's cash box."

Her thickly mascared eyelashes fluttered. "I don't know what you're talking about."

"Let's suppose you heard Rory's end of the conversation the night I called. He left the house immediately, so you went across the back pasture to see what was happening. To your utter amazement, you saw Rory leaving and Churls locked in the pen with his pit bulls. It's possible his threats alarmed you. Did you pop in the house to take a hunk of hamburger meat from the refrigerator and shove it into the pen? Then, while Churls was occupied, to put it mildly, you went into the house and broke into the cash box?"

"How would I know there was a cash box?" she said haughtily. "Churls was a filthy, nasty man. I wouldn't set foot in his bedroom, no matter how much he offered me!"

"Bedroom?" Deputy Amos echoed.

"Or wherever he kept it," she mumbled, folding her hands in her lap and attempting to look as if she were sitting on a pew.

None of us was fooled.

"Very good, Mizz Malloy. Who shot Daryl Defoe?" the sheriff asked, puffing contentedly as if he had solved one mystery and was merely teasing us before he unraveled the next one. The fat man with the orchids couldn't have done it better.

"I think," I said slowly, "he's been afraid to talk because of his status with the army. Once it's made clear that he's been exposed, he'll admit that he came to the same conclusion I did about Deputy Amos. His mistake was to go to NewCo to look under the porch, and be caught doing it. Deputy Amos shot him and left him in the pen, but then panicked when he saw Jan's car go by his house and came back to determine if Daryl was able to talk." I gave the accused a sad look. "You came too quickly. Jan hadn't been off the telephone for more than a minute when you showed up."

Sheriff Dorfer's beady look was hardly sad. "Guess

235

ballistics might want a look at your weapon, Deputy."

Amos sank down in the middle of the pit and covered his face with his hands. His shoulders shook, and the noises coming from him bore a disturbing resemblance to the wuffly barks of the mutilated dogs. He might have achieved the age required to join the sheriff's department, but he was still way too young. Bethanna, on the other hand, looked much older than her years as she took a nail file from her pocket and began to work on her scarlet nails.

14

Sheriff Dorfer's men took Deputy Amos and Bethanna to the county jail for further discussion. He remained on his bench and I on mine, both of us gazing at the pit bull arena.

"Mizz Malloy," he began, then stopped and shook his head.

"I should have called when I learned the girls had been tricked by those goons, but I was with Lieutenant Rosen. Then Deputy Amos said he'd call and we went on to NewCo."

"And you didn't trust me." He fired up a cigar and sent a swirl of blue smoke into the dark recesses of the rafters above us. "Thought I was the one involved in pit bull fights, didn't you?"

"The idea occurred to me."

"Thing is," he continued in a genial rumble, "Deputy Amos was supposed to be investigating Newton Churls real quiet like. There were some rumors that dogfights were taking place in the county. Guess there was a reason why he never came up with anything."

"I think it has to do with Bethanna's car and designer jeans."

He took a last puff on the cigar, then flipped it into the hole. "I should have looked a little harder for those stolen animals you were so worried about. My apologies, Mizz Malloy."

Mizz Malloy was not in the mood to graciously accept his apology; she was busy remembering where her daughter and Inez were at the moment. "We've got to get a locksmith, Sheriff Dorfer. Nick and Nora aren't vicious, but Caron might be if she stays in that pen much longer."

"We're seeing to it right now. They should be along any time. I'm a little bit unclear why they were out at NewCo and how they ended up with the stolen animals."

"I think Deputy Amos will admit he took the dogs and cat here after he locked Churls in the pen. He knew the only way to stop me from"—I coughed ever so discreetly—"meddling was to return the animals. Churls was going to take them to the Guttler sale, and even warned Yellow Hair and Baby Bear to frighten me if I appeared. They were too dim to realize there was no need to worry about me if the animals weren't there—or maybe they attacked me for the hell of it." I thought about the arm around my neck and shivered.

"Didn't seem to slow you down," Sheriff Dorfer commented as he felt around in his pocket, sighed, and gloomily looked at the smoldering cigar butt in the hole.

"Of course not. They probably weren't too happy when Amos told them to leave the animals in the pen so he could make an anonymous call to me. They decided to collect a ransom."

"Well, they Didn't." Caron marched across the floor and shot me a withering look. "They were extremely rude and one of them smelled worse than—than canned dog food and kibble. They drank whiskey all the way out here, made unamusing remarks, and actually laughed when they locked us in that dreadful place. They stopped laughing when they realized the money was in my pocket. Nick and Nora protected us."

"Where are Nick and Nora now?" I asked.

"They're in a cage in the backseat of Peter's car. Patton went with some deputy, and another was still trying to coax that satanic cat into a box." She crossed her arms. "Are we going to stay in this filthy place all night, Mother? I have homework, you know."

"Biology homework?"

"Mostly algebra," Inez said from behind me. "I do, too, and I have a paper due in history."

Sheriff Dorfer winked at me as he left. I took a minute to compose myself, and said, "I don't think you need to worry about homework, girls. Unless I misinterpreted Mrs. Horne's intentions, you'll both be expelled in the morning."

"Because of the frogs?" Caron said, although without any of the explosive indignance I expected. "Who cares about a bunch of frozen frogs?"

"Did you steal them?"

Her lower lip crept out and her chin trembled as she said, "What would I do with frozen frogs?"

"I asked Mrs. Horne that same question," I admitted. "Will you swear on your Mousse ticket that you did not steal the frogs?"

"Oh, Mother," she said as she went past me and out of the barn. Inez gave me a timid wave as she followed the martyr.

By the next afternoon, the situation seemed under control. Vidalia and Colonel Culworthy had been overcome when their pets were returned; Vidalia had hugged the deputy so tightly that he'd stumbled over a hydrangea, and the colonel had produced a

239

word of gratitude along with a bone-crushing hand-
shake.

I had a long telephone conversation with Jan,
who'd sounded tired but encouraged by Daryl's re-
covery from the bullet wound. He'd been transferred
to the psychiatric wing, where soft-spoken doctors
could ease him out of his mental cage in the jungle.

There had been no call from the high school earlier in the day, and Caron and Inez stormed the store
at their usual hour, spiritedly arguing the politically
correct posture of attending Rhonda Maguire's
slumber party since she was, Caron shrieked, "Such
a bitch!"

"But the guys are coming over after the concert,"
Inez said somberly. "Even Louis Wilderberry. Rhonda made this big show of stopping him in the middle of the hall after algebra."

Caron glanced at me, then grabbed Inez's arm and
dragged her behind the self-help rack. "What'd he
say?" she whispered loudly enough to be heard from
the campus.

I couldn't hear Inez's response, naturally. From
the intensity of Caron's sputters, however, it was not
difficult to presume the boy under discussion had
not made the acceptable reply.

"Enough!" I said. "You're not going to the concert
unless you go to Miss Emily's and take care of Nick
and Nora. Don't forget the African violets. We're
completely out of topics of conversation."

Caron stalked into view, with Inez trailing after
her. "We're going; we're going. We were merely discussing a Certain Conversation at school today."

"What did Mrs. Horne have to say?" I asked, not
willing to explore the delicate topic of Louis Wilderberry's hypothetical whereabouts after the concert.

240

Inez blinked. "She said we couldn't have lab, so we're supposed to draw the interior of the frog and label it."

"And there's no breakthrough in the case of the frozen frogs?" I persisted. "No one has any idea who took them?"

My daughter was not yet ready to assume the mantle of a master criminal. Her freckles were dark splotches on her suddenly pale face, and she ducked her head. "They'll probably turn up later in the week," she mumbled. "Come on, Inez. Let's go feed the dogs and chitchat with the violets. You can tell them all about Rhonda Maguire's fat ankles."

They grabbed their books and started for the door.

"Where will the frogs turn up?" I said with all the maternal sternness I could rally, considering the nature of the stolen items.

Caron glanced back at me. "Oh, you know. Somebody's locker, most likely, when they're nice and ripe." She and Inez sailed out the door, resuming their squabble. I was too stunned to pursue them.

To add to my stupor, Arnie came by shortly after that, already equipped with a bottle. "Yo, Senator," he said as he sat down on my stool and tried to type on the cash register.

"Yo, Arnie," I said without enthusiasm.

"I got fired." He took a drink, wiped his mouth on the cuff of his coat, and gave me a calculating look. "Don't suppose you need an aide?"

"Arnie," I said with a saccharine smile, "I'll tell you a big, dark secret if you'll answer one question."

"About the capital gains legislation? I was just saying to myself last night in jail, I was saying, Arnie, if—"

"A different topic entirely," I said quickly. "Did

one of the sheriff's deputies keep you supplied with booze so that you couldn't answer questions about the night you went to NewCo?"

He finished off the bottle, then gave me an enigmatic look that reminded me of Caron. "You know, Senator, now that I am distanced from the inconvenience of incarceration and able to look back objectively, he did. I just thought to myself that he wanted to keep me from discussing the capital gains reform."

"So what are you going to do, Arnie?"

"Thought you were going to tell me some secret, Senator?"

"I'm not a senator."

"Wowsy, Senator, this is a setback of astounding proportion," he said with (believe it or not) a solemn hiccup. "I had my heart set on an office with a view of the Washington Monument. I must rethink my career options." He slid off the stool and saluted me with the empty bottle. Buttoning his coat to protect him from the eighty degree wind roaring down the railroad tracks, he staggered toward the door.

"You didn't take the puppies to NewCo?" I said to his back.

"Check with that deputy, Senator." Arnie went out the door, but I had a feeling I hadn't seen the last of this proverbial bad penny.

Peter came by that evening. Once we'd settled into the sofa, I asked him if Yellow Hair and Baby Bear had been apprehended on their way back to Guttler.

"The state police stopped them not too far across the line," he said, attempting to distract me with a lazy smile and a meaningful look. "Want to cross a state line for immoral purposes?"

"Were they charged?"

"If you're willing to make numerous court appearances in Guttler, they might be charged with the assault." Mr. Suggestive arched his eyebrows. "Are you sure you want to talk about greasy rednecks? Let's talk about that hammock in Tahiti. The dogbane will be in bloom. I shall murmur bawdy bits of doggerel in your ear as the dog days drift by in a swelter of passion. We shall lie doggo in paradise, our discarded books dog-eared, both lost in a catatonic stupor of cathartic—"

"What about kidnapping?"

He gave me a disappointed look. "Their story is that they worked for both Churls and Amos. They really didn't hear about Churls's death until yesterday, when Deputy Amos told them to put the dogs in the pen. They claim they were merely being helpful when they called Caron and Inez, told them where the animals were, and gave them a ride to NewCo. No money exchanged hands."

"They were so inept that they're going to get away with it? What kind of—" The telephone rang, interrupting what was going to be an eloquent condemnation of the entire legal system.

"Oh, Claire," Miss Emily gushed, "I am thrilled I reached you. I have such exciting news."

"You now own a casino?"

"Well, I did make a tidy sum playing blackjack. It's really such a fun game, and all you have to do is count to twenty-one. No, this concerns Mr. Delmaro. I did tell you about him, didn't I?" She giggled and continued, saying, "I might not have mentioned that he's a widower. Sandra was most upset when we disappeared after dinner. We should have told her, but we slipped away to one of those little wedding chapels. It was ever so exciting and romantic, and now I'm Mrs. Arthur Delmaro!"

"Mrs. Arthur Delmaro," I repeated numbly.

"The group's having a party for us tonight, with a cake and punch. Tomorrow the bus starts back for Farberville, but Mr. Delmaro and I shall remain behind in the honeymoon suite. He's already instructed them to chill the champagne. He can be so extravagant," she confided coyly.

"This is wonderful news," I said with what conviction I could. "Give Mr. Delmaro my congratulations."

"Then you don't mind?"

"Of course not," I murmured. "I'm thrilled for both of you, and I'm sure you'll have a lovely . . . honeymoon, Miss Emily." I took a breath as her words began to sink in like frozen frogs in a lake. "How long will you stay in Las Vegas?"

"Not long. Mr. Delmaro says he knows an incredibly quaint village in Mexico that I must see, and then who knows? As long as I know Nick and Nora are being well cared for, why—we might just do something crazy! They haven't been any trouble, have they?"

I closed my eyes and willed myself to tell her the truth. I tried to find a way to gently refuse her. I remembered my promise to myself to be more assertive, to give my attention to the shabby remains of my business, to worry less about dogs and more about my daughter's academic future when Rhonda Maguire opened her locker on Friday. I gritted my teeth as I listened to Peter's muffled chuckles.

"No trouble at all," I said.